Happy Hour

Happy Hour

ELISSA BASS

Archway Publishing books may be ordered through booksellers or by contacting:

Archway Publishing
1663 Liberty Drive
Bloomington, IN 47403
www.archwaypublishing.com
844-669-3957

Because of the dynamic nature of the Internet, any web addresses or links contained in this book may have changed since publication and may no longer be valid. The views expressed in this work are solely those of the author and do not necessarily reflect the views of the publisher, and the publisher hereby disclaims any responsibility for them.

Any people depicted in stock imagery provided by Getty Images are models, and such images are being used for illustrative purposes only. Certain stock imagery © Getty Images.

ISBN: 978-1-6657-5674-7 (sc)
ISBN: 978-1-6657-5676-1 (hc)
ISBN: 978-1-6657-5675-4 (e)

Library of Congress Control Number: 2024903147

Print information available on the last page.

Archway Publishing rev. date: 04/02/2024

For Tammy, Leanne, Kathleen, and Karen:
the four pillars of my foundation

CONTENTS

PROLOGUE

KK

Everyone keeps telling me I need to get out.

They keep saying I have to get out of this house.

And it's weird because I know they're right, but every time one of them says it, it just paralyzes me more, just makes me burrow deeper, and compels me to keep the blinds down 24-7.

Because that's exactly what I kept saying to him that night everything fell apart. What I started out whispering but ended up screaming over and over and over, long after he was actually gone.

"You need to get out," I kept repeating.

"You have to get out of this house," I shouted.

"*Get out*," I screeched as I followed him out of the bedroom and down the stairs. I stood in the open front door and watched him get into his car and back out of the driveway, gravel flying.

And yes, it apparently worked like a charm on him, since he never came back, and we never fixed things, and I ended up totally alone in this same damn house.

Why would it work on me?

Jay

My phone dings.

MOTHER. Jason, it's your mother.

Sigh. I know it's you, Mother. You're literally in my contacts as "MOTHER."

ME. Hello, Mother. What's up?

MOTHER. Your father talked to Raymond O'Neill, and he has an opening at his company that would be perfect for you. He can talk to you next week.

God forbid there would be pleasantries. Or maternal chitchat. No "Are you getting enough sleep, dear?" or "Are you eating?" I think the most maternal thing she ever did was push me down her birth canal and out of her vagina.

ME. I'm great, Mother. Thanks for asking. How are you and Ted?

I don't call my father "Dad" or "Father" or "Papa." I call him "Ted." I figured out when I was eight that for him, our relationship was largely transactional. Spend money on me, get results. So from then on, I've called him by his name. I have no idea if it bothered him then or ever. He reveals nothing to me.

MOTHER. Your father will send you Raymond's contact information. You can schedule the meeting through his assistant. And we can have dinner afterward. You can stay with us overnight.

ME. I'm not going to do that.

MOTHER. *Typing*

MOTHER. *Typing*

MOTHER. *Typing*

I can't help but smile. She's strategizing, trying to figure out the best way to force me back into the world I left while at the same time showing me what a colossal fucking disappointment I am. I almost can't wait to see where this lands.

MOTHER. It's been long enough. This "break" you've been on. I'm assuming your head is straight by now. Isn't that what you said? You needed to "get your head on straight"?

I don't reply. Because I know she's not done.

MOTHER. *Typing*

MOTHER. *Typing*

MOTHER. *Typing*

Oh, this is going to be good. I swear she should just save these rants on her Notes app because it's only a slight variation of the same damn diatribe every time. Just copy and paste, Mother. Save your thumbs all that stress. Also, I'm not a kid. Don't tell me what to do.

MOTHER. Jason, we are at a loss here. A true loss. We spent more than $200,000 on your education. Your father used his considerable influence to get you a job that anyone else would have killed for. A great company. A great position. You are wasting your brain. You are wasting your talents. Talents that we spent considerable time, effort, and money nurturing.

MOTHER. You have been given every opportunity, and yet you refuse them. I told your father last week that he needs to send you an invoice for everything we spent on your education since you have decided to waste it all. If you are going to throw it all away, then you need to pay us back. Because we have had zero return on our investment. It's nearly impossible to show our faces at the club and have to suffer through everyone asking how you are. They whisper it. It's mortifying. It's disappointing.

And there it is.

I don't bother to reply. We're trapped in this loop of me not wanting what they want and them not understanding why I don't want what they want. The definition of insanity, right? Einstein knew what he was talking about. Is it so difficult to understand that I simply don't want to hate my life?

I power off my phone, shove it in my bag, and pick up my board. I start my new gig this afternoon at a local place called Dockside. They do an off-season happy hour, so I'll have to be there at three to make sure the bar is fully prepped and ready. The owner seems cool. I have time to try to catch a few good ones before I need to head in.

I start to paddle out. Here we go.

1

KK

My whole life I was scared to be alone. I have no idea where it came from. I just know that from the first time I realized I wasn't alone, I was afraid everyone was going to leave me.

As a small child, I would wake up in the middle of the night, eyes popping open, sitting bolt upright in the dark, convinced everyone was dead—my parents; my big sister, Bitty; and after he was born, my little brother, Harley.

I'd climb out of bed and drift down the upstairs hallway, stopping first at my parents' bedroom, where their door was ajar so they could hear a child in need in the middle of the night. I'd stand in the gap and hold my breath so I could hear them breathing.

Sometimes I stepped just inside and peeked around my father's nightstand so I could get visual confirmation of chests rising and falling.

Assured, I moved on to Bitty's room. Her name is Elizabeth, but that was too much for my toddler pronunciation skills, so I called her "Bitty." It stuck. I'd go right into her room, right to the bedside, and peer at her, listening to her breaths and watching her eyeballs move under her closed lids.

After Harley was added to the mix, I went into his nursery and held onto the crib bars as I pressed my face in between to watch him sleeping. Sometimes he opened his eyes, saw me, smiled sleepily, then stuck his thumb in his mouth and rolled over.

Only then, when my rounds were done, did I climb back into my own bed and fall asleep.

Is it ironic that now all I want is to be alone? I've never been good at knowing what actual irony is—so maybe it is. Or maybe it's just pathetic. Like the rest of my life.

BITTY. Good morning, beautiful.

ME. WTF?

BITTY. Oh, good. You're awake. I wasn't sure you'd be up. Can't quite figure out your schedule these days.

ME. I'm up. Or at least awake. And why the fuck are you texting me good morning?

Bitty. I see all these videos on TikTok that say one way to show you care about someone is to text them good morning.

Me. Oh, sweet Jesus, Bit. I think that's for husbands and boyfriends. Not sisters.

Bitty. Oh. Hmm. Maybe. Regardless, good morning! What are your plans for the day?

Me. What day is it?

Bitty. KK! COME ON. It's October 14. The year of our Lord 2022.

Me. Oh, good. The plan for today is to wallow in self-pity and set fire to more of his things.

Bitty. I'm taking sarcasm as proof of life. Also … what fire? What things?

Me. I guess I forgot to tell you I found a job.

Bitty. A job! That's awesome! Who's the client?

Me. Ha. Fuck no. I'm not in the working world. More of a purpose, I guess. I set a timer for thirty minutes, collect a bunch of his shit, take it out back to the firepit, pour a fuck ton of lighter fluid on it, and drop a match. An old-fashioned wooden match, of which, it turns out, we have a whole drawer full—boxes of them.

Bitty. Hmm. I'm going to categorize this as healthy processing. At least it's an actual activity that requires you to move. Just going to pretend it's fine. Totally fine. Nothing to worry about there. Fire is good.

ME. I'm making a list of shit that definitely doesn't burn in case I decide to turn this whole thing into a Ted Talk.

BITTY. OK. Well, I need to get a move on here, or I'm going to be late for work. Text me a photo of the fire. I'm definitely invested in this now. Loop in Haw. I'm sure he'd be onboard too.

ME. OK.

ME. Oh, and, Bit, thanks for checking in. I appreciate it.

BITTY. ♡

June 1972

Bitty, KK, Matty, and Chickie are on the jetty, fishing for crabs. Being only three, Harley is on the beach with Grandma. Kay is chatting with the other ladies, who all have one eye on the kids and one eye on each other. Their third eye is keeping track of the comings and goings at the beach so they know whom they can gossip about and whom they can't.

Harley fusses with Kay since he wants to be on the rocks with the big kids. She keeps handing him a shovel, and he keeps throwing it back at her. But he will not win this battle. She has decades of experience. Two generations' worth.

It's a great beach for kids. A long-ish stretch of sand, accessible from the street by a gate that's manned by a sullen, pimply-faced teenager during lifeguard hours—nine to four. Two long jetties, one on each end of the beach, provide a relatively calm area for little kids to splash and play. Past the jetties, the water is rougher, and that's where the surfers hang. There's a longstanding and unspoken agreement between them and the moms that they won't cross each other's paths. The surfers go in off the jetty closest to the big parking lot. And they aren't allowed between the jetties from Memorial Day to Labor Day.

Currently out on the shorter of the two jetties, the "big" kids (Bitty is seven, and the other three are five) crouch down, peering intently into the water in between the boulders. Bitty and Matty are each holding a length of twine that disappears into the murky depths, dangling the raw chicken legs that are meant to lure their prey. Crabs cannot resist raw chicken legs. Or hot dogs. But today's menu is poultry.

KK is clutching the bucket, about one-third full of seawater, with some seaweed to add ambiance. Chickie is empty handed but full of advice.

"I think they are under there," she says, pointing to a spot where no chicken legs dangle.

"Did you see one?" KK asks eagerly, moving closer and crouching lower. They have come up dry so far. There is some muttered concern about overfishing by kids who got here earlier. But Mom wouldn't let them come to the beach until after Harley's nap. Now it's three o'clock, practically nighttime, for Pete's sake.

Matty and Bitty carefully maneuver their bait, per Chickie's instructions. Silently, they wait.

Suddenly, a hard tug on Matty's string. "You got one!" the three girls yell. Matty is both startled and overjoyed, and so he overreacts, whipping his arm up and out, so his twine, chicken leg, and crab go soaring overhead. The crab lets go, and perhaps for the first and only time in its life, it flies, landing in the water on the swimming part of the beach with a small splash.

KK screams, grabs the bucket handles, and leaps to her feet. She starts to run across the jetty, jumping from one boulder to another to cut across toward the beach. But the wet algae on the rocks is like ice under her bare feet, and down she goes, screeching and disappearing from view between the boulders.

Silence. Bitty, Matty, and Chickie freeze.

"Is she dead?" Matty whispers.

Then they hear crying. "Come on," Bitty says, standing up and taking her two younger friends' hands. "We have to go save KK."

It is Bitty and Harley who save me.

Actually, that might be too strong a point since I'm pretty sure I wouldn't have died. Like, dead died. I certainly was dead inside though.

I have been lying on the beach house couch for five (or so) days when she and Harley show up and break my stupor.

I'm lying on my back, staring at the ceiling, when I hear a key in the lock. Then I hear the bolt move, and then someone bangs hard into the door as if they expect it to open but it doesn't.

Apparently, I never locked the door after he left that night. So my siblings actually lock themselves out before they figure it out and let themselves in.

The door swings open. From where I'm lying, I can see their two shadows in the sun splash on the hallway rug. Based on this visual, the Girl Scout in me surmises it is afternoon because the front door faces west.

"Jesus Christ. What is that smell?" I hear Harley say.

"Oh, God, Haw. Is she dead? Is she fucking dead in here?"

That's Bitty, always going immediately to DEFCON 1. Thermonuclear war.

"KK?" Harley calls out. "K, honey, are you here?"

I roll so my back is to the entryway. They must've heard the upholstery crinkle. This couch is torture, so uncomfortable. I probably have a full body rash by this point.

I hear their footsteps.

"Is she dead?" Bitty whispers.

"No," I say, and they both scream a little.

"Jesus. You guys, what do you want?" I ask, turning to face them but not sitting up.

Bitty screams again. "What the fuck happened?" she shouts, shoving Harley toward me.

"I'm getting a divorce," I say.

"Oh, thank God," Harley says. "Twenty years too late, but let's not quibble. Who needs a drink?"

2

So that was August. Which was my month to have the house, which is why it took them a few days to decide to check on me.

And I guess the only reason they were clued in that quickly was because he had suddenly blocked them both from all his social media. And I wasn't answering any texts, asking why he had done that. And then their calls to me went straight to voicemail.

So Bitty got on a plane, and Harley picked her up at Logan, and they drove to the beach to find me lying on the living room couch. The smell was a combination of beach house mildew, me unbathed, and food rotting in the kitchen.

It's now October. I'm still at the beach house. But now I shower. I also clean the kitchen and methodically collect and burn his stuff. I still don't go out.

In September, Bitty set me up on Instacart. She orders for me every week. Harley pays all the bills associated with the property, but that's nothing new. That's been his job since our dad died years ago. They got me a cleaning person who comes every other week.

They even worked out something so the local library brings me two books a week. Spicy romances. I think that was them trying to be funny. I read them though. I leave the finished books on the porch on Thursday mornings and collect the new ones off the steps that afternoon.

It's not a life, but I don't care. I stopped caring a long time ago. I just hadn't noticed until that night in August.

But that Tuesday morning when Bitty texts me like the good boyfriend she's always wanted to be, I suddenly have the urge to take a walk. We call this house the "beach house," but it's not actually on the beach. It's about a ten-minute walk down the hill to the sand. The old house sits up high because our great-grandfather, who built it, was a sea captain. He built his house at the top of the bluff so his wife could watch for his boat to return. Not all men suck.

It's chilly, so I throw on a big hoodie over my fleece vest and stuff my feet into my All Birds, which have been sitting by the back door since I kicked them off that August day. That was the day when I returned from my quick grocery run, my world half turned upside down by what I found under the front seat of his car.

I reach for the ChapStick I know is in the sweatshirt pocket. I always have a ChapStick; I keep some everywhere. It's a genetic trait I inherited from my father. He always had a ChapStick— and a tissue and a tiny, retractable box cutter—in his front left pants pocket.

I go out the back door and head down the hill. In the distance, I can see the surfers out on the water. Our beach is famous for its off-season waves.

It is one of those fall days when the sky is so blue you think it has to be fake. The water glitters. It's blinding if you stare too hard. There is no one on the beach, just piles of towels and clothes and surfing gear. The waves look decent. They are all outfitted in full winter gear, so they all look the same—floating ninjas.

The surfers' cars are parked in the lot, which is private from Memorial Day weekend through Labor Day but open the rest of the year. I stand on the breakwater and watch them for a while. One or two catch a decent swell.

By the time I get back home, I am winded. At my age, three months with zero physical activity are going to have repercussions. Do I care? Not really. But the fresh air and the sun feel good.

I open the family group chat, dubbed "Pains in the Ass" by me at some point.

> ME. I took a walk.

> HARLEY. Yay!

> HARLEY. *gif of Winnie the Pooh waddling down a forest path*

> BITTY. You got out of the house!

> ME. Please stop saying that. You know it triggers me.

> HARLEY. *gif of the Wicked Witch's feet under Dorothy's house*

ME. Jesus, Haw, do you have any words?

(Side note: Yes I am/was the giver of nicknames. I couldn't pronounce Rs for the first five years of my life, so Harley became Hawley, and that became Haw.)

HARLEY. Proud of you, KK. You're healing.

ME. Ha. Doubtful. Feel like an open, gaping, infected wound.

BITTY. Haw, you are banned from any memes in response to that comment.

June 1988

The Jamaican nanny taps lightly on the door, and when she hears "Come in," she softly turns the knob and enters.

She's carrying the two-month-old, his crotch near the crook of her elbow; he lies belly down, his tiny legs on either side of her solid forearm, his arms dangling, and his face turned so one cheek rests on her palm.

In her other hand, she holds a small baby bottle with a cap over the nipple.

"The babe is clean and ready for his bedtime bottle," she says cheerfully, advancing toward the woman draped on a velvet-covered chaise, reading *Marie Claire*.

"You may give it to him and put him down," the woman says without taking her eyes off the page.

"But …," the nanny begins.

"Eralia," the woman says sharply, her eyes flicking briefly before dropping back down to the magazine. "Put the baby to bed."

"Yes, ma'am," she says, beginning to back up before she turns and leaves, pulling the door shut behind her. She places the bottle on an ornate side table in the hallway and shifts the infant so his tiny body is pressed against her chest, his little head on her shoulder. His huge, pale blue eyes look up, catching her deep brown ones. He sighs a deep baby sigh.

"I know, little man," Eralia says, picking up the bottle and moving toward the staircase. "I know. I'm sorry. We can try again tomorrow."

3

A few days later, as I stare out the window at the surfers down below, my phone dings.

CHICKIE. Mama, are you at the house?

ME. Why?

CHICKIE. I saw lights on the other night, which was weird, since you guys close it up Columbus Day weekend, so I drove by and saw your car.

ME. Liar.

Chickie is my age. She's been my best beach house friend since we were in grade school. When we were kids, we spent the whole summer here with our mom and grandma, and so we had a tribe of summer beach friends. Chickie is a townie, born and raised here. Her grandfather opened Dockside, a clam shack, on the harbor a thousand years ago. Her dad turned it into a restaurant/bar, and when Chickie took it over seven years ago, she converted it from seasonal to year-round.

It was a smart business move since there's not much open off season here, and the locals show their gratitude by packing her winter weekend happy hours and buying up her early-bird specials. Off-season Dockside is open only for dinner, Monday through Saturday, with happy hour every day, four to six. Closing is at nine.

> CHICKIE. OK, fine. Bitty texted me. And also in all seriousness, fuck you for not telling me what happened. I thought you had just gone home early in August.

So yes, that was shitty of me.

And cowardly.

Not telling my best beach friend—or anyone for that matter—what had happened was a byproduct of the downward spiral I've been in for the last five years. Hadn't really shared with anyone my depression, my low self-esteem, my anxiety. Easier to just withdraw. Be invisible.

> CHICKIE. Come to happy hour.

> ME. Too peopley.

> CHICKIE. It's after Columbus Day! It's dead here. Have a drink and a snack.

> ME. Indigenous Peoples' Day.

CHICKIE. What?

ME. We don't say Columbus Day anymore. We say Indigenous Peoples' Day.

CHICKIE. Come lecture me in person.

July 1975

This is hands down the greatest summer ever. Now eight years old, Chickie, KK, and Matty are allowed to ride their bikes to get ice cream and to the five-and-dime to get candy *unsupervised*. Life will never get better than this.

But on this day, Matty is imprisoned in the house. He got in trouble yesterday because he was not a good listener at the beach when Margie said it was time to come in from the floating dock. Matty was holding court on the raft with a group of kids, making them laugh with his jokes and shenanigans, and Margie had to call him five times before he swam to the beach. So today he has no privileges. In fact, he is polishing a mountain of silver in the dining room. Margie thinks up the most terrible punishments.

But Chickie and KK are free as birds, and they have a pocketful of change for the candy counter. They lean into their banana seats and ride fast and furious, legs pumping up the hills and coasting down, the brightly colored handlebar streamers whipping their arms as they race.

They each have two dollars in quarters, dimes, and nickels, which should buy them enough sweets to definitely feel queasy and maybe even throw up. They agree before they leave that they will save two pieces each for Matty. They're sad he can't come but only briefly. Then they just feel freeeeeee.

Free, that is, until KK's front tire hits a rock, knocking her off balance. She loses control, and her bike pops up over the curb, across the sidewalk, and runs smack into a fence, which she flies over, tumbling through the air until she lands on the grass on the other side, splayed like a flattened scarecrow.

Chickie watches the whole thing happen in what seems like slow motion. She slams on her brakes and skids to a halt. The world is silent.

"KK?" she calls as she gets off her bike and drops it onto the sidewalk. She walks to the fence and leans over it. "KK?"

"Mmmmph," comes the reply. Chickie hops the fence and kneels by her friend's side.

"You OK?"

"Do I look OK?" KK asks, turning her head so her face isn't smashed into the lawn.

"I don't see any blood."

"Do you think anything is broken?" KK asks. "Do you think I can move?"

"Are you girls OK?" a lady calls out from a car window. Chickie looks over and sees a station wagon stopped in the road and a concerned-looking mom type with her window rolled down.

"Do I tell her we're OK?" Chickie whispers.

"Yes, jeepers. If my mom finds out I crashed, she won't let us ride alone anymore."

"We're fine!" Chickie hollers to the lady. "Just resting!" She waves madly and says out of the corner of her mouth, "Sit up, KK, or she isn't going to believe me."

KK moves her hands to her sides and lays them palm down on the grass, slowly pushing herself up. She twists, sits on her butt, and waves, calling, "Just resting!"

The woman considers them for a few more seconds and then pulls away, rolling up her window as she goes.

Chickie turns to her friend. "Are you sure you're OK? I don't care if we lose privileges. I want to make sure you're OK."

KK runs her hands over her body. "I think I'm good. Is my bike broken?"

Together they get up and climb over the fence, Chickie nimbly hopping and KK gingerly swinging one leg after the other. They pick up KK's bike and examine it closely, but it appears—miraculously—intact.

"You should've seen yourself fly," Chickie says. "Like Superman. Through the air. Actually flying. Since you aren't dead, it was way cool. I can't believe you didn't even cry." She licks her fingers and reaches over to KK's face, where she rubs dirt off her cheek. Then she uses the hem of her T-shirt to wipe it dry.

"Yuck," KK says.

"Making sure you're good," Chickie says. "You ready?"

Together they mount their bikes and push off, pedaling slowly at first toward the store. Soon enough, they pick up speed.

I don't go to happy hour that day. Or the next. But the day after, I walk down to the beach again and watch the surfers. I stand by the jetty, letting the rocks cut the wind a little. My hood is up, and my hands are jammed in the front pocket. I roll my ChapStick in my fingers like a fidget spinner.

There are about a half dozen of them on the water. As I get ready to flee back to the house, a tall man makes his way in, carrying his board under one arm. He stops when the water is around his ankles and reaches up behind him to tug off his hood. He shakes his head, and long hair sprays water. It makes me smile.

He turns his head and looks right at me. His eyes are ice blue. Like almost silver. Jesus. Is he a werewolf?

Maybe he sees my smile. Maybe he has hypothermia and is delirious. Maybe he has the sun in his eyes.

He smiles back at me. So I turn and practically run away.

Back at the house, I impulsively grab my keys and bag, and get in the car. I head to Dockside. I need a half-price drink.

I lose my nerve though, and instead of going to happy hour, I drive around the block by Dockside four times and then go home and crawl into bed.

The next day I make it to the parking lot. Even pull into a space. But then I back out and head home.

The day after that, I park, get out, and make it inside. It's just after four, and there are two old townies sitting halfway up the bar and one couple at a high top. Otherwise, it's empty. Two bartenders are wiping glasses and finishing prep.

I walk straight through to the restaurant, out the restaurant's front door, and back to my car. My phone dings as I hit the fob to unlock it.

CHICKIE. I fucking see you, KK. Get the fuck in here.

ME. I'm dizzy. I need to go home and lie down.

I start to open the door when I hear my name screamed across the lot. Chickie is outside the bar, holding the door ajar with her foot while she wipes her hands on her apron.

"KK, I swear to God I will drag you by your hair."

I sigh. I don't have the energy to fight this battle. I relock the car and walk toward her.

"Good girl," she says. "Come on, I'll get you set up. Got your book?"

I nod. She takes my hand, entwining our fingers so I can't easily shake her off and make a run for it. But I don't. She leads me to the far corner of the bar by the windows. It's clearly the safest space for someone who doesn't want things to be too "peopley."

She snaps her fingers, and a teensy woman who looks about sixty-seven months pregnant sways over behind the bar with a smile. She drops a napkin and raises her eyebrows.

"She wants a pinot grigio, an ice water, and a glass of ice," Chickie tells her.

She shoves my ass on the bar stool, hangs my purse straps over the back, pulls out my book (*Ugly Love*), and turns my whole body so I'm facing the bar.

"Drink your drink. Eat an app. Read your book. Then you can go home," she says. She starts to walk away as the bartender comes back with my wine. "Bring her the pesto flatbread," Chickie says to her. Then she turns back to me.

"This is Susie. She will take care of you. Text me when you are ready to leave." She steps back to me, close, and hugs me hard. "I love you, Mama," she whispers in my ear. "You can do this."

And I do. I force myself into tunnel vision so I see only the wine glass, the plate, the book page, and the pregnant belly of the bartender. I drink the drink, I eat the food, I pay the check, I go home. I do it.

4

July 1990

The Fourth of July at the Club is always a huge deal. Jason, his mother, and the latest iteration of the Jamaican nannies have been out on Long Island since the first. They have opened the house and prepared for the busy summer season. Well, busy for Irene anyway. Jason is only two, so his stamina is low. He needs naps and snacks to keep up with the society whirlwind.

Irene will have people for brunch at eleven o'clock in the morning on the Fourth in advance of the Club's celebration later in the day. At that quaint affair, everyone will dress in red, white, and blue; and all are required to bring blueberry pie. So fun, right? Everyone just loves it, and the challenge is always on for the ladies to make memorable blueberry pie. They absolutely slave over them! Or someone in their kitchen does, anyway. Who sweats the details?

There will be Bloody Marys at the Wells's brunch and then gin and tonics and Tom Collinses at the club. The grilled dinner is always fabulous, and then there will be croquet and badminton for the kids until the fireworks. All the adults will be drunk by then, of course, so it's up to the club staff to make sure none of the children wander away or drown off the docks. It can be hair raising at times, for sure. They will earn their tips.

This nanny's name is Femi, but honestly, they've gone through so many of them that they don't even try to remember names anymore. Irene calls them all "Nanny." Jason does, too. He has taken a real shine to the latest. She sings to him in a beautiful, lilting voice, teaching him lullabies, Jamaican songs, and even some popular music she heard on the radio. The boy loves to sing.

She has dressed him in a little seersucker suit with short pants, white socks, and Buster Brown shoes. Irene's plan is for the family Christmas card photo to be taken this morning, since all three will be in the same place at the same time. It rarely happens, and Irene seizes the moment. She is a top-notch planner.

The photographer is out on the lawn, positioning the two Adirondack chairs and the giant stuffed teddy bear so the sun will be the most flattering on Irene's sharp features. The woman lives on black coffee and apple slices. She hasn't eaten a sandwich since before she was married. She is a master of pretending to eat whatever it is she serves at any of her many sumptuous get-togethers. No one knows, she's certain.

Edward "Ted" Wells—Irene's husband and Jason's father—is a titan of Wall Street. He arrived from the city last night and has yet to emerge this morning. Femi knows that Irene is already annoyed, and she works hard to keep Jason out of his mother's way. It's really not too much of a challenge. Femi isn't 100 percent sure that Jason even knows Irene is his mother.

I used to go out all the time. *We* used to go out all the time. And then shortly after my forty-ninth birthday, menopause arrived. I swear to God I woke up one morning ten pounds heavier, all in my belly. My skin turned ashy. I had high blood pressure for the first time in my life. Hot flashes appeared out of nowhere, starting in my chest and spreading up my neck, turning my face purple. Actual sweat dripped off my forehead. Multiple times a day.

Sleep became a chore. It took me forever to achieve it, and I woke two or three times in the night, drenched in sweat. I had insane dreams. My eyes popped open at 3 a.m. or 4 a.m., and that would be it; I'd be awake for the day.

I looked and felt like shit. I Googled, I went down crazy Reddit rabbit holes, and no matter what I tried, nothing helped. Melatonin, lavender, black cohosh, magnesium, Chinese teas, chamomile tea, dandelion tea. My primary care doctor would nod her head sympathetically and say these issues might last years. Years.

She put me on lisinopril.

Then the thirty-something-year-old physician's assistant told me—while cranking the speculum to pry open my vagina—that she might not get a sufficient sample for my Pap smear because at my age, often the tissue in the cervix is the consistency of parchment.

Parchment. There's pretty much no coming back from that.

I lost all interest in sex, mostly because the act of sex itself became physically painful. That was probably the final nail in my twenty-five-year marriage, and it was a rusty nail at that. Not only did we stop having sex, but he didn't even sleep in the same bed with me for the last year or so because all my "tossing and turning and sweating" disrupted *his* rest.

So we reached this new normal in our marriage, in our relationship, where we were together in the sense that we lived under the same roof and went out to dinner occasionally with friends, but on all other occasions, we were separate.

Yet, even knowing that, I was baffled when I found that iPhone under his car seat on that August day.

I never told Bitty and Harley the whole story. The day they found me and during the few days they stayed to get me and the house put back together, we didn't really talk about "it." Or "him."

I told them it was bad; it was over, and I needed a lawyer. But they didn't pry, and I didn't provide details. I'm sure they figured I would share eventually, and besides, they were balls deep in the immediate crisis of bringing me back to life.

Now, two weeks after they left in mid-September, I sit at the kitchen table, staring into my long-cold cup of coffee when I hear chaos in the front hall.

"God *damn it*," a deep male voice says, followed by thumping, banging, and crashing. "*Fuck*."

"Matty?" I call.

Silence. Then footsteps. Then a big, wide smiling face pops around the kitchen door frame.

"Hi, Mama," he says. "I had a little issue with my stuff in the hallway. The door was open, so I let myself in."

Jesus, I have got to focus on locking that damn door.

"Don't be mad, K," my oldest friend says, blasting me with his megawatt smile while at the same time giving me his meltiest eyes. "Come help me. I brought everything for an epic sesh. Just what Dr. M ordered."

Matty is, of course, Dr. M. His name is Matthew, but I have called him "Matty" since the day we met, and professionally he goes by Mateo. Even his mom has to call him "Mateo." But he does the hair of all her friends at the assisted living place, and they love him.

I know Chickie must've called him to let him know I was in a full-blown meltdown/life crisis.

I follow him into the hall. There are hair care products everywhere, and his big, roly-poly carrier thing is tipped over on its side. In the front doorway is another roly-poly thing, and on the porch is one of those dollies you see congressional interns haul through the Capitol hallways, laden with (in those cases) someone's tax returns and (in this case) what looks like everything you need for a real-deal pedicure. Soaking tub, towels, lots of tools, lots of polishes, lots of tubes and jars.

"Ta-da!" he says loudly and brightly, doing a little ball-chain shuffle thing with his feet. "Imma cure you of whatever ails you!"

And that is apparently what I needed to hear to open my floodgates.

Tears squirt from my eyes, and sobs heave from my chest.

He stares and opens his arms wide. "OK, Mama," he says. "First, we dehydrate. Then, we rebuild."

Twenty minutes and fifty tissues later, we are in the kitchen, and I am sitting on a stool as he brushes me out. "So …," he begins. "Do you want to …"

And I know it's time. It's time to tell the story. It's been like this boulder in my belly since that night, and it's been crushing my chest, squeezing my gut, and burning my eyes. And Matty is the one I need to hear it.

We met when we were four. Our moms were in a neighborhood playgroup. Well, my mom was, and then Matty's family moved in two houses down, and they showed up one Wednesday afternoon. There were eight to ten kids in the group, and it started at four in the afternoon, and the moms drank wine while we trashed whichever house we were in.

Matty took an immediate shine to me, maybe because I was on the quiet side, a little shy. I was more an observer than a participant. If there were toys, I could drag them to the perimeter of the madness; I would do that and quietly play while chaos reigned around me. He would join me.

Then we were in the same kindergarten class, and that sealed our fate as besties for life. He liked to play with dolls, and so did I. He liked to brush my hair, and I liked him to brush it. At some point, he nicknamed me "Mama." He never explained why. But only he and Chickie are allowed to call me that. Bitty and Harley have lifetime bans.

As we moved through elementary, junior, and then senior high school, he would braid my hair, cut my hair, perm my hair. He picked out all my clothes. In return, I would fight whoever tried to bully him. Literally fight. I got suspended twice.

Ride or die, Matty and me.

In the summer, we took Matty to the beach with us. I think it was a relief of sorts, for his mom, as his journey of self-discovery was, well, flamboyant and included many bad decisions that occasionally involved law enforcement. And having an eight-week break from his mother—as much as they loved and supported each other—was good for him as well.

Matty, Chickie, and I lived the dream at the beach during those childhood summers. And as teens, Chickie's father gave us jobs at Dockside. At night we would run amok, get drunk, fall in love over and over, and laugh our asses off. It was the late '70s, early '80s after all. Life was simple.

Chickie and I went to college, and Matty went to Los Angeles— where he became Mateo and started styling celebrities. A cocaine problem and a bad breakup brought him back to New England, and he landed in Boston, where he opened his own shop. He charged outrageous prices and catered to the elite. We stayed close, but as the years went by, our relationship morphed into mostly texts and calls. I can't remember when I last saw him in person. Other things got in the way.

"So …," he prompts. "Can we talk real quick about this hair before you tell me what that mother-fuckety fucker did?"

"I don't want to talk about my hair. I'd rather relive that night than have you run down everything that's wrong with my hair."

"KK. This hair."

"I know Matty. Trust me, I know. It's terrible. Do whatever you think needs to be done, short of shaving my head. I no longer have the cheekbones to support that."

"Oooo goody," he says, clapping his hands. "First, we color, and then we cut. Also, we are totally growing out these bangs. It was forty-five years ago that Aaron Greene called you 'Tennessee Tuxedo.' It's time to move past that. It's forehead time. And then I am giving you a facial because holy shit, Mama. Oh, and I brought wax, and I'm sure your toes are like talons."

"Are you sleeping over?" I ask.

"Oh honey, you know I am. Because after all this is done, we are getting drunk."

5

August 1972

You would think that by living at the beach in the summer, the laundry would be easy. Live in bathing suits, right? Well, yes, but also wrong. Living with an eleven-year-old, two nine-year-olds, and a seven-year-old at the beach results in tons of laundry. Every day. Tons.

First, consider the towels. Beach towels. How do kids destroy beach towels the way they do? How can they spend two hours at the beach and turn their towels into crusty, sandy, filthy piles of cotton? They are evil magicians.

Then there are the clothes. Outside all the time, they get just as dirty, crusty, and filthy as their beach towels. Sometimes there are three changes of outfits per day per child.

Then there are Margie's clothes. The ass of all her shorts is always dirty from sitting with the kids on the grass or the sand. She sweats through her blouses. Frequently. Ugh.

And yes, this equation includes *two* nine-year-olds because Margie somehow gets roped into bringing Matty with them to the house every single year. For the whole summer. When she first proposed this idea to his mother a few years back, she thought one, maybe two weeks tops. It would be fun, and the added diversion would help the kids get along better among themselves. But that first time, Matty's mom showed up on leaving day with two suitcases plus a box of food. "Treats for the kids as thanks for doing this," she explained as she dumped everything and practically ran back to her car. "See you at the end of August!" And a new tradition was born.

Sweet Matty. That little boy is a lot. Loud. Rambunctious. One might even say flamboyant. And the ideas he comes up with! The games he makes up for them, the way he has everyone lining up to do "fancy jumps" off the floating dock. "Mrs. R," he yells, "give us scores like they do in the 'Lympics!" And at night she can hear Matty and KK giggling in her room long after lights out, long after the last warning to be quiet. Not to mention the crazy hair styles he gives them, braids all over their heads or thirteen ponytails. So even though she's tired and spends a lot of time washing and folding mountains of his laundry on top of everyone else's, she doesn't begrudge him one minute of time with them. He is family.

As is Chickie, Margie thinks, as she looks out her second-floor bedroom window, watching as the four kids hike up the path. Chico Madeira's little girl, Chickie, is the same age as KK and Matty. They are peas in a pod, these three. Chickie never hesitates to accept any of Matty's challenges. Vote for them to be the Two Most Likely to Be in the ER This Summer.

Margie laughs as she watches her tribe walk up the hill. Chickie and Matty are playing some game where they are trying to hop on one foot the whole way. They keep tipping over and laughing. KK is clearly tired and not joining in, just watching with a smile and holding Harley's hand. And then there's Bitty, tall for her age and oh so skinny, following behind, carrying a tote bag in each hand. Her regal girl. The boss of this group. Always taking responsibility.

"I needed to run to the store." This is how I begin the story of that day, that August day. "I was planning to make chicken galantine, and I realized I forgot to get the tongue because I had to go to a different market to pick it up."

Matty makes a gagging noise. For all his high living, he's a burger-and-fries guy. But *he* always liked it when I made complicated fancy recipes, and so I would slave in the kitchen. For *him*.

"His car was blocking mine in the driveway, so I grabbed his keys. Halfway to the store, I reached for my car ChapStick." (Matty snickers, because I have staged a ChapStick for every location in my life—car, purse, nightstand, by the back door, beach bag, makeup bag, desk ...) "And that's when I remembered I wasn't in my car, so I dumped my purse on the seat to grab that ChapStick. And of course it rolled off the seat and disappeared. So when I got to the market, I parked and hopped out to look under the seat. I had my hand under there, rooting around, and all of a sudden, I found an iPhone.

"I pull it out. It's not his phone, because his phone is silver, and this one is black. Also, his phone is a 12, and this one is a 13. So I'm thinking, *Whose phone is this?* I throw it in my purse, and I go get the tongue and drive home.

"But I can't stop thinking about that phone. I don't say anything to him. I keep it in my purse, and I make dinner, and we eat, and he literally doesn't even comment on the fucking galantine. Then I go upstairs to read, and he stays downstairs, watching TV. And then I hear him go to bed."

"You hear him go to bed?" Matty tilts his head at me. He's busy painting color on my hair and wrapping sections in foil.

"Oh, yeah. Right. We hadn't been sleeping in the same bed for a while. He said my night sweats and insomnia were killing him."

"Sensitive," Matty says, flattening his lips together.

"Anyway, I wait a while, and when I think he's asleep, I go downstairs and get the phone out of my purse and go into his room. I click the side button and put the phone to his face."

"*Mama*!" Matty screeches, making me jump a mile and knock the little pot of color out of his hand. "What are you, Jason fucking Bourne? Using his face to get into the phone!"

"Yeah, I'm brilliant. Or really stupid. You can decide in a minute.

"So anyway, it opens up, and I go back into my room and shut the door. The phone has all these dating apps on it. I open one, and there he is. He's got a profile on Tinder. I open another. He's got a profile on Bumble. He's on eHarmony. He's on Match. He's on OurTime."

My hands are getting shaky. I grasp the edges of the stool to steady myself. "Breathe, Mama," Matty says.

I heave a big sigh and take in a bigger breath. "I open the Instagram app. It's not the account I know about. It's different. It's post after post of him … on dates. Fucking dates. With all different women. In all kinds of different places. It goes back about a year. Big, smiling selfies with happy ladies. Young ones. Older ones. Pretty ones. Everyone is having a great fucking time. In the most recent ones, there's about a dozen of them. It's all the same woman. They are clearly a couple."

"Fuuuuuuuuck," Matty whispers, pausing in his foil wrapping. He puts his hands on my shoulders.

"Yeah," I say, tears starting to roll down my face. "I open the texts, and it's him and this woman. Trish. He literally has her named Trish the Dish in his contacts. I feel like I'm going to puke, so I sit on the bathroom floor, and I read all the texts. They're a couple. They're in love. They're making plans. She knows he's married. She knows about me. She knows my name. She makes fun of me. He makes fun of me.

"He is waiting to leave me because he wants his 'last summer' at the beach. She's 'trying to be patient' because he can't see her while he's here, but he begs her to hang on because he wants to 'wring everything out' of his last time here in this house he 'loves so much.' He loves the house so much. The house. My house.

"I'm on the bathroom floor and my whole body is shaking. Like I have a fever, you know? Looking back, I kind of feel like that night was a fever dream. Parts in slow motion and parts all speeded up and jumpy. I'm jumpy. I don't know what to do. I don't even think I'm hurt. I think I'm mad. Mostly because he's so focused on this house. He literally listed stuff he was going to take with him when he left. *Steal.* He was going to steal stuff from my family's house. My family's *home.*"

I am wracked with a sob, and I run out of breath. Matty puts his hands on my upper arms and helps me stand up. He leads me to the sink, tips my head down into the basin, and starts peeling the foil off the strips of my hair. He runs the water, and when it's warm, he begins rinsing and massaging. He's silent. I'm silent. What is there to say?

Then: "Do you want to hear what I think?" he asks quietly.

"Not yet," I reply. "Just take care of me for a while, and then, after I'm drunk, you can tell me."

He does the color. He does the cut. He gives me a facial, dermaplaning, a clay mask, salmon DNA serum. I don't even know what else, I swear he makes up names for stuff. He waxes me. He tints my lashes and my brows. He's taking clothes off me and putting clothes back on me. I sit on a chair in the living room, and he soaks my feet and gives me a pedicure. He paints my toes. As they dry, he goes out to his car and returns with a Yeti cooler. He unpacks it on the living room floor, and the next thing I know, there's a fresh margarita in my hands, salted rim and all.

We adjourn to the back porch. It will be dark soon. Down the hill in the distance, we can see surfers bobbing on the water. He wraps me in a fleece and plops down next to me.

"Before I tell you what I think, I want to know what *you* think," he says.

"What more is there to say? I told you everything."

"No, Mama. You told me what happened. You told me the facts of the case. I want to know what you think about all of it. I mean, obviously you threw him out. That happened. Your marriage, your relationship ended. Facts. Now tell me about your feelings."

I blow out all the air in my lungs. What do I think? I haven't really thought about what I think. I mean, I'm hurt, right? My thirty-year relationship ended. Badly. Messily. Suddenly.

"You mean, like, do I think it was my fault? Of course, I think it was my fault. I've let myself look and feel like shit for the last six years. Was that fair to him? No. Of course not. I gave up on everything, and then he gave up on me."

Matty tips his glass back, emptying it into his mouth. "Drink up, Mama," he says. So I throw mine back too, and he fills us back up. Without a word, we both chug those, and he makes two more. We sit in silence until about half the bottle of tequila is gone. We move from sitting on the porch furniture to lying on the porch floor, making a nest with all the pillows and blankets.

"It wasn't your fault," he says, tilting his head toward me. I look over, and I might be seeing one and a half of him. "You aged. He aged. Your relationship needed to change as you both did, but neither of you was willing to make the effort. You fell out of rhythm with each other, and you were both too lazy to try to get it back."

"Ouch," I say to him, hitting his arm with my again-empty glass. He fills me up. We abandoned the salt early on.

"I hate my fifties," I tell him before I take a sip. "I think back to my thirties and my forties and how great they were. I loved that time. I felt confident. I felt good. I felt like I had everything under control.

Then *bam*—nothing is under control. In fact, everything is so out of control that I feel like everyone is looking at me like I'm crazy. And no one will help me. They all just nod sympathetically and encourage me to ride it out.

"Everything used to feel so effortless. Now it's like everything is so—I don't know—effortful?"

"Effortful. I don't think that's a word," Matty mutters. His eyes might be trying to close.

"How about exhausting? That's a word," I say. "Every single fucking thing in my life exhausts me. Including staying happy in my relationship, staying happy in my marriage, staying interested in anything. When I found out what he had been doing, I thought, *Cool. Now I can just finish becoming invisible. It will be so much easier than all this bullshit.*"

I hear nothing. I look over at my oldest, dearest, sweetest friend who showed up today and ripped off my cocoon for me, showing me his love language of caring for the outside of me in the hopes that it will heal the inside of me. He's asleep.

July 1977

The Fourth is so fun. Parade, food, fireworks. And the adults are so hammered that no one ever tells the kids to go to bed. Or brush their teeth. Or be quiet.

Anyone who wants to march in the parade can, and KK, Matty, and Chickie spend days decorating the Radio Flyer wagon they use to haul gear to and from the beach. They let Harley "help," but mostly he annoys them; and when he gets bored and wanders away, they remove whatever additions he has made and replace them with their own.

The wagon is draped in flags and covered in glitter paper and red, white, and blue streamers and pinwheels designed to spin as they move. A massive amount of duct tape has been put to use. The kids have matching shorts and shirts in patriotic colors. They will throw candy to the spectators.

Matty of course has added several boas to his look, and he joins the girls when they paint their nails red, white, and blue as well. All three have patriotic tiaras. It will be so grand.

The morning of the holiday dawns hot and sunny without a cloud in the sky. The kids are old enough to go to the parade by themselves—Harley included, as long as they promise not to lose him. Bitty announces she is staying home this year, that she is "too mature" for such childish endeavors. But she watches them from the front porch as they head out, a frown on her face.

When they get to town about fifteen minutes later, everyone is milling around the square, waiting for the grand marshal's red convertible to start the festivities. The grand marshal is always some old person who sits in the back of the car and waves. This year it is a lady, and she is wearing a hat the size of Rhode Island.

The four kids skirt the edges of the crowd, looking for a clear path to where the parade will start so they can take their places in line. Chickie is pulling the wagon, Matty is next to her, and KK and Harley are two steps behind. KK is firmly holding Harley by his shirt.

Suddenly, there are five big boys in front of them. "Hey, fairy," says the biggest one, a redhead named Travis. His brother is a lifeguard at the beach. Travis isn't smart enough to be a lifeguard. He's barely smart enough to be alive. He's twelve, but he's still in the fifth grade. He pokes Matty in the chest and then slaps his tiara off his head.

Chickie halts the wagon. Matty bends to pick up his tiara, and Harley moves closer to KK, putting his thumb in his mouth, even though he's eight and not supposed to do that anymore.

As Matty reaches for his tiara, one of the other boys grabs a handful of the boas that hang around Matty's neck and yanks hard. Matty loses his balance and falls onto the sidewalk. He raises his face to look at the boys, who are now pressing in around him, cutting Matty's friends out of the circle.

KK puts her hands firmly on Harley's shoulders. "Stand on the other side of the wagon, near Chickie," she tells him. He does as he's told. Seeing him where she wants him, she turns back to the circle of bullies. Their backs are to her. They are all focused on Matty, who sits silently on the ground.

Taking two big steps, KK plants her feet and shoves the boy in front of her, using all her strength. Because he's focused on Matty, he is caught off guard and off balance. He goes flying headfirst across their small human circle, crashing into the boy across from him. They both fall. *Two down*, KK thinks. *Three to go.*

Matty turns to her, surprise on his face. He realizes he has an opening and scrambles quickly away on his hands and knees, rising only once he is on the other side of the wagon with Harley. Harley takes Matty's hand.

The three remaining boys are startled, and KK wastes no time. She pulls her right arm back and swings wide with all her might, closing her open palm into a fist seconds before she makes contact with the closest boy's neck. She wanted to hit him in the face, but she's not tall enough. Instead, she clotheslines him, and he staggers back, choking.

"What the fuck," Travis mutters, watching as three of his friends are taken out and the fourth one quickly retreats, distancing himself from whatever trouble might unfold.

KK turns her attention to Travis just as he turns his attention to her.

"Stupid little bitch has to protect her faggot friend, huh?" he says, stepping toward her.

KK tips her chin up and glares. She doesn't move, seemingly daring him to come at her.

He takes two more steps toward her, smiling. "I guess I will teach a bunch of lessons today," he says, clenching his hands into fists.

And that's when Chickie hits him from behind with the baseball bat. Takes him out at the knees. He drops like a stone to the bottom of a lake.

A couple of adults have noticed there's something happening among this group of kids, so Chickie tosses the bat into the wagon and starts to haul it toward the parade's starting point. KK grabs Matty's hand and pulls him along, and he in turn pulls Harley. When they think they are a safe enough distance away, they stop.

KK bends at the waist and puts her hands on her knees. Her heart is still pounding. "Jeez, Chickie, a bat? Where'd you get a bat?"

"I always throw it in the wagon when we go to the beach," Chickie says. "My dad keeps one behind the bar at Dockside, and he says you never know when you'll need it. It's always good to be prepared."

KK starts laughing as Matty comes up to her and Chickie and puts his arms around them both. "Thank you," he says, his eyes filling with tears.

"No crying," KK and Chickie say simultaneously. Chickie adds, "And no need to thank us. You'd do the same."

"Well, I'd probably get the shit kicked out of me before I could save you, but the thought would definitely be there," Matty says, his sob turning into a laugh. They hug for a minute and then step apart.

"Come on," KK says. "Let's get in line. And Haw," she says, looking sternly at her little brother, "not a word of this to Mom or Daddy."

My ears are ringing. Or maybe the angels are calling me to heaven. Either way I want it to stop. My head is killing me.

I try to open my eyes, but they seem to have been glued shut by tequila. Next to me, Matty is thrashing his arm around in a vain attempt to stop that fucking ringing.

Matty's phone is under me, vibrating and trilling. I pull it out and shove it at him, and he swipes to see Chickie's scowl.

"You two motherfuckers aren't dead," she says.

"I wish we were," Matty mumbles, putting his head on my shoulder so I can see Chickie on the screen as well. Based on how bad his breath is, mine must be deadly.

"Well, you were pretty entertaining last night," she says. "Check your videos. I got a *lot* of texts."

Oh God. I find my phone under my pillow and swipe over to my photos, then tap videos. There are eleven new ones, ranging from six seconds to over three minutes. I click one in the middle of the bunch.

"*Desperately Seeking Susan* is the greatest film ever made," Matty is screaming.

Next to him, I'm laughing and saying over and over, "Spa king. Hello? Spa king of New Jersey!"

I click to another one. We are singing "Crazy for You" by Madonna. Clearly, we went down the Madonna rabbit hole after Matty woke up from his little margarita-induced nap.

We look back at Chickie on his phone. "Sorry, babe," I say. "If it helps, we would love you to come over here and kill us right now."

"I'll do you one better than that," she says. "I'll go get you guys McDonald's Diet Cokes. See you in twenty."

When she arrives, we guzzle the giant sodas as if they are filled with the nectar of life. Which, if we're being honest, is exactly what a McDonald's fountain Diet Coke is. Lifesaving.

"Did we solve everything?' she asks.

"Uh, maybe?" Matty says. "I'm having a little trouble remembering."

Chickie starts to say something, but then she sees the perfect pyramid of spent half limes we carefully constructed on the kitchen island last night, and she laughs so hard she crumples to her knees. We drop down next to her, and we all hug each other hard and long, and if I'm being honest, I do feel better. Lighter. Able to breathe.

Did we solve everything? Nope. Did we solve anything? Probably not. Does everything feel effortless? Hell no. Do I feel seen and loved? Absolutely. And that's what I needed the most.

6

CHICKIE. Sup?

CHICKIE. Mama, you there?

CHICKIE. KK, what are you doing right now?

ME. Sitting with sorrow.

My phone trills. It says, "Chickie FaceTime Video." I decline. It trills again. I decline.

CHICKIE. Answer your goddamn phone, K.

ME. I'm fine Chickie. Just leave me be.

The phone trills again. *Shit.* I answer it because if I don't, she will drive over here.

Her face fills my phone screen. "Mama, what's going on?" she asks, her worried eyes scanning my face. "Where are you sitting?"

"On the porch," I say, tilting the phone down so she can see me on the wicker loveseat, wrapped in fleece blankets. By this time in October, the ocean breeze is definitely leaning toward cold.

"Why? What's going on? Wait. Do you have Sam Smith playing? Are you crying?"

"Yes. He's my spiritual adviser. And yes." I pause. I check out my face in the little box at the bottom of my screen. I look like shit. Blotchy. Snotty nosed. Dark circles under my eyes.

"Papers came today. By courier. It's done," I explain. The world's fastest end to a thirty-year relationship.

She blows out air. "Come to happy hour."

"Ha. No thanks. Just going to wallow. I need to. I just need to be really sad for a bit. I'm having a kind of a wake here." I flip the camera and show her the bottle of wine, already half gone, and the slab of cheese on the table in front of me.

"Are you drinking from the bottle and just biting off chunks of that cheese?" she asks.

I flip the camera back to me and nod. Fresh tears roll down my face.

"OK, Mama, I am giving you today. But tomorrow you are coming to happy hour, four p.m. sharp. Don't make me come get you."

"OK, Chickie. I will. I promise. I just need today."

"I love you, KK. You are *loved*. By so many people. You fill hearts. You bring joy. *You. Are. Loved.*"

I give her whatever version of a smile I can muster in this moment, a slight nod, and I click off.

I just need today.

June 1992

"Hey, little buddy! What's your name?"

The tall young man dressed in white shorts and a blue short-sleeved pullover crouches down so he can be eye to eye with the four-year-old standing before him. The little boy holds a tennis racket in his two hands. He doesn't reply.

The tennis pro looks up at the young woman standing with the boy. "His name is Jason," she replies in a vaguely European accent.

There are no more Jamaican nannies. Ted Wells discovers as his boy begins to talk that the child has a decidedly Caribbean lilt to his voice, and that is that. In their stead is an au pair, last name Gundersen, first name no one cares to remember. Jason calls her "Gunny."

The little boy reaches up for the nanny's hand. Once she takes it, he feels brave enough to look the tennis pro in the eye and smile shyly.

"Jason, huh?" the pro says cheerfully. "Well, I'm gonna call you my little 'Jay Man.' How does that sound? Good? You ready to learn some tennis today? We are going to have fun, my friend."

The pro straightens and smiles at the nanny. "My name is Jack," he says, holding out his hand. "It's nice to meet you. I guess we'll be spending a lot of time together, since I see Jay Man is scheduled for a lesson every morning."

The nanny smiles. "I am Freyja," she says, shaking his hand.

Jason looks up at her. "Gunny," he says firmly.

The tennis pro looks at her questioningly. She gives a little laugh. "He calls me 'Gunny,'" she says. "My last name is Gundersen."

"Ah," Jack says. "Gunny. I like it. Good thinking, Jay Man. She looks like a Gunny, doesn't she?" Jack holds out his hand to Jason. "Come on, buddy. Let's go play some Jailbreak. Work up a sweat." He points to benches under a tree at the side of the court. "You can wait there in the shade," he says. "Unless you have somewhere else to be during his lesson."

"No." She smiles at him. "I have nowhere else to be. My job is to be where he is."

"Cool," Jack says, giving her the once-over. She's dressed in pressed khaki Bermuda shorts, sneakers, and a short-sleeved blouse. Her long blonde hair is pulled back in a ponytail. Both she and the little boy smell like sunscreen.

Gunny bends down to Jason. "You go with Jack for your lesson," she says. "Afterwards we will get some lunch. I have water if you get thirsty. Have fun." She pats him on the butt and rises. "Have fun," she says to Jack as she begins to walk toward the bench. She gives him a wink.

"Oh we will," he says. "No worries there."

True to my word, I walk into Dockside at four the next afternoon. I can't help but laugh when I see a glass of white wine, a glass of ice water, and a glass of ice cubes at my usual spot over by the windows at the end of the bar. There's also a set of cutlery rolled into a cloth napkin, a small plate, and a scrap of folded paper that says "Reserved, Assholes" in Chickie's distinctive scrawl.

I put my purse straps over the back of the stool and pull out my book. The same book because my purse book takes a while to get through since I read it only when I'm out and about and need a distraction. I flip open to my bookmark, take a pull of wine, and lean back in the chair, eyes on the page. Tunnel vision activated.

"Hey there," a low, soft voice says. I look up into those pale blue eyes. The werewolf eyes. *Shit. It's Surfer Guy.*

"I'm Jay," he says, smiling. "Do you need anything else right now? Want to order some food?"

I'm mute. I've literally lost the ability to form words. I take another big drink of wine.

He looks at me for another couple of beats, then knocks his knuckles on the bar twice. "OK, just let me know," he says as he turns to walk away. The old townies are up around the corner of the big mahogany bar, and their drinks already need replenishing.

Surfer Guy comes back about twenty minutes later. I've spent that time prepping myself. I will speak.

"Flatbread? Hummus plate?" he asks. "Another pinot grigio?"

"I'm good," I say. "Thanks." He starts to turn.

"Where's Susie?" I ask.

He spins back to me and places both hands on the bar, one on each side of my place setting. Big hands. *Whew.* Long fingers. *Hmm.*

"Baby," he says. "She had her baby. In fact, her water broke right here last night. Lots of excitement. Lots of, uh, water."

"Oh, that's great," I say. "Boy or girl?"

"Boy," he says, taking a minute to rearrange my glassware in front of me. He switches the ice water with the wine and then picks up the glass of ice and chucks the half-melted cubes into the sink. He fills it with fresh ice and puts it back down. "That's why Chickie isn't here. She went over to Susie's place to get things ready for them when they go home tomorrow."

I stare at him. "Chickie's not here?"

"No, she won't be in till later. But she told me all about your setup. I hope I got it right."

For some reason the thought that Chickie isn't at Dockside throws me for a massive loop. I can feel panic starting in my throat. I have to go.

"Can I have the check?" I manage to squeak out.

Those blue eyes narrow. "Everything OK?" he says.

"Fine. I just need to go," I reply. Without waiting, I grab a twenty from my wallet and toss it on the bar. I stuff my book in my purse and throw the strap over my shoulder. I spin the stool and hop off. Without another word, I head out the door. I can't get home fast enough.

ME. I panicked.

CHICKIE. I heard.

ME. Shit really? What did you hear? Was it from Surfer Guy?

CHICKIE. Surfer Guy?

ME. Your bartender. He surfs. At the association beach. I've seen him.

CHICKIE. Really? Hmm. Yes. Jay said he mentioned I wasn't there and that you threw twenty bucks on the bar for a four-dollar tab and ran.

ME. Your happy hour prices really are the best.

CHICKIE. Don't divert. What happened? Sometimes even when I'm there I don't actually see you.

ME. I don't know. The mere thought of your presence is anchoring for me.

CHICKIE. I'm not sure if you've had too much therapy or not enough. Come back this afternoon. I'll be in the kitchen.

CHICKIE. Jay was asking about you.

I stare at my phone.

ME. I'll be there at four. I like my reserved sign.

July 1976

The Fourth this year is utter chaos, what with it being the bicentennial and all. The Cape is insane although not nearly as bad as Plymouth. Tourists pour into that town, which is off the Cape, to visit the *Mayflower* and celebrate the dawn of America as well as its two hundredth birthday.

Margie is exhausted. Which is why she tried to convince Rod that he should not bring his mother down for her "annual two weeks" the weekend after the holiday. She needed to catch her breath. And not having her own mother with her at the beach—Kay died two years earlier—made it all exponentially harder.

But there is no deterring Rod or his mother for that matter.

So he brought her with him when he arrived that Friday, and he left her behind when he drove off Sunday evening. He gave Margie an extra kiss before getting into the car. He knew she was miserable with his mother there. Apparently, that wasn't enough to make him stay or take the old bat back with him but still. She slightly appreciated him acknowledging her pain.

So here she is, sitting at the breakfast table in her dress and pearls and sensible shoes, waiting for her coffee and soft-boiled eggs with toast. Like Margie is running a goddamn bed-and-breakfast instead of living in her own home.

As a monster-in-law, Kristina's glare/scowl combo cannot be beat.

"Good morning," Margie says pleasantly, plastering a smile on her face. "I'll get everything going."

It is seven thirty. The kids are also wiped out from all the festivities, so Margie doesn't expect to see anyone soon except …

She hears the slap of little bare feet on the linoleum and turns to see a tousled and grumpy Harley walk into the kitchen. "Morning, Haw," she says to him, her smile turning genuine. He always wakes up slowly. And slightly annoyed. He'd been that way since birth.

"Harley," Kristina says firmly, "come give your grandmother a kiss."

Margie knows that is the last thing this five-year-old wants to do right now, but she also knows intervening will be futile. So she turns back to the stove and puts the eggs on to boil, setting the timer. They must be *soft*. She turns on the burner under the percolator as well. Coffee can't come soon enough.

Harley pauses briefly and glances at his mother, but he gives up the fight before he even starts it. He slouches over to the old lady and stands as limply as he can while remaining upright. She grabs him by his skinny shoulders and pulls him in, smothering him in her ample breast. Then she releases him. He stumbles backward.

Margie fights a laugh. She catches his eye, points to the family room, and whispers, "Cartoons." He disappears.

"Would you like to do anything special today?" Margie asks her mother-in-law.

Kristina has never liked her. She thinks Rod "married down" when he tied the knot with Margie. This always grated on Margie's mother, Kay, because it was their family who descended from sea captains, for God's sake, men who built and sailed ships across oceans, who lived in mansions overlooking the sea, who were respected and revered in their community. They have roots going back generations.

Rod's grandparents came over from Europe and were given a random name when they entered Ellis Island. His grandfather and father had a dental supply business in Worcester. I mean, they did OK, but it was nothing great. They weren't rich. Rod is handsome, has a good job, and treats Margie well, but he's no … catch. She's the catch.

"What is there to do?" Kristina asks.

"Well, the kids will want to go to the beach, but we could head downtown and browse the shops if you'd like. Maybe grab some lunch?"

Kristina sighs. "I came here to visit with my grandchildren."

Margie sighs. "Well, yes, but you hate the beach."

"I don't hate the beach."

The timer dings, and Margie grips the slotted spoon a little too tightly to pull the eggs out of the boiling water. She places each one in an adorable, little china egg cup; butters the white toast, which has popped from the toaster; and carries the plate over to her mother-in-law.

"Would you like to go to the beach with the kids? I can drive you down. They always walk, but I can drive you."

Kristina peers out the window. "It might be too hot."

"I have an umbrella."

"OK, fine then. I will go to the beach with the children."

Margie pours a cup of coffee from the pot on the stove and brings it to Kristina. She smiles and says, "Perfect!" But Margie knows Kristina will last about thirty minutes on the sand, even under an umbrella, and then she will begin complaining. The complaining will morph into criticizing, and that will morph into outright character assassination. And then Margie will load the old bat back into the car and drive her back to the house, and then they will go downtown, browse the stores, and grab some lunch.

She better go up and wake Matty and KK. Time to get the show on the road.

When I get to Dockside at 4 and get situated, it turns out my other anchor—my book—isn't in my purse. I feel the panic rising, but I also feel Chickie's energy emanating from the kitchen. I can do this. I can have a drink without my book. Without my tunnel vision. I gulp the wine and add some ice cubes to the glass.

"Food tonight?" that low voice asks quietly as those big hands appear on the bar in front of me.

I look up. *Fuck, those eyes. Seriously. Those hands are distracting. How is he real?* His hair is amazing too. It's long on the top and sort of swooshed back and then thick and curly down to the nape of his neck. Dark brown. Almost black. Made to have hands tangled in it.

Wait. What?

"Maybe in a bit," I say, reaching into my glass of ice for more cubes, hoping that will keep my face from bursting into flames.

"Where's your book?" he asks, grabbing the now-empty highball glass and scooping in more ice.

I wave my hands around vaguely. "I forgot it, I guess."

He smiles and walks away. I look down and realize I am gripping the edge of the bar so hard my fingernails are white. Am I having fun yet? Why am I doing this to myself? I itch to text Chickie.

A minute later, a copy of my book is placed carefully on the plate in front of me. It has a bookmark in it from the local indie store. I look up. Surfer Guy shrugs.

"I saw you reading it and decided to check it out," he says. "It's pretty good. There's some hot stuff in there."

Ignoring the urge to simply dump my glass of ice down the front of my shirt, I pick up the book and open it, searching for where I left off. "I think I'll have the hummus plate," I say.

He knocks his knuckles on the bar twice and turns away. "Coming right up," he says, looking over his shoulder at me.

Did we just become best friends?

7

Do I have a routine or a pattern? Which one is considered healthy?

Over the next few days, either my healthy routine or my unhealthy pattern emerges. I walk down to the beach and watch the surfers from a distance. Then I walk into the village and grab a latte at Beechwood Café, the only year-round coffee shop. Back at the house, I burn something that belonged to him, putter around, shower, put on actual pants, and at four I go to Dockside.

One big reason why I can function semi-successfully in the outside world is that after his visit, Matty got me a prescription for a low-dose estrogen patch from one of his Boston clients who is a doctor. After I was done being angry that none of my own medical professionals had offered up this potential salvation, I started wearing them. Within two weeks I felt significantly better.

Surfer Guy is always "my" bartender. Chickie hasn't found a replacement for Susie and is having waitstaff hop behind the bar if it gets busy, which it never really does because it's late October and we are a beach town.

At this stage in our relationship (dear God, I know I don't actually have a relationship with this beautiful man. He's probably half my age, and we don't even call each other by name), we make whatever conversation is a little deeper than small talk. I'm not sharing how my life blew up, and he's not sharing why he works as a winter bartender in a summertime town. We talk about Netflix and spicy romance novels and what time high tide is.

It's nice. He makes me smile. I think my blushing is at a minimum.

On this day, when I arrive at four, there's a man sitting on the stool next to my reserved space. Really? There are twenty-four seats at this long L-shaped stretch of varnished mahogany. There are only three other people seated sporadically down its length. Lots of options. And yet here he is, next to me.

I take my seat and hang my purse strap over the back.

"Well, hello," the man says. Maybe he's my age? He's got grayish, thinning hair, the last remnants of a summer tan, and small hands. He's got a martini in front of him, nearly full, so he hasn't been here long.

"I was wondering who the celebrity was," he says, "who gets special reserved seating and already has three drinks waiting."

I give him a small smile and start to reach into my purse for my book. Surfer Guy appears and engages his signature move, hands on both sides of my place setting, leaning his face over the bar toward me. Except I notice that the hand on the side of Mr. Chatty Martini is moved closer to that guy than to me. Like my bartender is staking out space.

"How about a flatbread tonight," Surfer Guy says.

"Maybe in a bit," I say.

"Put her drink on my tab," Chatty Martini says.

Surfer Guy knocks twice on the bar and walks away. I open my book, and Chatty Martini opens his mouth. Yada yada yada—I'm not listening. I've had years of experience tuning out men my age. Gold medalist.

He's still talking, and I'm still reading when a flatbread appears. Surfer Guy places the plate to the side of my place setting, pretty close to directly in front of Chatty Martini. His (big) hand then grasps the stem of the man's martini glass and slides it down a whole space, stopping when it's in front of the next empty stool.

I am sitting very still, watching what's happening through my eyelashes as I pretend to keep reading.

"Just making some space here," Surfer Guy says to Chatty Martini with a big smile. "You know, like, breathing room? So she can eat in peace? I appreciate you."

I may have stopped breathing. There's a loud banging in my ears, which may or may not be my heart frantically pumping blood to my brain so I don't pass out.

Chatty Martini sucks in a loud breath and slides his butt over to the next stool. He takes a long pull on his drink. Surfer Guy knocks twice on the varnished wood and heads down the bar to take an order.

As soon as he's gone, Chatty Martini leans over to me and says in a low voice, "That's really nice."

Thinking he's admiring my flatbread, which is topped with fresh tomatoes and caramelized onions and really is a thing of beauty, I look toward him with raised eyebrows.

"Your son. It's really nice that he looks out for you while you have dinner at the bar. You know, keep you safe from getting hit on. He's been keeping an eye on you the whole time."

My brain truly must be deprived of oxygen because I swear to God I thought he said, "My son." *My son.* My motherfucking *son?*

I raise my eyebrows even farther. "Son?" I croak.

"It's really nice," he says again. "He's a good son." He sits back up in his new seat and sips more of his cocktail. He pops one of his olives into his mouth.

My eyes sting. My nose stings. The roar in my ears is so loud. It's like there's a train in my head. There's a burning in my chest. I fumble with my wallet and drop my credit card on the bar because I seem to be out of cash. I push my stool back. At the loud scraping sound, Surfer Guy turns his head toward me. He's way down at the other end, chatting with one of the old townies.

I make one second of eye contact with him, and then I'm gone.

Ｙ

August 2006

Jay zips the last duffel closed and surveys his bedroom. There are plastic milk crates full of books and toiletries, a massive bag with all his lacrosse gear, and some trash bags filled with sheets, towels, and blankets.

Like everything else in his family life, Jay pulls it all together himself. Why should this be any different? He's been asking his parents for years to call him Jay, but they refuse. He is Jason to them.

He's leaving from the Manhattan apartment, but his mother is still on Long Island. He assumes his father is at his office in the city, but Ted Wells hasn't spoken to his son or even acknowledged his existence since the day Jay broke the news that he was going to Bates College.

"No, you're going to Harvard," Ted said, pushing back his chair from the dining room table and standing.

"That's where most US senators went to college," his mother chimed in. This wasn't even really true, but Irene was going to believe what Irene was going to believe.

Jay figured this wasn't his final 'fuck you' to his parents, but it might end up being the biggest. When he chose lacrosse over tennis in middle school, when he worked at the Long Beach surf school on Long Island in the summer instead of as a tennis instructor at the club, when he opted for the mail room during his internship with his father's company—those were all decent "fuck yous."

But secretly applying to Bates College in Lewiston, Maine, under early decision—whew, that was mammoth. Like, all capital letters level. Like, F-U-C-K Y-O-U. And then accepting the acceptance? And using his own money from his supersecret checking account to pay the admission fee? DEFCON 1, definitely.

"No, Ted, I'm going to Bates. And I'm going to play lacrosse," Jay replied, also pushing back his chair and rising to his feet. Irene remained seated, but she gulped from her wine goblet. Drained it, in fact.

Jay wasn't sure if he had been hoping for a fight, but as usual, he didn't get one. His father turned and left the room. That was back in April.

Ted hasn't said a word to him since. Not that Jay has seen much of his father, but still. The man's grudge-holding ability is world champion level. Aspirational.

That leaves Irene to do all the chirping, and, good Lord, that is endless. The litany of disappointments Jay has visited on his parents since his birth. Over and over again. He likes to think he is immune to it, that he tunes it right out, but in the deepest recesses of his heart, it hurts. He's still a kid, for God's sake.

Whatever. Jay shakes his head and takes a long look around his childhood bedroom, full of tennis, surfing, and lacrosse trophies. Medals hang from hooks. Jerseys from past teams. Photos of a smiling Jay with teammates or by himself with a championship cup in his hands. Nothing of Jay with his parents. Just teammates.

Carl took all the photos. Years ago, he pulled out a little camera from his navy sport coat pocket and offered to take a photo of Jay on the winner's riser, and he has done it ever since.

Carl is Jay's driver. He takes him to all his surfing competitions, his tennis matches, and his lacrosse games. When tournaments are out of town, Carl sleeps in the car because Ted never offers to put him up in the hotel where the kids are staying, and Carl can't afford it on his own. He tells Jay it's fine; he's slept in lots of worse places.

He is Jay's biggest fan. His only fan, really. Maybe his only family. Carl hypes him in advance, comforts him after losses, celebrates his wins with visits to the Wendy's drive-through. He can talk about the skill levels and abilities of Jay and his teammates, and he knows the strengths and weaknesses of the opposing teams. He makes sure Jay has sunscreen and water and Subway sandwiches at the surfing competitions. He even took him to the store to get a new wet suit when he outgrew the old one.

Today, Carl will drive Jay to Maine, help him unload the car, get him set up in his dorm, and then make the long drive back to New York. Jay hopes Carl isn't going to lose his job with the family now that he is off to college. But with Ted, you never know. There are no feelings behind Ted's decisions. Just economics.

I'm on the couch. My arm is over my eyes, which are closed. Nothing is stinging anymore; there's no more roaring train noise. The flames inside my chest have gone out. It's dark out, and there are no lights on in the house. The dark is your friend. It doesn't judge you. It helps you hide.

I feel like this piece of furniture has become my place of penance. I've yet to figure out why I keep getting punished by God or the universe or whatever the fuck is in charge. Punished for aging ungracefully?

For trying to find a new normal? For hating what's happened to my body? For feeling invisible for so long?

I wonder how long it will take Bitty and Harley to find me this time.

I hear a soft knock. That was quick. Their K-dar must be on high.

"Hello?" Deep voice. Well, more like low. Little gravelly. Not Harley. Sure as hell not Bitty.

"Katherine?"

Hmm. Literally no one calls me "Katherine." Are there still door-to-door salesmen? Seems late for sales but maybe.

The hallway floor squeaks. Maybe I'm about to be murdered. Would that really be so bad?

"Katherine?"

I sit up, reach over to the side table, and turn on the lamp. And then I really sit up. Like super straight.

Surfer Guy is in my house. Tomorrow I am spending quality time teaching myself how to close and lock my fucking front door.

"Oh hey," he says. "Hi. There you are. The door was open."

"No one calls me that," I say.

"Sorry?"

"Katherine. No one calls me Katherine. Everyone calls me 'KK.'"

"Oh," he says, looking down at something in his hand. "It says Katherine on your credit card. I've heard Chickie call you 'KK,' but I've also heard her call you 'Mama,' so I wasn't sure which name was right. Figured Katherine was safest."

I don't say anything else. I just sit there, staring at him like a goddamn idiot. Then I lie back down and cover my eyes with my arm again. "You can just leave it on the table," I say. "Thanks. Chickie can sign my name to the bill. Give yourself a great tip."

I hear him walk over to me, and then I hear the coffee table creak. I peek under my arm. He's sitting on the coffee table, leaning his elbows on his knees, facing me. He's tapping the credit card on his palm.

"Are you OK?" he asks quietly.

"I'm fine," I whisper, because isn't that what we are trained our whole lives to say? We're fine. I'm fine. Everything's fine.

But then a traitorous tear rolls out the side of my eye and down my face and lands on the couch cushion.

"I don't believe you," he says. "Tell me what happened. What did that asshole say to you? I threw him out."

I sit back up. "You threw him out? Why?"

"Well, because he obviously did something that upset you," Surfer Guy says. "He kept insisting the two of you were just talking, but I know something happened. I saw your face. So I tossed him and told him never to come back."

I cover my face with my hands. If I weren't already the most mortified I've ever been, I would be the most mortified I've ever been.

"All he did was provide me with a reality check. Which I obviously needed."

He looks at me with a furrowed brow, waiting for an explanation.

"He congratulated me on having such a good son, who looks out for me while I have dinner at the bar. He thought you were my son. And it made me understand that I was being foolish, that I was embarrassing myself by sitting there every night, chatting with you. That I was maybe even flirting with you a little, and you're clearly so much younger than me, and you were just humoring me and being nice and watching out for me. And I'm pathetic and stupid. I put on mascara for God's sake. I'm stupid. I'm pathetic.

"Thank you for bringing me my credit card. I'm sorry for all this embarrassment."

He just sits there, looking at me with those piercing eyes. Then he runs a hand through his hair and blows out a huge breath. "I was flirting with you too."

8

I'm starting to think I need to have a doctor check out this ear-roaring thing. Maybe I'm having a stroke. I pause for a second to see if I smell toast.

"I like you," he says, leaning forward so that his face is directly in front of mine. His knees widen as he moves his whole body closer. My eyes widen. The roaring in my ears sounds like Niagara Falls.

I break my gaze from his and look down. His thumb and fingers grasp my chin and force my face back up to his.

"I do," he says. "I like you. I've been flirting with you. I can't help it."

I have no idea what to do. He's making me look at him, he's making me blush, he's making my brain overload, he's making … wait, hold on, let me … yep, he's making me wet.

"Why?" I manage to squeak out.

He lets go of my chin and shrugs. "Honestly, I don't know. There's something about you, something I want to find. Chickie has a photo of you and her pinned on the wall by her desk. I can't stop looking at it. I want to find that woman in that photo. I want to get to know her."

I know the picture he's talking about. It was taken on Block Island, where we went to celebrate our thirty-fifth birthdays. We're on the deck of the National Hotel, and every inch of space on the table in front of us is covered with beer bottles, cocktail glasses, shot glasses, dirty napkins, and dirty plates. It's nearing sunset, so the light on our faces is rosy gold. Chickie's arm is around my shoulders, and her head is thrown back, her face pointing straight up. She's wide-mouth laughing.

I'm leaning slightly forward, turned toward her, and I'm smiling the biggest smile—so many teeth showing, my lips parted as I try to catch my breath. Matty took the photo, and for twenty years we have tried to recall what exactly was so funny. We were all so drunk, utterly and completely shitfaced, that we just can't remember. Chickie and I are tanned and gorgeous. So happy and full of life. I have the same photo framed on my dresser upstairs. I, too, would like to find that woman.

"How old are you?" I blurt out.

He sits back a little and says, "Thirty-four."

So the good news is, he's older than I thought. The bad news is, he's only thirty-four.

"You weren't even born when that photo was taken," I tell him.

He shrugs again. His hair does this amazing thing when he lifts and drops his shoulders. It kind of shakes all around his head and then just falls back perfectly into place. Apparently, I'm a huge fan of shrugging. And his hair.

"How old are *you*?" he shoots back.

"Fifty-five."

And then I wait for the inevitable "Oh," the moment it hits him that I am pathetic, that whatever little thing was going on between us during those happy hours is, in fact, a huge "ick." I silently coach myself, *Whatever happens next, don't flinch. Don't cringe. Stay upright. You can fold after he's gone.*

I maintain eye contact because if I don't, whatever progress I've made in the last few weeks will have been for naught. I'm so ready to be invisible again.

"Well, you clearly suck at math, since I *was* born when that photo was taken. In fact, I was fourteen. I had braces and zits. I had yet to kiss a girl, but I could already surf, and I was a genius on my skateboard," he says sharply. He looks at me for a long minute. He looks kind of annoyed, but then … oh my … the shrug.

"Would you like to come watch me surf tomorrow morning? It's going to be really early because of the tide, but the sunrise should be spectacular. You could meet me at the beach, or I could swing by and pick you up since it will still be kind of dark."

Wait. What? Also, I need to breathe, or I'm going to pass out for sure.

He keeps staring at me, his eyes watchful but at the same time kind. Soft.

I breathe in and then out.

"Sure," I say, looking right back at him.

"Cool."

He pushes his hands off his knees and stands, heading toward the hallway and the front door. "I'll pick you up at six. Dress warm."

He knocks his knuckles twice on the living room door frame before he disappears around the corner. I hear the front door open and close. I hear it click shut. "Lock the door," he calls from the porch.

What. The. Fuckety. Fuck.

May 2004

The score is tied.

Jay is drenched. Absolutely soaked with sweat. His lungs are on fire, and his legs are shaking. As a middie, he has run himself ragged on the field today. Other than that goal in the first quarter that he assisted, the Columbia Prep Lions have been held scoreless by the defense.

On the upside, his team's defense has played superbly, and their goalie has been close to flawless. Not flawless, though, since there was a goal in the third quarter.

So they are tied, 1–1, and there are six minutes left in the last quarter. Jay doesn't want to go into OT. He wants to win this championship outright in regulation time. He's a junior, but he's been on varsity since he was a freshman. It's his first time in the final.

He's entirely focused, and yet somehow the noise from the bleachers intrudes. Movement catches his eye, and he turns slightly to look toward the Columbia Prep varsity lacrosse fans. Across the rows of people, giant heads are bouncing up and down on sticks. They are photos of the varsity players, enlarged to massive proportions. "Fat heads," he heard someone call them. His eyes scan quickly, and he sees the faces of all his varsity teammates. The only face missing is his.

One of the moms approached him in the parking lot the night before while he was waiting for Carl to pick him up. Jay didn't know where to look. He could see she was carrying his giant face on a stick under her arm.

"Jay? You're Jay, right?" said the nice lady with a big smile. She is Monroe's mother. He knows who all the mothers are. He has watched them out of the corner of his eye for years as they dropped off and picked up his teammates and handed out tubs of cut-up watermelon or handfuls of Go-gurts or ham sandwiches. He knows who they all are.

And he knows that they know who he is, and he isn't positive, but he can guess—assume—that they talk about him, the kid who has no one. He sometimes wishes that years ago he invented a story (a plane crash, a car accident, an avalanche in the Swiss Alps, or maybe even 9-11) and told everyone he was an orphan. At least then they can look at him with sad *Oh, he's an orphan* eyes instead of sad *Oh, no one loves him* eyes. Those eyes are tough. Jay hates pity. He doesn't allow himself to feel it, and he doesn't want it anywhere near him.

Anyway, Monroe's mom—who makes the best ham sandwiches because she puts pickles in them—handed him his giant face on a stick and patted his arm.

"I wasn't sure if I'd see your mom," she said cheerfully, her smile blinding him. So many teeth. "So I thought I would just give this to you. So excited for the big game tomorrow! Go Lions, right!"

"Mom!" Jay heard Monroe scream for his mother. "Come on!"

She gave Jay one last look and turned away as Monroe jogged toward them. "Hey, Wells, see you tomorrow!" his teammate called. He grabbed his mother's arm and gave her a tug. "Mom," Jay heard him say to her, "I told you not to do that. His parents don't care."

"Well, I didn't want to take a chance," she said. "In case they did come. I mean, it *is* the championship. The first time in a decade! It's so exciting. I'm sure they'll come."

Monroe looked back over his shoulder and realized it was likely Jay heard every word. He gave his teammate a small smile and yanked his mother's arm again, and they moved across the parking lot.

Jay sighed and looked around. Carl must be stuck in traffic. He was starving. And tired. And wound up for the game tomorrow. He spotted a trash can under the light pole near him and made his way over. He dropped his gear bag to the ground and clenched his giant photo face between his two hands. Grimacing, he bent the cardboard the photo was mounted on as hard as he could until it folded into itself. Taking the stick in one hand, he tipped it upside down and put it headfirst in the trash can. He jammed it down as far as it would go until he couldn't see the stick anymore.

He brushed his hands off and saw Carl drive into the lot. He grabbed his gear and walked toward the car. He didn't look back.

I've been up since four. Or possibly never went to sleep. Am I going on a date?

Of course not.

I like you, he said. He. Likes. Me.

Me.

Jesus, am I fourteen years old?

There must be some mistake. Probably another fever dream like that crazy one I had in August when I used my Jason Bourne-like skills to open that cell phone and everything melted down. I mean, I know Matty left me the estrogen patches and great hair and smooth skin and a strong eyebrow game and a million products I have been using conscientiously twice a day since, but … there's no way the thirty-four-year-old surfer god/hot bartender wants to take me on a sunrise date.

He feels bad for me because of the humiliation I suffered at the bar. It's a pity invite. Which, honestly, whatever, I'm going. I haven't felt this interested in anything since … since … well, let's just say a while. Ages. Eons. I'm interested. Curious. Intrigued.

I pull two Yeti travel mugs from the cupboard and fill them with coffee. The least I can do is bring him a nice, hot drink, right? *Oh God, like a grandma would. Is that a grandma thing to do? Or a mom thing? I need to text Chickie.*

No. Stop it. Jesus. Get out of your head. It's a terrible place to live. And absolutely no texting Chickie. I don't need that level of positive energy in my life right this second.

I pour some oat milk in a small jar and throw some packets of stevia into the bag next to the coffees.

Then I see headlights in the driveway.

It's still dark, but I can tell the dawn is thinking about starting to wake up. Out over the water, the sky is a shade paler at the horizon.

I open the front door as he's making his way up the steps. Can't even wait for him to knock. I guess at my age there's no hard to get. There's barely even hard.

Guess what? My ears are roaring. The only thing louder is the thumping of my heart.

Yep. I'm fourteen.

He's got his wet suit on the lower half of his body, with a big hoodie covering his torso. The hood is pulled up and over a backward baseball hat. He walks up the steps and to the door and comes to a stop right in front of me. Inches away. He's tall. I have to tilt my head back to see his face. "Hey," he says quietly.

"Hi."

"Ready?"

"Yes, let me just grab my bag."

"I have blankets for you," he says, reaching to take the bag from me when I come back. He gestures for me to go ahead of him down the stairs, and I hear the door click firmly shut.

It's a quick drive down to the beach. We carry all the non-surfing gear to the sand, and he gets me set up in a mass of blankets. Then he hauls in everything he needs for his morning surf. The sky is turning cotton candy pink, with some purple swirls and hints of blue. He drops down next to me, reaches into a small cooler, and pulls out two Yeti travel mugs. "I brought coffee," he says.

I reach into my bag and pull out my two Yetis. "So did I."

We look at each other and laugh. He pulls out a small jar with milk in it and another one with what I'm assuming is sugar. And a spoon. I pull out my small jar of milk and my packets of stevia.

"You win," I say, shoving his shoulder with my shoulder. "I forgot a spoon."

He slings his arm around my shoulders and pulls me in. "Great minds," he says. "No such thing as too much caffeine."

"Aren't you going in the water?" I ask as we both gingerly sip from a mug, cautious because the coffee is still Yeti hot.

"Not till after we watch the sunrise," he says. His arm has stayed around me. He must have the wingspan of a condor, since his hand is dangling down to my elbow. Occasionally his fingers rub my fleece there.

"How many layers do you have on?" he asks, exerting a little more pressure in an effort to feel the actual limb. I used to run hot all the time, but since I started the estrogen patch, my body temperature has reset.

"Three," I manage. It's a miracle I form words because I can't even begin to explain what the fuck is happening inside me just from these casual touches. I might explode. Or die. Or have an orgasm, which would be embarrassing. I think I'd rather die.

I clear my throat, watching as a beautiful set of swells rolls in.

"I feel bad," I say. "You're missing some good waves."

He turns his head and looks at me. "We're watching the sunrise," he says.

And so we do. And it is, as he predicted, spectacular. Pinks and purples and blues and swirly clouds and a ball of fire coming over the horizon.

Then he finishes suiting up, grabs his board, and paddles out. We are the only ones on the beach.

He surfs for about an hour. He's beautiful to watch, agile, quick, strong. Even when he falls off, he looks good.

When he comes out, he does that same thing where he tugs off the hood and shakes his head, water spraying. He pushes his hair back with one hand and drops his board on the sand.

"You OK?" he asks before I can get a word out.

"I'm great. That was awesome. You look so good out there."

"Thanks," he says. "I love it on the water. It's the best feeling. It's quiet and serene while you wait for your wave, and then it's fast and loud as you ride in. Perfect."

As he's talking, he reaches back and grabs the long tab that allows him to unzip the suit. He begins to peel it down his body, pulling his arms out before stretching it down his torso. He yanks it down over his butt and then down both legs, letting the black neoprene pool around his feet. He's wearing nothing but a pair of compression shorts and a smile.

Aaaaand I'm done.

He makes eye contact. "You OK?" he asks again, his smile so big.

I look away.

He laughs, grabs a towel off the pile, and vigorously dries off. Holy shit, I am not sure I can take much more. I shake off my blankets and start to stand up.

"What are you doing?"

"Aren't we leaving?" I ask. "Won't you get cold?"

"I have dry clothes," he says. "And we have tons of blankets." He gives me a side eye. "And body heat."

I sit back down because it's that or fall down.

He wraps the towel around his waist, reaches up under it, and pulls off his compression shorts. It's a trick every kid learns at summer camp. Then he pulls on gray sweatpants because of course he would and then a long-sleeved Under Armour shirt and his hoodie. He rummages back around in his cooler and pulls out a white paper bag. Then he drops down next to me and bundles us both up in a fleece cocoon. He starts pulling things out of the bag. Croissants. A Danish-looking thing. Something big and sticky with white icing.

"Breakfast," he says with a little flourish and another huge smile.

Jesus fucking Christ, I am on a date.

When we pull into my driveway about forty-five minutes later, there is one of those big Pods storage containers on my lawn. It wasn't there when he picked me up.

"Expecting a delivery?" he asks as we get out of the car. I carry my bag up the porch steps and pull a piece of paper off the door held with tape. It's an invoice for the storage pod. $1,700.

Son of a bitch.

As part of the divorce, he bought me out of our house. I was actually kind of a bitch about the price, and I rejected his first seven offers. Harley, who is a lawyer, and his husband, Keith, who is an accountant, advised me. They researched appraisals in our neighborhood and recent sales. Of course, he kept lowballing me because why not, but eventually I got the amount I deserved.

"What's in it?" Jay asks.

"My life, I think. It looks like my ex-husband has sent me all my things."

"Hmm," Jay says. "Want me to help you with it?"

"Ha. No thanks. I'm going to pretend it isn't here until I need my winter coat and have to open it up. It's part of my current life strategy."

He shrugs. "OK, cool. If you need help, let me know." He climbs the porch stairs and once again stands very much in my space. "Are you coming to happy hour?" He brushes back some stray hairs that have escaped my ponytail.

"Do you want me to come to happy hour?" I ask. *Am I flirting?*

He smiles. "Yes." He bends his head down toward me. "Very much."

"Well then, I will see you at four. Thank you so much for this morning. It was really fun. It was special."

His head moves a little closer. "I want to kiss you," he whispers.

I close my eyes, waiting to feel his lips, waiting to see if I will be struck by lightning, waiting.

And waiting.

After a minute, I open my eyes. His face is right there, a small smile on his lips. "Do you want me to say, 'Go ahead'?" I ask.

"Yes," he says.

So I do. And he gives me a gentle, soft kiss, slightly more than brushing my lips. He reaches down and squeezes my hand, then turns and heads down the steps, giving me a wave over his shoulder. He knocks twice on the porch railing. "See you at four," he calls.

And that, ladies and gentlemen, was my first date since 1992.

9

Our happy hour conversations get a little deeper, a little more personal. But he doesn't ask me about the storage pod or the divorce or the state of my being, and I don't tell. If no one needs a drink, he spends all his time down at my little corner, with his hands splayed on the bar, caging in my place setting. It's like he's marked his territory.

One afternoon I come in at four to find only ice water and a glass of ice at my place.

I hop up onto the stool as he walks the length of the bar to greet me.

"Am I abstaining?" I ask.

"No, I wanted to mix things up a little. Chickie said you love tequila and margaritas, and I want to make my signature one for you."

He walks back to the liquor shelf, pours and mixes, shakes, then returns with a gorgeous reddish-orange cocktail in a salted glass.

"Blood orange," he says. He waits while I sip, his eyes glued to my mouth.

"It's delicious," I say. "Thank you."

I end up staying longer than usual, and when I pay my tab, Jay comes around the bar and grabs my coat off the back of my chair. "What are you doing?" I ask.

"Walking you to your car," he says.

"But you have customers."

He looks down the bar. "Jerry," he says, his voice raised a little. "Do *not* eat all the maraschino cherries. I will be right back."

Jerry, the only other customer and a lovely old barfly, gives Jay a little salute with his middle finger and focuses back on his beer.

We walk out to the parking lot. My car is thirty feet away.

"Worried about me in this high-crime area?" I ask.

"Nope," he says, throwing his arm over my shoulders and tugging me close. "I just really wanted to kiss you."

Oh my.

We get to my car, and I click the fob to unlock it. "Good to know you can lock some things," Jay says as I reach for the door handle. He puts his big hand over mine, stopping me from opening it. He puts his other hand on my waist and turns me toward him. He takes a step closer to me, and I take a corresponding step back, so my spine is pressed against the car.

Oh my.

Now his hands are on the car roof, and his arms have boxed me in. He leans in close. "May I?" he asks.

This time I'm ready. "You may," I say, smiling.

His lips swallow my smile whole, and his tongue gently pushes its way into my mouth.

Oh. My.

My hands take on a life of their own and rise up to both sides of his face. His hands go in the opposite direction, sliding down my neck, my upper arms, and then moving to my ribs. They keep going south, and I pull back slightly and suck in my stomach. He pauses for a second, looks at me, and then resumes his tongue's exploration of my molars.

When his hands continue their fluttery march across my belly, I suck in another breath.

He really pulls away this time and grasps my chin in his fingers. "Don't do that," he says.

I try to look away, but he holds my chin in place. He looks hard in my eyes. "I mean it, Katherine," he says. "Don't do that. Don't try to change your body like that."

I force a laugh that sounds incredibly fake, even to my ears. "Don't tell me what not to do," I say as I put my hands on his shoulders and gently push him away. "Thanks for a great night, but I'm going home now."

He stands there, rubbing his thumb over his lower lip, as I get in the car, start it, and back out of the parking space. As I pull away, I offer a small wave.

He doesn't wave back.

UNKNOWN NUMBER. Hey.

UNKNOWN NUMBER. It's Jay.

UNKNOWN NUMBER. From Dockside.

ME. How'd you get my number?

UNKNOWN NUMBER. We have mutual friends.

ME. 👀

UNKNOWN NUMBER. You didn't come to happy hour.

UNKNOWN NUMBER. Everything OK?

ME. Everything's fine.

UNKNOWN NUMBER. Can I stop by when I get off shift?

UNKNOWN NUMBER. Just to say hi. I won't stay long.

Unknown Number. Katherine.

Me. Sure, that's fine.

Unknown Number. Cool. See you in a bit. I'm assuming the door will be unlocked?

Me. Never assume.

After that little text exchange, I race upstairs, brush my teeth, put on deodorant, mascara, a clean T-shirt, and nicer yoga pants. So I'm trying? But not *really* trying. I mean, it's easy to just be not gross, right? I feel like my bar is pretty low.

He gets here around ten, simultaneously knocking and letting himself in because, you know, unlocked door. He finds his way to the back of the house, to the family room that's off the kitchen. I'm lying on the giant sofa, half watching *Heartstopper*. He's wearing a T-shirt under a zippered hoodie and jeans, so he must've changed at the restaurant before leaving.

He finds me and immediately lies down on the couch next to me, using his elbows and knees to move me over to make room. I'm flush against the back cushions, lying on my side facing him. His hand brushes my cheek, and then his lips brush my forehead before moving to my mouth.

"Not asking permission anymore?" I ask.

"I can if you want me to," he replies. "But I'm hoping we've reached an understanding."

"Yeah, what's that?" I say, curious as to what he means.

He runs his nose down along the side of mine and then across my jawline. My breath is shallow. He nuzzles my ear and murmurs, "We like each other, right? So kissing is understood."

Before I can answer, he manifests his understanding with a deep kiss that stops my heart. Then restarts my heart. Then stops it again. Without thinking, I'm kissing him back, my mouth open, my tongue seeking answers from the back of his throat. He groans softly, and his hand moves to the back of my head, massaging my scalp and tangling my hair.

My hands slide up his chest, clutching his shirt as I pull myself even closer to him. He moves one hand down my neck, his fingers leaving a trail of heat, then across my chest to cup my breast through my shirt. Without thinking, I pull back a little and suck in my breath.

He looks at me, almost sternly. "Katherine," he says. "I told you. Don't do that."

I give him a weak, slightly apologetic smile.

"Don't tell me what not to do," I say.

He moves away, sitting up and pulling me with him.

"I'm serious," he says. "Why do you do that? Every time I touch you, it's like you stop and try to suck everything in."

I move my eyes away from his and stare at the floor. The silence gets awkward quickly.

"Katherine."

I sigh. *Here we go.* "I don't like my body."

"What? Why? That's crazy. You're beautiful."

I'm quite possibly going to cry, and I really, really don't want to do that because honestly, it's nice spending time with him, thinking about him, kissing him, and touching him. It's really nice. I don't want that to end. But this conversation will very likely do just that.

I take a deep breath. "I used to like my body," I explain. "I mean, yes, I was always criticizing it, wishing it were five or ten pounds lighter, wishing I were three inches taller, wishing my ass was rounder. But really, it was a good body. It was mine."

He's holding my hands in his, and I know he's looking intently at my face, but I can't look up from the floor.

"OK," he says.

A tear pops out of the corner of my eye, rolls down my cheek, and plops onto the back of his hand.

"Menopause wrecked me," I say. "It changed my body, and it fucked with my head. I literally felt insane. I felt like I was a teenager again, going through puberty, getting my period for the first time, having all these new feelings and emotions, except it was going backwards. You know? Like my period was stopping. I gained all this weight even though I wasn't doing anything different with food or exercise. My insides felt like they were drying up. My brain was foggy. I was hot all the time and not in a good way. Burning up from the inside. In a way that made me want to throw myself out a window.

"Things were sagging and bulging and puckering that never had before. I had this buzzing in my ears.

"And every time I tried to talk to someone about it, my doctor, my husband, my sister, my friends, I just got these looks of pity and nodding of heads and pats on the back. With great advice like 'Ride it out' and 'This too shall pass.' Or 'Have you tried black cohosh? That worked for me.' Even Chickie and Bitty, when I talked to them, they couldn't really relate because they hadn't had as bad a time. Bitty's menopause lasted less than a year, and Chickie basically stopped having her period, and that was it.

"And I used to love sex. But then, all of a sudden, sex hurt. Like, really hurt. And I didn't want to do it anymore. And he had zero interest in trying to figure out how to get back to where we had been, so we both just shut down. Like I know my marriage ended last month, but really it ended about five years ago. I felt invisible. Like nothing."

It's quiet except for *Heartstopper*. I can hear my breathing, which is kind of ragged as I try not to break down. Another traitorous drop of water leaks out of my eye and follows its brethren to the back of Jay's hand. His thumbs are rubbing soft circles on my palms.

I pull a hand away and wipe my cheek. I look up at him, finally. "It's OK," I say, trying to give him a supportive smile. Fairly certain I might look like a serial killer right now but whatever. *A* for effort.

"You don't have to stay. This is dumb. I'm too old for you. I appreciate the attention you've shown me. It's been really nice. And I love talking to you about stupid stuff and that you started reading spicy books. I love watching you surf. Thank you for that date. But you can go. This won't work. I knew it all along, and now you do, too."

I expect him to get up and head for the door, but instead he puts his hands around my waist and scoots me over so that I am straddling his lap. He cups my face in his hands and pulls me close. We are inches apart. I can feel his breath.

"I see you," he says. "I've seen you since the first time I saw you on the beach. Since the first time you came into the bar. Now I want more than just seeing you. Now I want to know you. Now I want to know what's in your head and what's in your heart and where you came from and what made you who you are. I want to know who you are going to be. I want to know who you are with me.

"I don't care how old you are. I don't care how old I am. *That's* something I *don't* see. You intrigue me. You make me want to know more and stay longer. We can go slow. We can take our time. Whatever works for you. I will do whatever it takes to make it work for *us*. I want to see what us looks like. Let me stay."

He is looking hard at me, those werewolf eyes blazing into mine. His hands are firm around my face. His thumbs are lightly stroking my cheeks.

I close my eyes for just a second, and when I open them, his eyes are still right there. On me. I cup my hands around his jawline, my fingers splaying around his ears.

Here we go.

"Can I kiss you?" I whisper.

He smiles. His whole face smiles. Those ice-blue eyes go half lidded.

"Yes," he whispers. "Please."

10

November in town is practically postapocalyptic. Even with no snow, it's cold. The die-hard surfers still go out, but their sessions are shorter. With the time change, the window for catching good waves can be pretty small as they juggle tides and wind direction and sunlight.

It's a Tuesday night, and Dockside is really dead. I'm the only one in the bar, and Jay and I have been whispering and holding hands and laughing together in my corner, him leaning in from behind the bar and me leaning in from my stool. There were a couple of tables in the dining room, but it's after seven now, and everyone's gone. The waitstaff all went home.

Chickie pops her head out of the kitchen. "Guys, I'm closing. Kitchen's all set, and the dining room is cleared. You don't have to go home, but you can't stay here."

I laugh at her Semisonic reference. Jay cocks an eyebrow at me and then turns to her. "I'm happy to lock up," he says, "if you want to leave ahead of us."

Chickie looks at Jay, who is smiling at her sincerely. Almost Boy Scout-ish in his desire to assist her. Then Chickie looks at me. Then she looks back at Jay. Then she shakes her head, disappears for a second, and comes back with her purse. She lives upstairs from the restaurant; her apartment is over the dining room with amazing views of the harbor. So it's a short commute.

"Lock up," she says, giving Jay a hard stare. "Set the alarm."

She moves to the side door, which will take her to the outside staircase leading up to her apartment. She takes one look back over her shoulder and scowls. "And don't break anything."

Jay huffs a laugh. "'Night, boss," he says. We hear the door click shut behind her.

"What are you doing?" I ask him as he moves around behind the bar, flipping light switches and making different parts of the room go dark one by one. He leaves the wall sconces on so there's a soft yellow glow across the room. He goes to Chickie's exit and slides the bolt, then he goes to the bar door, and I hear that bolt lock into place. I spin my stool around so I am facing him, my back to the bar.

He comes toward me with a look on his face that both excites and terrifies me. Since our confessional conversation a few days ago, we've had some intense parking lot make-out sessions but nothing more. Making out that included definitely teenage-level pawing of each other but fully clothed.

"Just something I've been thinking about," he says as he gets close to me, nudging my knees apart with his hips. His hands go around my waist, and he yanks me toward him until I am on the edge of my seat. Literally and figuratively. Pressed up hard against him. And that's not the only thing that's hard.

Wait. What? Jay is hard. Erect. I can feel him through his pants.

Did I do that? Did I make him hard?

He takes my hands and wraps them around his neck. "Yes," he says, moving in to nuzzle my neck, pushing my hair out of the way with his nose. "You did that."

Oh, so now he's a mind reader? I'm in trouble.

His nose, his mouth, his hands feel like they are everywhere all at once. We are pressing ourselves up against each other, creating friction wherever we can. He peels off my fleece and pulls my T-shirt out from my yoga pants as I untuck his black work shirt. My fingers brush up against his belt buckle, but I hesitate.

"Katherine," he murmurs in my ear, sucking the lobe into his mouth, "yes. Please."

Fever dream. This has to be another fever dream, but this time I'm just going to go with it and try not to wake myself up. He sighs, and one hand cups my breast under my shirt.

His thumb rubs my nipple, which is standing at attention. I unbuckle his belt and pop the button above his zipper.

He groans and pulls back a little. *Oh shit. I've done something wrong.* "Sorry," I mumble. "I'm so bad at this."

He chuckles. "It's not you, babe. Trust me. I just need you in a better spot."

And just like that he grabs me around my waist and pops me up onto the bar. Now we are eye to eye. His mouth finds mine, and his hands go behind my back, pulling me forward until I am again flush against him. And his erection. Instinctively, I wrap my legs around his waist and begin to unbutton his shirt. He sighs.

"That's what I'm talking about," he says.

His fingers make their way to the waistband of my leggings, and I feel a surge of panic. I work hard not to follow my instinct and suck in my belly, but the panic involves more than the thought of him touching my muffin top. Can I even do this? It's been a long time since I've had sex. It's been a long time since I've wanted it.

Stop it, I tell myself. *This is what I want. I can do this.*

Even so, I opt for a diversionary tactic, and I grab his zipper and pull it down. His cock pops out, tenting his boxers. I reach in and wrap my hand around him, freeing him from his fabric prison.

Jay puts his forehead against mine. "Katherine."

"Let me," I say. "I need to."

He closes his eyes. My hand strokes his erection from bottom to top, and my fingers flutter over the head, which is already slick. I bring my other hand down and cup his balls. His hands press against my back, holding me steady and keeping me balanced on the bar.

I find a rhythm, stroking up and down, slow then fast, hard then soft, front then back, while gently massaging his balls, which I can feel tightening.

"Babe," he says.

"Let me," I say again. "Just let me."

His hands move under my shirt, and his fingers push hard into the skin on my back. *That's going to leave a mark*, I think as I move my mouth over his and not so gently bite his bottom lip.

He shudders, his fingers digging into me, and then he comes all over my hand and his abs.

We are still. I'm breathing hard; he's breathing hard. I kiss him one more time and then reach behind me, searching blindly for the stack of bar napkins I know is there somewhere.

He pulls his head back a little, and those werewolf eyes search mine.

"That wasn't what I envisioned," he says. "I wanted to—"

"I know," I interrupt him, finding the napkins and bringing a pile of them forward to start sopping up the mess I made him make. I give him a little smile and a soft kiss. "I needed to."

June 1985

This is the summer with a plan.

They are eighteen. Well, KK and Matty are eighteen, while Chickie's birthday is around the corner. They graduated from high school. They are leaving at the end of August for college. Well, Chickie and KK are. Matty is moving to LA to live with his mother's cousin, who is going to help him find a job as a stylist for a studio. She has connections, apparently.

The only thing left uneven among the three is virginity. As in, KK still has hers. Matty has been giving and receiving hand jobs since he was thirteen and blow jobs since he was fifteen, and while that is as far as the details go among them, no one is considering him a virgin.

Chickie lost hers during her sophomore year to a boy whose name is no longer spoken. Leave it at that.

And KK is determined—and has so announced—that there is no way in hell she is starting college with an intact hymen. So this summer, KK has to get laid.

And that is the extent of the plan. So far.

Matty and KK have been at the beach house for a week. They arrived and jumped right into their jobs at Dockside, with no time to even think. The season is starting, the tourists are arriving, and damn it, they want lobster rolls, Long Island iced teas, and white zinfandel.

KK and Matty are barbacking and table running, and Chickie is "assistant manager," which just means she is glued to her father's side and takes the brunt of his moods. Summer hasn't even really started, and Chickie is already packed for UMass. She. Can. Not. Wait.

It is a rare day when all three are off together, but this Tuesday, the stars align. They are sitting at the end of the jetty at the beach, smoking a joint. It's close to five, and all the families are long gone from the sand. The lifeguards are locking up their gear and securing their chairs. The breeze is cool though the sun is warm.

"So who should it be?" KK asks. "He has to be cute."

"Who do you think is cute?" Matty says, taking a deep drag and passing the joint to Chickie.

"She thinks Brad Wiley is cute," Chickie says.

KK nods. "He is. I love his hair. There's so much of it."

"Didn't you make out with him last year at that party on the dune?" Matty asks.

"No, that was Ponce. Mike Ponce. Who mauled my boobs, by the way. Jesus. Kind of drooly too."

They laugh. Among the three of them, they probably have tasted the lips of every male in town between sixteen and twenty. Sluts and proud of it.

"So, how will we make it happen?" Chickie asks. "You don't want it at Black Rock because you don't want your first time to be in the back seat of a car. Or on the ground."

"Speaking from experience?" Matty asks, leaning back on his elbows.

Chickie silences him with a stare.

"Sorry," Matty says. He turns his face toward KK. "What's your dream, Mama? Goose down mattress and eight-hundred-thread-count sheets? Tent next to a babbling brook? Sand dune at sunrise?"

"God, I don't know," KK says, flicking the teensy bit of joint that's left into the ocean. "Why did I wait so long? I just want to get it over with. The first time sucks anyway, right? So does it even really matter? Romance? Mood? Location?"

"Comfort matters," Chickie says, suddenly interested in her cuticles.

Matty huffs and gets to his feet. He takes three steps and sits back down next to Chickie. He hugs her tight to his side. She smiles at him but then looks away.

"Fuck," KK says, hurling a chunk of clam shell against a nearby boulder. "Let's just figure out a way to get me and Brad Wiley in the same place at the same time. He won't say no, right? He likes me. Right? He likes me?"

"Mama, of course he likes you!" Matty says, possibly a little too loudly. The joint has kicked in fully, and they are pretty high. The weed this year on the Cape is strong. "Everyone likes you. We will make it happen. No worries at all. You will leave Cape Cod and enter Tufts University as a seasoned sexual being."

"I don't need to be seasoned. I just need to not be a virgin."

Matty huffs again. "Same thing, Mama. Same damn thing."

Tonight's cocktail is something called a "gin bramble," and holy shit, is it good. I have two of them, and I'm a little buzzed. I don't arrive at Dockside at the start of happy hour much anymore. Hell, sometimes I don't get there until after happy hour is over because Jay likes me to stay until he's off shift. So I'm paying full price for those drinks and apps, all in the name of making out with a hot surfer bartender.

He's got me pinned up against my car in the parking lot again, and his mouth is devouring mine as his hands cup my breasts under my coat, sweater, shirt, and bra. Winter layers make it challenging to get to second base.

ELISSA BASS

"Can we go back to your house?" he mutters. "There's way too many clothes involved here." His cock is rock hard against my belly.

Remember how I said going through menopause was like reverse puberty? My new relationship (*wait—is it a relationship?*) has me planted firmly in adolescence. Our physical interactions are hovering in the ninth-grade range, with major kissing, heavy petting at second base, and thwarted attempts at sliding into third.

"Katherine," he says. "Your house."

I grab his wrists and pull them out from my shirt. I pause to catch my breath as he looks at me expectantly.

Here we go.

"I'm scared," I say.

Jay steps back. "Of me?"

"Of ... us," I say. "Doing things. More things. Together."

I can feel my blush rising on my cheeks. Yep. I'm definitely fifteen years old right now.

"What things?" he asks gently. He dips his head so he can see my eyes.

"Sex," I say. "I'm scared to have sex. Because sex has been terrible— truly terrible—for quite a while, and then, well, I haven't actually had sex for more than a year. Like, nothing. Haven't even wanted to have sex."

"Do you want to have sex now?" His eyes flit between my eyes and my lips.

I nod.

Vigorously.

"I'm just not sure I can, uh, have it successfully. Like, uh, not terrible. For you. Or me. Or both of us." I stop talking. I'm guessing he won't want to walk me to my next class after this mortifying conversation.

He leans in and kisses me hard. His hand moves swiftly down my side, and his fingers slide underneath the elastic waistband of my leggings. I gasp, but he doesn't stop, and sweet Jesus, those fingers are now inside my panties, moving very purposefully. He slides one finger in and up into my center. Then he pulls it all the way back out and takes one step back from me.

He holds that finger up in front of my face, and it glistens off the parking lot lights. Wet and shiny. From me.

Jay smiles. "I think you're underestimating yourself," he says. Then he puts that finger in his mouth and sucks it clean.

"Now can we go to your house?"

Oh my.

11

Things I Didn't Know I Wanted:

1. Being in an actual bed instead of in a parking lot
2. Being naked in the bed with full access to all body parts
3. All body parts
4. Cuddling
5. Talking while cuddling

The sex is great. I mean it's great for me. I'm assuming it's great for Jay since he keeps wanting to do it and because of the absolutely filthy things he continuously whispers in my ear. But the cuddling and the talking? Off-the-fucking-charts spectacular.

I think I'd forgotten about intimacy. And its many iterations.

There's physical intimacy, in which you lay yourself literally bare to another human. In which you make an effort to provide physical pleasure to another, to make each other feel good.

Then there's the emotional part, in which you also spend time making sure the other human's heart is good, that he or she feels safe, cared for, liked (loved?), respected, and appreciated.

Then there's the intellectual, in which you spend time and effort stimulating the other's brain through thoughtful conversation and strong listening skills. Hearing, responding, inquiring, validating.

I haven't had any of these in at least six years and, if I'm being honest with myself, ten.

With Jay? Hat trick.

On this night, he arrived a little after nine. We ate some food, we drank a glass of wine, we made out in the kitchen, and then we made love in my bed. Now, we're lying on our sides, facing each other, fingers entwined on the mattress between us.

"Can I ask you something?" I say, untangling my fingers from his so I can stroke his hair.

"Of course."

"Why is your hair always perfect?"

He laughs. "What do you mean?"

"I mean it's always perfect. It has this perfect shape and perfect waves, and it moves around and yet always remains ... perfect."

"It must be the saltwater. I don't really wash it much, and when I surf, I don't usually even rinse it out afterwards. It's just salty, crunchy hair."

"My turn," he says.

I raise my eyebrows.

"Do you work?"

That makes me laugh. "I guess that 'sort of' is the best answer to that right now," I say. "My career was in marketing. I worked for some good firms in Boston over the years and had a reputation as the queen of taglines. I enjoyed what I did and made good money.

"When I got laid off in 2020, I said I was going to freelance, but that's a bitch to get going, so it sort of stalled. And as everything else slowly went to shit, the work just fell by the wayside. Of course, now that I'm not married anymore, I can't sponge off—his words, not mine—his insurance or income. What he gave me for my half of our house will keep me afloat for a while, but I will have to figure out something eventually."

"Now me," I say. "Why do you knock twice on things?"

"My grandfather," he says, pausing to fix his pillow and then adjust mine for me so our faces are even with each other. "It was a thing he always did when he was making a point. He'd say his piece, and then he'd knock twice. Like, 'Period.' I picked it up from him, but mine is different, I think. When I do it, it's more like, 'Thank you. Next.'"

I smile at his Ariana reference. "OK, your turn."

"Oh, this one's easy," he says. "Why do you have so many names?"

I cover my face with my hands. "Well, my legal name is Katherine Kristina for each of my grandmothers. They tell me that right from the start, my dad called me KK, and it just stuck. Matty called me 'Mama' pretty much from the moment we met when we were four, although he's never explained why, and I'm not sure I've ever actually asked. Chickie calls me both. You're the only one who calls me 'Katherine.' Why do you call me 'Katherine'?"

He does a half shrug. "I like having my own name for you," he says. "It's a beautiful name. It suits you."

"OK, me again," I say.

"Wait," he says. "I have one more, real quick." He pulls the covers down and runs his finger over the shiny plastic disc that's adhered to my skin at the base of my abdomen, near my right hip. "What's this?"

I frown. "It's my estrogen patch."

He quirks a brow.

"It tames my menopause symptoms," I explain, feeling slightly embarrassed. "It's a prescription, and it alleviates the hell menopause was putting my body through."

He leans down and kisses it lightly. I swear to God I hear him whisper, "Thank you," but I might be wrong.

"OK, now it's your turn," he says, his eyes meeting mine.

"Why are you a winter bartender in a summer town?"

He doesn't answer right away, and I panic, thinking I went too far. Maybe he's two steps ahead of the law. Or maybe it's just none of my business.

"After college, I got a job in finance. The company paid for my MBA, and I was fast-tracking it on Wall Street. I was making a shit ton of money for the C-suite and another shit ton for myself. I was good at it, at numbers, at seeing the deals and how they should go. I kept trying to convince myself I loved it, the excitement of making the trades, cashing the checks, buying the penthouse apartment. I was that guy in that cliché blue suit from that Instagram account. Every day."

I interrupt. "NYCsuits! I love that account."

"Ha, yeah," Jay continues. "And then one day I walked out of my apartment, and there was a homeless girl—well, a woman, a young woman—and she had her whole setup in this little cut-in on the side of my building. Sitting on some cardboard spread out over a sidewalk grate. I gave her twenty bucks as I passed by, and she said 'Thanks, Jay.'

"I stopped and looked at her. She was a mess. Dirty, wearing layers of clothes, smelling bad. Her teeth were gray. Her hair was literally in giant knots on the back of her head, and her fingernails were black.

"'It's Jasmine,' she says to me. 'Jasmine Simonds. From Bates. We took freshman seminar together.'"

He shakes his head. "Jasmine Simonds was a dance major. Gorgeous. So talented. I knew her a little at college. Our social circles would intersect. I had heard that after graduation, she went to dance in New York.

"And there she was, camped on the street outside my building.

"I took her to the bodega and got her a sandwich and some water. I tried asking what was going on, what had happened, but she didn't want to talk. She thanked me for the food and took off."

"Jesus," I say. "Then what happened?"

"I'd see her periodically, sporadically, sometimes at my building, sometimes elsewhere on the block, sometimes in the subway. She always said hello, gave me a big smile. I always gave her twenty bucks. I kept asking her to let me help, find her a place to live, get some stability into her life. She'd always give me that big smile and say, 'No thanks, Jay. I'm cool.'

"And then one day she was gone. I asked around, the guy at the bodega, the doormen on the block, but everyone just shrugged. She disappeared. I made some calls to the police, social services, gave them her name and a description. Then I got a call that there was a body at the city morgue that matched the report I had given."

He pauses. He blinks a few times. Reaches out his hand and brushes my hair back behind my ear. Rubs my cheek. Twines his fingers with mine.

"It was her. They didn't think it was murder or anything. They didn't think it was suicide. Maybe it was drugs, but they never tested for that because they didn't want to spend the money. Because she was homeless, and who cared, right? They said she just died. She died in a parking garage. And she had nestled herself away behind some long-term parked cars, so she was dead for days before anyone found her.

"They gave me her personal stuff, not her clothes or sleeping bag or anything—I'm guessing they burned all that shit. But there was a box that was duct-taped closed inside a gallon-size plastic bag. And they gave it to me because there was no one else to give it to. I brought it home and cut it open, and inside it was another plastic bag, and that was filled with newspaper clippings about her performances, reviews of things she was in that mentioned her. Dating back to college. Even from back then. There was a little clipping cut from a larger article, just a paragraph, that noted that Jasmine Simonds had been replaced as principal dancer in some show because of an injury.

"And there was a card, like a notecard with watercolor flowers on the front, and inside was this little old lady handwriting. It was from her grandma, and she was writing to say she was proud of Jasmine for having the lead in the modern dance spring showcase and how she knew she would go on to become a big star on Broadway. And it was signed, 'You are the sunshine of my life, Jasmine. Love, Grandma.'"

Jay takes a deep breath. He has tears in his eyes.

"And honestly, to this day, I still don't fully get it, but I realized I couldn't do it anymore. I couldn't feed this broken, fucking system we live in that allows people like me to live fifty-seven stories above the city and look down on it, and every single fucking thing I need is available to me, while people like Jasmine die unnoticed in an underground parking garage. Because we were basically the same person, and who gets to decide that shit, you know?

"So I quit. Sold my apartment and moved to Rhode Island, to Narragansett. Rented an apartment, got a job bartending. My parents were beside themselves, said I was throwing away all my education, that I had wasted all that money they had spent on my college. We don't talk a lot, and I'm sure that's why. They're still angry.

"I've moved around since then, just focused on surfing and trying to live in a way that doesn't hurt anyone else. Wherever I am, I connect with a homeless shelter or meal center or something, and when I'm not bartending, I volunteer whatever they need. To help, you know? A friend of Chickie's who owns a place in Newport told me she was looking for a winter bartender, and the waves here are decent this time of year. So here I am."

We lie there for a minute, and then I scoot as close to him as I can get and wrap him in my arms. I hold him tightly, and he rests his face in the dip between my neck and shoulder. I feel him sigh. Then he starts kissing me, moving up to my ear and down across my jawline, and I start kissing him. He rolls us so he's on top of me and nudges my legs apart with his knee, and then he slides inside me, all the way.

He holds there for a few beats and then begins to move in and out, and instinctively my legs wrap around his waist, and I lift my hips to meet his. His silver-blue eyes are glued to mine, and I feel like he's looking for something. I'm not sure what or if I could give it to him if I knew, but we find a rhythm. It's the quietest sex I've ever had.

When it's over, he stays on top of me, heavy, and I let him. When our breathing is back to normal, he rolls to my side and pulls up the covers. I look at his beautiful face, his eyes closing as sleep begins to overtake him.

"Jay," I whisper.

"Mmm?"

"I would've liked to have seen you in one of those suits."

He smiles a tiny, sleepy smile, and he's out.

Y

Bitty flies in for a few days, so Harley and Keith and Matty drive down from the city. For some reason, they all decided we should do hot yoga at a studio a couple of towns over. I have never been so drenched in my life. It's as if someone held me under in a bathtub.

Sweat is pouring off me. I'm not sure why anyone would think that I—a woman who spends a considerable amount of money sticking estrogen patches on her body so I don't feel hot or insane—would want to do this. But here we are.

I look over at Chickie, and her face is a shade of purple I have never seen before. Her entire body is shaking as she attempts to hold this pose, I think it's called Screaming Eagle or Frightened Bat or some such bullshit. Whatever. I already gave up on this one, and I am simply bent over at the waist, hands on my knees, watching the sheen of sweat drop from my face to the mat.

Behind me, the fucking Yoga Four are making their eagles scream perfectly. And while they are sweating buckets, they have the most annoying looks on their red faces, like they are in a state of serene, fucking nirvana or something. I hate them.

"I'm going to either puke, pass out, or fall down," Chickie hisses at me.

"Just quit like me," I whisper back.

Suddenly, I feel pressure on my lower back, at the base of my spine. I twist to look up. The yoga teacher (Brian? Barclay? Bougie?) has two fingers pressed to my soaking-wet tank top. "Come on," he says to me, "I know you can do this. Let's try again, and I will help center you."

The last thing I want to be right now is centered. Second to the last thing I want right now is a stranger touching my disgusting, sweaty self. My eyes move up to his face. and I swear I am not making this up—he winks at me.

But hey, I can't be rude, right? So I sigh, wipe my face with my clammy palm, and straighten. He lightly touches my elbow, keeps his fingers on my back, and waits as I stretch out one leg, point some toes, bend a knee, and teeter precariously on the edge of sanity.

Next to me, Chickie goes down. Hard.

Bougie startles and drops to her side immediately.

"Are you OK?" he asks anxiously, moving around to her other side.

When he's not looking, she mouths to me, "You're welcome." I snort, and a considerable amount of snot comes out of my nose and splats on my mat.

That's it. I'm done. There are only a few minutes left in the class, so I grab my water bottle and my mat, and I head to the door.

Chickie is right behind me. We sit on a bench in the hallway and wait for the others. The sweat is drying on our skin, and we are even grosser than we were when we were trapped in the hot box.

Her arm is over my shoulders. "Was that guy hitting on me?" I ask.

"Oh yeah," she says. "Gumby was making eyes at you the whole class."

"Gumby?" I say.

"Yeah. He's flexible as shit. You know, now that I think about it, maybe you should've gone for it. There's a lot to be said for flexible."

I snort again. "Listen, I can barely keep up with what I have going on right now with Jay. I don't need to add ankles behind my ears to the mix. Or ankles behind his ears."

She looks at me out of the corner of her eye. "How is it going with—what do you call him?—Surfer Guy?" she asks.

"It's good," I reply, not meeting her gaze.

Her shoulder nudges mine. "Mm-hmm," she says.

"Please don't make me talk about it," I beg her as my face turns red again, this time from embarrassment and not Heart Attack Yoga. But then I can't help myself. "Does he talk about me?"

Chickie laughs. "To me? No, not really. I mean, back in the beginning, he asked me about you. He was obsessed with that photo I have of us hanging at my desk. Was always looking at it and asking me about it. And he asked me what your deal was."

"My deal?"

"Yeah, you know, like were you married, divorced, widowed?"

"Did you say, 'No, just fucked up'?"

She squeezes me to her. "Of course not, Mama," she says. "First, because we are all fucked up. And second because on the scale of 'not at all fucked up' to 'what the fuckety fuck' fucked up, you only rank in the middle. And third, he's a little fucked up himself, I think. I get the vibe off him that he's one of those guys who's searching for something, you know? Like a purpose or something."

As a bar/restaurant owner in a summer tourist town, Chickie has vast experience with all of life's various misfits. She can read people really well. Her instincts are usually dead on. I realize this is the most in-depth conversation we've had about my relationship with Jay.

"He's OK, though, right? For, uh, for me, I mean? Like, I'm OK?"

"I think he's OK. I mean, I don't know what exactly you're thinking about this whole thing or what you're looking for, but I think you're OK."

I nod and look away. I, too, don't know what I think about this whole thing, this Jay-and- me thing. Just then the studio door bursts open, and the Yoga Four prance out, red faced, invigorated, and satisfied.

"Well, now that that's out of the way, let's go drink," Matty says. "Margs?"

There's an activity I can get behind. No centering needed. Just ice and salt.

12

August 1983

It's hard to know which decision was the wrong one.

Was it the beer?

Was it the bottles of Mad Dog 20/20 and Tequila Sunrise that were being passed around?

Was it the first joint?

Or the second?

"I think it was the second joint," Matty says, staring up at the stars in the clear night sky as the fire pops embers straight up into the air.

"I think it was the Mad Dog," Chickie says. "Nothing good ever comes from drinking something purple." She too is lying flat on her back, staring at the sky.

"I think it was everything," KK says. She's leaning against a big rock, her legs straight out in front of her. Every once in a while, an ember lands near her, but she doesn't even notice.

"I think I'm gay," Harley says. He's cross-legged on the other side of the circle. He's dead sober. The deal with his sister and her friends is that he can hang, but he cannot partake. Even though he's only fourteen, he can also in a pinch drive them home if they are too wasted to do it themselves. This is the summer everyone gets his or her license, sixteen and freeeeeeee behind the wheel of a car, though absolutely no one is using good judgment.

They are at Black Rock, the name the townie kids gave the never-finished industrial park at the edge of town. Just off the high-way, the property had been cleared and the skeleton of a road built before the economy nosedived and everything stopped. It is the perfect party place. They can have a fire, and no one can see it. They can get wasted, and no one will know. They can get laid and … well, of course everyone will know about that, since there are no secrets in a small town or at the teenage party hangout place. But still. You can get laid.

Most summer kids aren't welcome at Black Rock. It's a townie thing. But being with Chickie is like having a Golden Ticket. It's midweek, so it's quiet. There's one other group off to the side. They are on mushrooms and are having their own issues right now.

"Did you guys hear me?" Harley asks.

KK shakes her head. "Yeah, Haw, we did. We don't care, honey."

"But I *want* you to care," Harley replies.

Chickie struggles to a sitting position and then leans over and yanks Matty upright as well.

"Harley, baby, it's not that we don't care," Chickie says, putting emphasis on *care*. "Of course, we care. What KK means by that is, it doesn't change anything. You are who you are with or without declarations."

"Do you think I'm gay?" Harleys asks them.

"Haw, it doesn't work like that," KK says. "That's something only you can know."

Harley looks at Matty. "When did you know?"

"Oh honey, you can't use me as a guidepost," Matty says. "I knew I was gay in the womb. Like, never a question. I could barely breast-feed. Thank God my mother switched me quickly to a bottle."

Chickie snorts. "Jesus, Matty."

"I don't know if I want to be gay," Harley says, his voice cracking.

KK flips herself over so she's on her hands and knees and then slowly pushes to standing. She gives herself a minute to find her balance and then oh, so carefully, she makes her way around the fire circle to Harley. She less than gracefully sits next to him and puts her arm around his shoulders.

"Dude, we are pretty fucking wasted right now," she says. "I'm not sure this is the best timing for you to make a major life announcement, never mind asking us to help you through it. I can barely keep my eyes open."

"We shouldn't have smoked that second joint," Matty says.

"We should not have drunk that Mad Dog," Chickie says.

Harley wipes his cheeks with his palms. "Are you seriously asking me to apologize for the timing of my coming out?"

"Oh, Jesus, *no*," KK says. "I'm just saying … actually I don't know what I'm saying. Here's what I should be saying. I love you. We love you. We will love whoever you love. Forever and ever. That's how family works. So, we don't care that you're gay—or you may be gay—or you're slightly gay. We will be here for you no matter what. Matty will give you advice. Chickie will hype you up. I will throat-punch whoever needs to be throat-punched. 'Kay?"

KK hugs her little brother. Matty and Chickie wave from the other side of the firepit and then lie back down.

Harley stares into the fire, but he has a little smile on his face, book-ended by his tear-stained cheeks.

Before we go out drinking, we all must shower, and of course, Matty puts on his Mateo hat and insists on styling all of us. He even brought me an outfit from his favorite boutique in the city, skinny black pants and a wraparound cranberry-colored top in some sort of insanely soft material that clings to me in all the right ways. The V-neck makes my boobs look amazing. Even Harley says so. Black suede booties with a heel give me a little extra oomph.

Jay texts me, asking what's up. I tell him to meet us after he gets off shift at Dockside, and that's how we find ourselves in a karaoke bar a couple towns over at 11 p.m. The five of us are pretty lit by the time Jay arrives.

"Oh, scrumptious," Matty says as Jay walks in and sees us crowded around a high top in the back.

"Settle down," I caution him. "Do not scare him away."

This is the first time Jay meets Matty, Bitty, Harley, and Keith. Obviously, Chickie knows him and knows him well, but I have no idea what she has told the others. I haven't asked, and she hasn't said. There are handshakes and hugs all around. He squeezes in next to me and slides his hand around my waist. "You look incredible," he whispers into my ear, kissing my cheek.

The group has had enough tequila to start signing up for karaoke except me because, while I love watching everyone else partake, I would rather be dipped in hot wax than stand in front of a bunch of drunks and sing off-key.

Harley and Keith do what they call their "famous" rendition of "You're So Vain," Bitty and Chickie sing Rozzi's "Best Friend Song," and Matty dips into the DJ's box of accessories, dons a giant cowboy hat, and absolutely crushes Darius Rucker's "Wagon Wheel," pointing straight at me when he croons, "Hey, Mama, rock me." A couple of more people get up and sing since it's getting close to midnight.

Suddenly, Jay grabs my hand and starts pulling me toward the stage. "C'mon, babe, it's our turn," he says. I try to yank my hand back.

"Uh, no, it isn't," I say. "I don't do this. Plus, we aren't signed up."

"I know the DJ," he says, continuing to haul me across the room, "and I texted him and told him I wanted the midnight slot. We're all queued up."

This cannot be happening.

But apparently it is.

Jay jogs up the couple of steps to the small stage and firmly brings me up beside him. The DJ gives him two mikes, and he hands one to me. He turns me to face the screen, where the lyrics will start scrolling, and he leans into me and says, "Get ready. It's going to start."

I can't tell if the room has gone quiet or the roar in my ears has drowned everything else out. I might faint.

Words start appearing on the screen. "You're first," he mouths at me, pointing.

Panicked, I put the mike up to my lips and say/sing the first words to scroll onto the screen.

"I'm a motherfucking train wreck."

Wait. What?

Also, the room explodes. Like everyone just goes crazy. Because this middle-aged woman and smoking-hot surfer dude are singing "Boyfriend" by Ariana Grande and Social House. They are clapping and yelling and stomping their feet.

"You go, girl," I hear someone scream, and I'm guessing it's Matty.

I lower the hand holding the mike to my hip and drop my head. Then I turn to look at Jay, who is smiling so big at me right now. He points back at the screen, where the words continue to scroll by whether I want them to or not. He closes the gap between us and puts a hand to my waist. He squeezes and gives me a wink.

So I turn back to the screen and sing. And as I make my way through the lyrics, Jay starts to dance around me, shaking his hips and grabbing my ass. He's smiling and nuzzling my neck and grinding against me, and the crowd is going bananas. Gwen Stefani-level B-A-N-A-N-A-S.

Then it's his turn in the song, and I learn two things:

1. Jay can sing. Like actually sing. He sounds amazing. What *can't* this fucking guy do?

2. Apparently, I love karaoke.

When he gets to *"Baby, I'm a train wreck too / I lose my mind when it comes to you,"* he yanks me to him. He dances with me, making me, for all intents and purposes, ride his thigh. We are gyrating like we aren't standing in front of two hundred drunk strangers. We pretty much do that for the rest of the song. When I sing the last line, *"Baby, we ain't gotta tell nobody,"* he snakes his free hand around the back of my head and pulls me in for an insane kiss, mouth open wide and lots of wet, sloppy tongue.

If you ever wondered what it looks like when someone brings down the house, that bar at that moment was it.

There's a knock at the front door.

Did I actually lock it this time?

"Jay? Come in, I think it's open," I call out from the kitchen.

"Babe, my hands are full. Come open the door for me," he yells back.

I make my way to the door and swing it open. "Fuuuuuuuck," I whisper.

This is hands down the most gorgeous sight I have ever seen. And I've been to White Sands National Park at sunrise.

Standing on the top step, leaning a shoulder against the post, with one ankle crossed in front of the other, is Jay. In a suit. A deep-blue business suit. *The* deep-blue business suit. White button-down shirt. Blue-and-silver tie. Top button on the shirt undone. Brown dress shoes. No socks. Usual messy hair. The blue of the suit makes his eyes a color I'm sure Pantone only seen only in a wet dream.

Fuuuuuuuuck.

"Hey," he says, cocking an eyebrow.

I slam the door. A few seconds pass, and I open it again. He's still there. But now both of his brows are raised, and his forehead is scrunched.

"You OK?" he asks.

"I might've—and let me stress might've—just had a teensy orgasm," I reply.

He bursts out laughing.

"You wanted to see me in a suit."

I take two steps toward him, grab that tie just under the knot, and yank him as hard as I can in the direction of the open door. "Yes. Yes, I did."

I haul him through the door and shut it firmly behind me. I purposefully turn the bolt and hear it click into place. His grin is huge, and he takes back control, grabs my hand, and starts toward the stairs.

We don't even make it halfway up. I make him leave on the shirt, tie, and jacket. I'm not sure who I am anymore.

13

HARLEY. Please come. It will be fun.

ME. No. For the millionth time.

MATTY. Mama … come.

KEITH. KK, seriously we wouldn't ask if we didn't mean it.

I am in the group text known as "K and The Gays." They are peer-pressuring me about Thanksgiving.

ME. Guys, I love you, but I don't want to spend a crazy, peopley Thanksgiving with you. Plus, I don't meet the criteria.

HARLEY. There are no criteria.

ME. Haw, it's Thanksgiving for gays.

KEITH. No it's not. It's Thanksgiving for people who make their own families.

ME. Guys, you literally call it 'Spanksgiving.' I've seen the photos. Provincetown Carnival is tamer. There are men in chaps. Only chaps.

MATTY. Those are the Pilgrims.

ME. Dude, your knowledge of American history is sad.

Harley wants me to come to Boston for the holiday weekend. I want to stay at the beach and eat a turkey sandwich. The town will be practically deserted because everyone heads inland to visit all the family that always takes advantage of them in the summer. Turnabout is fair play.

HARLEY. I don't want you to be alone. Bitty said she offered to fly you to Chicago.

ME. Let me be.

KEITH. KK, you know if you change your mind, you just show up, right? The door is open for you.

ME. I know, honey. Thank you. And I promise if I get too sad, I will make the drive.

It will be quiet. Really, really, really quiet. Chickie will have Dockside open Wednesday night because it's a huge party night, but then she closes the restaurant through the weekend. Gives her staff a chance to have some family time. She will spend the weekend with college friends in Maine. She's got no family left in town.

I won't do happy hour that Wednesday—it will be packed. Too much for me. My plan is to lie low, read, eat cheese, and binge-watch a half dozen shows. I don't know what Jay is doing. He hasn't said anything to me about the holiday weekend or having it off.

It's fine. I'm fine. Everything is fine.

August 2001

Jay is pulling the first of his two surfboards out of the back of the Ford Explorer when he hears his name. He turns and breaks into a huge smile.

His former nanny, Gunny, and his former tennis teacher, Jack, now Gunny's husband, are making their way across the parking lot toward him. Between them, holding their hands, is a small boy. The boy jumps and swings, making his parents stumble periodically as they walk.

"Jason," Jack says to the toddler, "stop it. Mommy will fall down, and we don't want that to happen."

"Why will Mommy fall?" the little boy asks.

"Because my gravity is off," Gunny says to him, using her free hand to rub over her pregnant belly. Baby number two is about three months away.

Jay props the board up against the side of the car. "Gunny!" he says. "I can't believe you guys came."

"Of course, we came," she replies, wrapping her arms around his ever-broadening shoulders. "I can't believe you are taller than me!"

Jay blushes and looks at the ground, then turns to pull his second board out of the back of the SUV. Carl, the driver, comes around the side and also breaks into a big smile. "Gunny!" he cries.

"Carl!" she says. "Oh, this is a great reunion. I've missed you guys."

Gunny hasn't taken care of Jay for about five years, since she got married. But she and Jay have stayed in touch. He didn't think she would come watch him surf in the Eastern Surfing Association's Annual Surf Challenge in Long Beach, but he invited her anyway. He is competing in the Boys U14 division for thirteen and younger. It's his first time in this competition, and he is nervous as hell. This is a pretty big deal.

Jack holds out his hand to Jay to shake and then to Carl. "Fellas," he says, "it's great to see you. I was sorry to hear you abandoned tennis for the cavemen of lacrosse, Jay." He claps the boy on the back and then bends to swing his own son into his arms. "Say high to Jay, Jason," he says.

Jay blushes even more and holds his palm up to the child for a high five. "I still can't believe you named him after me," he says, looking at Gunny.

"Well, you taught me everything I needed to know to raise a child," she says. "It made sense."

"I see there's another one coming," Carl says, pointing at her belly. "Do you know what you're having?"

"We don't," Gunny says. "But I think it's a girl because I feel totally different this time around."

"I think it's another boy," Jack says. "Jason does, too."

"I be a big brother!" the little boy says proudly.

Carl grabs one surfboard and motions to Jay to grab the other. "Let's go get you checked in, and then I can find a good place to watch with these three. Probably over there," he says, pointing at some dunes off to the side. "We can probably see good from there."

"We'll go stake it out," Jack says. "Jay, you've got water and stuff?"

Jay nods. "Yeah, I packed a whole cooler with drinks and food. I was hoping I'd do well enough to be here all day." He smiles shyly. He reaches into the back seat and grabs the duffel bag, which holds his wet suit, towels, and the rest of his gear. "I'll see you guys in a bit."

He starts to walk away with Carl and then turns back. "Thank you, guys. Thank you for coming. It … it really means a lot to me to have you here."

"Of course, we're here," Gunny says brightly. "We're always here for you, Jay."

The thirteen-year-old turns back toward the registration tent with Carl. Gunny and Jack exchange a look. Jack shifts Jason to his other hip and takes his wife's hand. "I know, babe. I know it pisses you off. There's nothing you can do. They won't ever change. As much as we can, we will be there for him. As much as we can. Come on, let's go grab some sand."

Gunny grimaces. "I just wish on my last day I had punched that horrible bitch in the throat," she says. Her husband throws his head back and laughs loudly.

"Throat punch?" little Jason says wonderingly, looking back and forth from Mommy to Daddy. His father laughs even louder as they make their way through the crowd.

My heart is pounding.

Sweat is about to start dripping off my forehead, and my chest heaves with my panting.

I know I need to pick up the pace, but I'm seriously worried I won't finish. Might die from cardiac arrest first.

I swing my arms up over my head and use the momentum to spin myself around, first noticing that my tiny Bluetooth speaker is vibrating itself toward the edge of the kitchen counter and—beyond that—seeing the outline of a large male figure standing in the doorway.

Both of those things make me shriek as I dive to try to catch my speaker before it commits suicide.

I miss. The speaker hits the Mexican tile floor and shatters into a trillion pieces. Jesse J, Ariana, and Nicki, who had been "Bang Bang"-ing their hearts out, abruptly go silent.

Jay steps into the kitchen, laughing. He's in sweats and a hoodie, and his hair is wet. He must've just come from surfing.

"Hey," he says, bending down to start to pick up the pieces of plastic scattered everywhere.

"Jesus, you scared the shit out of me," I say accusingly, also dropping to the floor to scoop up the remains of my dear, departed little speaker.

"Katherine, the door was literally open. Like, ajar. Be glad it was me. Also, what are you doing? And why do you have a dollhouse speaker?"

"I'm dancing it out," I explain, standing up to go get the dustpan and brush from the pantry.

When I come back, he's sitting back on his heels, waiting for me to explain.

"I'm dancing it out. It's a stress reliever. Chickie and I have been doing it since 2005. Way back we used to do it together, and, more recently, we do it on FaceTime. But she's got no signal in Maine, so I had to do it by myself today."

He grabs my phone off the counter and taps the music icon. "Bitches Be Manifesting," he says, reading the playlist name aloud. He starts scrolling.

"Hmm. Pink. Ariana. Lizzo. Selena. One Direction. Harry Styles. Miley. Whitney. Taylor. Madonna. Justin Bieber. Dove Cameron, interesting. Chaka Khan. This is quite the list. Why 2005?"

I tilt my head at him. "2005?"

"Yeah, you said you guys started doing this in 2005."

"Oh, right. That's the year *Grey's Anatomy* started."

"I still don't get it."

"On *Grey's Anatomy*, Meredith and Christina would dance it out whenever they got stressed. Chickie and I were all over that concept. We update the playlist all the time since we like to stay currently hyped up as opposed to OG hyped up."

"Ah," he says. "Makes sense. Why are you stressed today?"

"Yesterday was harder than I thought it was going to be."

His face softens, and he comes around to my side of the counter to pull me into a hug. "Katherine, didn't you go to Harley's? I just assumed …"

I shake my head. "I was invited of course, but no. I didn't feel up to all that. I just stayed here."

"Oh my God, I'm so sorry," he says. "I figured you were with your family. I spent the day at the meal center, serving Thanksgiving dinner. If I'd known you were here alone, I would've asked you to come. And we could've had a late dinner together."

Am I having hurt feelings because Jay never asked me what my holiday plans were? Absolutely. In his defense, did I share with him what my holiday (non)plans were? No, I did not. So of course, I can't hold this against him.

"It's OK," I tell him, giving him a quick kiss. "It was fine."

"God, I hate when you say that," he says. "Every time you say, 'I'm fine,' it means you are one hundred percent *not* fine. I mean, you had to dance it out. Not fine. Don't tell me you're fine if you aren't."

"Don't tell me what not to do," I say, pulling away from him and sweeping up the rest of the mess.

"All right, well, go jump in the shower or whatever because we have to go," he says, expertly changing the tone the conversation has taken on.

"Where?"

"Babe, it's Black Friday. We have to go buy you a new speaker. And not one made for a dollhouse. Real speakers." He slaps my ass and gives me a gentle push toward the stairs.

I start to head up, and suddenly he's right behind me.

"Actually"—he grins—"I think I need a shower, too, since I was just surfing. Then we can go. I mean, we've already missed the Door Buster sales, right? There's no rush."

I don't argue. I've never really been interested in a bargain anyway.

On Saturday we sleep late, and then Jay insists we dance it out while we are waiting for the coffee to brew. He is so happy about the Bluetooth speakers we bought for the house. Upstairs and downstairs. And he's got the music up so loud I think the ancient windows are going to shatter. He's all excited to add some songs to the playlist as well. With permission of course, he says. His enthusiasm is adorable.

Later, we are lounging on the family room couch under a pile of fleece. I'm stretched out with my legs across his lap, and he is sitting up but is so smooshed into the cushions it's hard to tell where his actual body is. He might well be a head and some legs. He is a champion cushion smoosher.

He's holding his book with one hand, and he has my foot firmly wrapped in his other hand. He's always touching me, like there's always some form of physical contact he instigates between us. It's 180 degrees from what I'm used to since; when I was married, I would be upstairs, reading or watching TV, and he'd be downstairs on his computer, doing whatever it was he did. Dating apparently.

But Jay always has a hand on me. I love that.

Wait. What? Did I just think "love"? About Jay?

No. I thought it about something *about* him. Not him. *I don't love him. Nope. No love here. Pay attention to your book, KK.*

He's reading one of his Mafia romance novels. He found a used bookstore a month or so ago, and he came back with an absolute mountain of spicy books for us. They were a dollar each. He prefers the Mafia ones, the biker gang ones, the ones in which she's fleeing her abuser, or it's a reverse harem. Those tropes all make me anxious. Mine are more mild enemies to lovers, fake boyfriend, hockey player stories. All with guaranteed HEA.

He lets go of my foot, and I see him moving his lips as if he's reading silently. He shakes his head in apparent frustration and reaches down into his backpack on the floor, pulling out a package of those little multicolored page tabs. He pops out a red one and sticks it on the page. I realize the book is littered with these tabs: blue, red, green, and yellow.

I poke him with my foot. "What are you doing?"

"These books drive me crazy," he grumbles. "I swear to God the descriptions of the sex. Half the time I think it isn't physically possible for their hands and mouths and dicks and buttholes to be in the places they say they are. Like it's Sex Twister or something."

I start laughing. "What are the tabs?"

"Oh, I mark the pages where I think, *No way can that work.*"

"And the colors?"

"So, blue for a shower or pool, red for no way in hell this can happen, green for outdoors, and yellow for personal experience."

"Personal experience?" I say, raising an eyebrow.

"Yeah, you know, positions I've done that I know work."

Oh my God, this guy.

"Seriously, Katherine, listen to this," he says, sitting up straight against the cushions. Oh, he's annoyed all right. He's unsmooshed.

"'He pulls away and rests back onto his shins. He lifts my ass high in the air while pulling my thighs against his chest. Then he hooks my feet behind his head. Holding me up, he rocks onto his knees and thrusts into me with abandon.'

"I mean, what the fuck?" he says. "Picture that. It's like, *what?*"

I can't stop laughing, but on the other hand, he has a point. I often feel like the lovers in these books have to be octopi to make some of this shit happen.

Jay grabs my hand and pulls me off the couch. He shoves the coffee table out of the way and motions to me to lie down. "Uh, what is happening?" I ask.

"We're going to try this," he says. When I hesitate, he adds, "Clothes on." I lie down.

"OK, so I'm here, on my shins," he says, marking the paragraph with his finger. "So lie on your back here, with your feet toward me. OK, so I lift your ass in the air—I'm assuming like this, with my hands underneath."

He pauses to move his knee over the page to keep the book open. My ass goes up.

"But now I have to … wait, what is it … oh right, pull your thighs against my chest. Do you think it's the front of your thighs? Wait, it must be, because the backs of your thighs aren't your thighs. They're your hamstrings. So it must be the fronts. So how the fuck do your thighs go against my chest if your ass is in the air?"

"Jay, you know I'm not in shape, right?" I ask, feeling my core beginning to quake.

"Hang on, babe. We're almost there," he says, barely paying me any attention. "Now, I have to hook your feet behind my head, hold you up, rock onto my knees, and thrust into you." He keeps one hand under my ass and uses the other hand to grab my feet and put them over his shoulders so they are behind his head. He has a shimmer of sweat on his brow. "OK, ready? I'm going to rock and thrust."

Except he rocks and loses his balance, tipping onto his side with my ankles crossed behind his head, taking me with him as he goes.

We lay there for a second, then we explode with laughter. "*See!*" Jay yells. "It's bullshit."

We untangle ourselves and lie on the floor. I turn my head and look at him. "Do you really like reading these, or do you do it for me?"

He looks back at me, his eyes flitting across my face. "Why can't it be both?"

I reach over and grab his book. "There are a lot of blue tabs in this one," I note.

"There are," he says, looking at me with interest.

"Want to go test some of the shower scenes?" I whisper.

"Oh, hell yes," he shouts, grabbing the book, grabbing my hand, and running up the stairs with me. An hour later, there's no hot water, the book is a pulpy, unreadable mess, and we are sound asleep under my down comforter from all the effort.

We are making dinner Sunday night. Without really thinking about it, we spent the entire holiday weekend together. From when he arrived Friday morning until now, we've been apart only long enough for Jay to go back to his apartment and get clothes. I don't know if this happened because he felt guilty that I spent Thanksgiving Day by myself or if we were just really enjoying being together. It's been nice.

Music from his phone is playing through the new speakers, and as we cook, he keeps dancing with me, singing to me, grabbing my ass, and spinning me in his arms.

I feel … happy.

My phone trills. "Matty FaceTime Video."

"Hey, Matty, what's up? Say hi to Jay," I say, turning the phone a little so we are both on the screen.

"Oh my God oh my God oh my God. I am so glad you are both together," he screams into his phone. *"Turn on the TikTok!"*

"Turn on the TikTok?" Jay says with a smirk. He watches as I start to pick up my phone. "You have TikTok?" he asks.

"What? Am I too old?" I snap back, immediately sorry that I've drawn attention to our age difference. "I created an account last year so I could follow the pug with no bones."

He turns off the music on his phone. "You can't open the app if you are FaceTiming," he says. "I'll do it."

We turn our attention back to Matty, who I realize is FaceTiming from his laptop. He's holding his phone up to the computer's camera. His hand is shaking. "Find this account," he says.

Jay types the account name into the search. "OK, got it," he says. "Now what?"

"The video is in the third row down in the middle. Play it."

Jay taps the video, and we peer at his screen.

"Holy shit," we say at the same time. Because … it's us. At the karaoke bar.

It's our "Boyfriend" performance. Not the whole thing, more like a highlight reel. I glance at Jay, who is staring intently at the screen. It starts with my opening line—"I'm a motherfucking train wreck"—and then pans to the crowd going ballistic. Then back to our performance. Whoever shot it was over to the side of the stage, about thirty feet back, so you can see us both. You can see Jay and his dancing shenanigans, and you can see the crowd reaction all at the same time. It's clearly bedlam but in a good way. Everyone is having fun, especially Jay and me.

I can't keep my eyes off myself. Have I ever watched myself have fun? Ever seen myself having a great fucking time? Is this what I look like when I don't have a care in the world? When I'm with someone I enjoy? Because if it is, I want to be like this all the time. I love the way I look. I love the way I'm looking at Jay. I *really* love the way he's looking at me.

The video ends with our "big finish" kiss and the audience screaming its appreciation.

We are silent. I actually forget that we're FaceTiming Matty until he clears his throat.

We look back at my phone. "You guys," he whisper-shouts. "It has more than a million views."

Jay and I look at each other, and our eyes are huge. It's like we are sharing a brain and a body right now. We look back at his phone, and he reads aloud: 1.1 million views, seven hundred thousand likes, seventeen thousand comments, twelve thousand favorites, and nine thousand shares.

"Look at the hashtags," Matty says.

Jay reads the hashtags: #cougargoals #cougardreams #yougogirl #agegap #livingthedream #karaokeheaven #capecodkaraokecouple

"*You guys are viral*," Matty shrieks.

Now *my* hands are shaking. "Am I a cougar?" I ask.

"No," Jay says.

"Yes," Matty says.

We all laugh. Jay puts his arm around me and pulls me in. "Well," he says, "if you are a cougar, you're *my* cougar."

14

"Jay, I need you."

I'm in the dressing room at the surf shop. I was able to get the wet suit about halfway on, but I am stuck with my arms three-quarters into the sleeves and the body part of it wedged under my boobs. I'm wearing a one-piece bathing suit underneath.

I am beyond self-conscious right now. I worked up a good sweat jamming myself into this fucking neoprene nightmare. Every terrible thing I think about my body? If those thoughts were a font, they'd be sixty-point **IMPACT** right now. I hate everything about myself. And I hate that I need him to help me, and I really hate that he's going to see me at my worst, physically and mentally. Most of the time, with his encouragement, I keep this shit at bay. But not today.

He pushes open the dressing room door and steps in, closing it behind him. He smiles.

"Ah, yeah, this is the tricky part," he says. "With practice, you'll be able to do it by yourself."

I lower my eyes. He moves around behind me, grabs both sides of the suit, and lifts me up, sort of shaking me as he does. He does this three times, and I'm in. He zips up the back and comes around to stand in front of me.

"Katherine," he says. "Katherine." He puts his fingers under my chin and forces my face up. I keep my lids lowered so I am still avoiding eye contact even if we are having face contact.

"Katherine." He's got that stern voice going. I really like that voice when we are in bed. I don't love it right now. He's about to make a point.

I meet his eyes. Those blue, blue eyes. "What's going on?" he asks.

"This suit makes me feel bad about myself."

"Why? Everyone has trouble getting into their wet suit. Everyone."

"I feel like if you stuck a big spoon right here"—I point to the side of my waist just above my hip—"and pushed really hard, I would explode out of this thing like a package of crescent rolls."

He laughs. Then he palms both sides of my face with his big, gorgeous hands and tips his head down.

"Really?" he whispers into my ear. "Because I'm literally trying to figure out if there's a way I can fuck you right now in this dressing room because you look so fucking hot in this wet suit."

Did I mention that Jay wants to teach me how to surf?

June 2009

Jay climbs the four steps and stands for a second in front of the screen door. He looks for a doorbell, but there doesn't seem to be one. He pulls the screen open and knocks on the wooden door.

He feels like an idiot standing there in his cap and gown with his academic cords around his neck, but that's what Gunny said she wanted. And he will always do whatever Gunny asks.

The door flies open. In the background, Jay can hear a child crying. But in front of him is Gunny, smiling, holding her arms out wide.

"Jay!" she cries. He steps into her embrace and feels himself immediately relax as her arms go around him.

"Gunny," he says. His eyes fill with unexpected tears. He tries to blink them away so she doesn't see them when she pulls back, but he isn't quick enough.

Turns out it doesn't matter; she's crying, too.

"You look so handsome," she says. "So accomplished. I'm so proud of you."

He graduated the week before from Bates College with highest honors. There was no one there for him. Carl died last year.

Gunny couldn't make the trip because she has a whole life here in Queens that has nothing to do with Jay and hasn't for a long time. But even though she's married and now a mom to four kids, she's stayed in touch. She wrote to him every week when he was at college. And she's seen him at least once every summer, usually catching him at a surfing competition.

"Are you all moved back?" she asks.

He nods. "Yeah. I'm actually going to live in university housing. It will just be easier."

"Have you seen your parents?"

He nods again but looks away. "Mm-hmm. We had dinner at their club the night I got back."

"And since?"

Now there's a head shake. Gunny notices how long his hair is. It sweeps up off his forehead and curls down to just above his shoulders. "No, not since. It's OK, though. You know. Whatever."

Gunny tries to smile but fears it looks more like a snarl. She still wants to throat-punch Irene Wells.

"Well, they must be thrilled that you are getting an MBA, right? And from Columbia! Ivy League. Boxes are checked."

Jay shrugs. "I guess. Hey, is Jack home? Can I see the kids? They must be so big now."

She takes his hand and pulls him inside. "Of course," she says. "Jason has been driving me crazy, asking when you are coming. He wants to show you his new lacrosse gear. His dad is not happy about that."

Jay laughs and steps inside the little house. "Ha, I bet," he says. "I'm glad I have influence over someone around here."

Jay says December is the best time to learn to surf because there are no people around. No one to crash into. Or fall on top of. Or in my case, drown next to.

I continue to really hate the way I look all suited up, but I am locked and loaded into the wet suit. I have neoprene booties on my feet, gloves on my hands, and a ridiculous hood over my head. I honest to God feel like Otis from Bloom County. Which made Jay laugh all day once I showed him a photo of Otis, because of course he had never heard of Bloom County. He continues to tell me I look amazing, and I apparently now have a praise kink.

We go surfing whenever we can fit it into his schedule, because Jay says for me it doesn't really matter what the tide is. We stay in the white water, never more than waist deep. For the first few times, I don't even try to stand up. He basically has me body boarding in the foam. I love his surf teacher persona because his face is serious, his concentration deep, and his hands all over me. Which is distracting and which, I think, raises my risk of drowning several notches. But I'm not complaining.

He says things like, "I want you to understand what the board can do and what you can make the board do," and I just want to stick my tongue down his throat.

Once we went out past the white water together on one of his boards. Oh, and he has five boards. *Five.* Surfboards. Nobody better talk to me about how many pairs of black shoes I have ever again. We sat together on his board, our backs to the beach, and just watched the waves come in. Jay talked and talked about watching the waves, learning which ones would be good to surf and which ones wouldn't, and how to decide which one you want. We sat there, bobbing on the surface, our legs dangling over the sides into the water, and he never took his hand off my waist while he talked into my ear and pointed to the swells. He took a selfie of us with his GoPro.

I still don't think I will ever actually stand up and surf a wave, but after a couple of weeks of this, I'm no longer terrified. I get what he says about the peace you feel on the water.

On this particular morning, I wake up earlier than usual, so I am extra jacked on caffeine. Jay texts and asks whether I can meet him at the beach instead of him picking me up as usual, so I squeeze myself into my wet suit, throw on a fleece and a hoodie, grab my bag (which has my towels, booties, gloves, and hood), and walk down to the beach. Jay's not here yet and, in fact, is close to half an hour late.

I'm actually getting ready to head back to the house when he comes running from the parking lot with my board. He shoves his feet in his booties, and I finish putting on the rest of my gear.

"Hey," he says, a little out of breath. No other explanation is offered. He starts walking toward the water with my soft board. After a minute, he realizes I'm not with him. He looks back over his shoulder.

"Coming?" he asks.

"Where's your board?" I ask. Today we were going to go out together on separate boards and see whether I can successfully choose a wave and ride it in. Not necessarily standing up, because I haven't actually done that yet outside of the white water, but just getting the feel for picking a wave and going for it.

"You can head out, and I'll run back and get it," he says, motioning me with his free hand to catch up.

"Without you?"

He rolls his eyes. *Rolls his fucking eyes.* At me. He has never done that before. Not to me anyway. Someone else in my life used to do it all the time. Most of the time, in fact. But never Jay. Until now.

"Come on," he says, dropping the board in the ankle-deep water. "You'll be fine. I'll be right behind you."

My eyes feel hot, and my nose feels prickly. No idea what is going on here, but everything feels off. So wrong. I don't want to go any farther, but I do. Because it's fine, right? Everything's fine. I'm fine.

He hands me the leash, and I wrap the Velcro around my ankle. Without touching me and without another word, he starts back toward the sand. I guess I am supposed to keep going into the water.

So I make my way through the white water, and when it's up to about my waist, I hoist myself onto the board like I now know how to do, position myself correctly, and start to paddle. I move out past the swells to where it's calm. It's definitely over my head out here. My heart thuds in my chest.

I turn the board so my back is to the horizon and I can watch for Jay to come back to the beach. There he is with his board, putting

on his hood and gloves. He picks up the board and starts to walk
out. Trying to be upbeat, positive, and totally not scared shitless to
be out here alone, I smile big and wave one hand over my head in
greeting. His eyes land on me, and then I see them grow huge on
his face. As wide open as they can be.

And then I hear a train come up behind me, and then the train runs
me over.

Of course, it isn't a train, silly. I'm in the ocean. It is the ocean de-
ciding it wants to kill me.

I realize this as I feel myself being slammed onto the bottom of said
ocean. It really hurts, this body slam onto sand and rock, and I gasp.
Which, being underwater, turns out to be a big mistake. Potentially
fatal.

I remember reading something once that said drowning is actually
really painful. That it hurts. It burns. One time when we were all
sitting around drinking and playing Would You Rather, the question that came to me was "Would you rather drown or freeze to
death?" I chose freeze to death because I had read that thing that
said drowning hurts.

And now I know it's true. Drowning hurts. My lungs feel like they're
on fire. Salty, watery fire.

I bounce along the bottom, and I decide to open my eyes. I look
for Daryl Hannah, because maybe she'll save me. I'm not cute like
young Tom Hanks, but a mermaid's gotta do what a mermaid's
gotta do, right?

I'm still attached to the surfboard by the leash, and it's basically dragging me. I realize that this is going to be it. I feel bad for everything I have put Chickie, Matty, Bitty, and Harley through over these last few months. It's been a lot. I'm a lot.

Suddenly, I am violently jerked upward, and then my head is above water. The sun hurts my eyes, and I begin coughing and puking up the ocean I swallowed. Salt water is apparently just as painful exiting as it is entering; my sinuses, throat, and lungs burn as I vomit out a gallon.

I feel a hard chest pressed to my back and a strong arm tight around my waist. I hear heavy breathing. I have zero strength and no words. I would like to go home now.

"Katherine," Jay says. He's kind of yelling. There's a weird buzzing in my ears. I'm so tired. He's half swimming, half lunging through the water, hauling me with him. "Can you stand? Can you walk? Jesus fuck, Katherine. Can you stand up?"

"Stop," I mumble.

He yanks the hood off my head. "What? What did you say?"

"*Stop.*"

He freezes. He plants his feet in what is now chest-deep water on him and carefully turns me around in his arms so we are facing each other. He pushes my hair off my face and cups one hand under my jaw.

"Jesus, Katherine, you scared the shit out of me," he says.

The buzzing is starting to clear from my ears, and the fog is starting to lift from my brain, although my arms and legs still feel like they weigh a thousand pounds each.

I scared the shit out of him?

Him?

"Let go of me," I say, even though I'm not 100 percent sure I can stand on my own. The water is just under my chin.

"What?" he says.

"Let. Go. Of. Me."

He's confused. *Join the fucking club, buddy.* I stare at him, those ice-blue eyes. He lets go.

I remain vertical. Maybe I'll buy a Powerball ticket later since I'm feeling so lucky right now.

I turn and start to walk away but immediately stumble because I am still attached to the surfboard by the leash. I catch myself, reach down, and rip open the Velcro, hurling it away from me. Free at last, I make my way toward the sand. I can hear Jay behind me, splashing to catch my board as it starts to float away.

I get to dry land and barely slow down as I walk up to the pile of our stuff on the beach, reaching down to grab my tote bag. I don't even bother to take off my neoprene booties. I just shove my All Birds in the bag and keep walking.

"Katherine, where are you going? Wait a minute. Katherine!"

Nope. No. No way. Not stopping.

Until he grabs my arm. Goddamn my short legs.

"Where are you going?" he says.

"Home," I say. "Let go of my arm."

"Why are you acting like this? I'm trying to make sure you're all right."

"Why am I acting like this? Why am *I* acting like this? Why are *you* acting like *that*?" My voice doesn't even sound like mine. I fight the urge to poke him in the chest. Or punch him in the throat.

"What do you mean?" He tilts his head at me.

I'm so tired right now. If I closed my eyes, standing here, I would fall fast asleep, I think.

"You left me alone, Jay. In the ocean. That you know I am scared of. On a surfboard. That you know I'm not comfortable on. You've been weird since you got here—late, I might add—and then you sent me out there all by myself. *All by myself. And I almost fucking died. So why are* you *acting like* that?"

He looks away from me, just for a second, and then looks back. In that flick of time, his face goes from confused/angry to just plain sad.

"Oh God, Katherine, I'm sorry. I'm so sorry. I wasn't thinking. I shouldn't have done that. You're right. That was really stupid on my part. I put you ... I put you in a ... you could've been really hurt. I would never do that."

"Well, you *did* do that," I point out. Because I can't *not* point that out.

He shakes his head and puts his hands on my shoulders. "Babe, I am so sorry. You're right, I did do that. I wasn't thinking. I was distracted. I got a text from my mother this morning, and I let it get to me, and I wasn't paying attention. Please know I would never put you at risk. I mean, I just did, but it won't ever happen again. I won't ever let anything like that happen again."

"I trusted you," I say, my voice cracking. Am I seriously going to cry right now? I hate myself.

"I know, baby, I know. I want you to trust me. With everything. I just let you down. Badly. I'm so sorry. Please forgive me. It won't happen again. Please." He moves his hands from my shoulders to the sides of my face. "Please."

I take a deep breath in and blow it out through my mouth. I lay my hands over his. "OK," I say. "OK."

"Forgive me?" he asks, leaning in and brushing his lips against mine.

"Yes," I say, pressing my mouth harder against his and opening it to allow his tongue to find mine. I feel a rush of heat through my center. Maybe almost drowning is foreplay.

We pull apart after a minute, and he pulls me back to our gear. "Let me get all this stuff, and I'll drive you back up the hill," he says.

"All right," I agree, reaching down to shove towels into his backpack.

"You know, I thought I might see Daryl Hannah when I was down there," I say.

He looks up at me, confused. "Who's that?"

I sigh and give him a hard shove. "Goddamn millennials," I say.

15

On today's "Jay-genda," which is what we call our plans for every Sunday when he is off work, is a trip to the tattoo shop Jay frequents. He has a new piece of art he wants done, and his guy Danny said he could squeeze him in. I am promised a mimosa brunch in Chatham if I come.

Jay has a truly incredible series of tattoos that run the length of his back. The main piece is an outline of a surfboard that goes from the base of his neck to the bottom of his spine. It's about five inches across. Within the surfboard are depictions of places and things that are meaningful to him, including the longitude and latitude of every place he has surfed.

One night when we are lying in bed, I touch each tattoo, and he tells me the story. There's the New York City skyline, the Bates College bobcat mascot, a martini and shaker, lacrosse sticks, a tennis racket and ball, a trophy, and lots more. There's even one that looks like a pen-and-ink drawing of a woman sitting hunched over on a sidewalk next to a building. It's Jasmine.

The surfboard is about half full of images. They fill the bottom, moving up his lower back. He says it's like that Drake song—"Started from the bottom, now we're here"—which of course I had never heard but which now has a place on the "Bitches Be Manifesting" playlist.

We stop at the Beechwood Café to get coffees, including one for Danny, and when we get there, he is just at the front door, unlocking it.

"Hey man," he says to Jay, his eyes flitting to me.

"Danny, this is my girlfriend, Katherine," Jay says.

Wait. What? Girlfriend? I have a label? We have labels? We're labeling?

"Hey," Danny says, giving me a once-over. I am immediately self-conscious and hyper aware of Jay's and my age difference. When it's just the two of us, I never think about it anymore. Even when I'm at the bar at Dockside, it's not really an issue because I feel like we're in our own little bubble there. A little cone of safety. It's only when we're in the big, wide world that I revisit it and wonder what people are thinking.

"Get yourself situated, Jay. I'll get my equipment set up," Danny says.

Jay moves me over to what is apparently Danny's station, on the far side of the room. He pulls his shirt off over his head and lies face down on the chair—it actually looks as if a barber chair and a chaise lounge had a baby—before rising up on his forearms.

"Babe, sit here by my head," he says, pointing to a stool on wheels. I roll it over as Danny returns and sets up his inks, needles, sanitization supplies, gel, and more. He opens a drawer and pulls out a piece of paper. "The one we talked about last week, right? The image you texted me?"

"Yeah," Jay says, looking over his shoulder. "No peeking!" he says, turning back to me. "It's a surprise."

"For me?" I ask, raising my brows in a question.

"Yeah," he smiles, reaching out and taking my hand. "For you."

I watch as Danny sprays a small area of Jay's back and then lays the transfer paper on his skin. He presses down for a few seconds and then peels it back. He pulls on latex gloves, picks up the little machine that holds the needle, and gets started. There's just a faint buzz, and Jay winces.

"Does it hurt a lot?" I whisper as I lean over so my arms are resting where his face is, putting my face next to his.

"Nah," he says, giving me a wink. "Just when he starts. Then it's fine."

We don't say much while Danny hunches over Jay's back. He has a piece of paper, a printout of an image I can't see, on the table next to him that he keeps glancing at for reference. I keep pushing the hair out of Jay's eyes and touching his cheek, and he just watches me and smiles. It takes about an hour.

"OK, man, all set," Danny says, pushing back his stool. "Do you want your girl to see first?"

I'm sorry, what? "Your girl"? I can't decide how I feel about all this labeling this morning. I mean, a part of me loves the validation, but another part is thinking, *Girl? Girlfriend? At my age?*

"Yeah, I do," Jay says, giving my hip a little shove and pointing his thumb over his shoulder. "Tell me what you think, Katherine."

I walk down the length of the chair and peer at the spot where Danny has worked his magic. The skin is red around the perimeter of the ink, and there's a little blood oozing in spots. It takes me a second to understand what I'm seeing.

It's a book. Specifically, it's *Ugly Love* by Colleen Hoover. It's an exact replica of the cover, the shades of blue in the background, the lighter blue of the letters, the air bubbles rising to the surface. It even says across the bottom in the teensiest font, "#1 New York Times Bestselling Author." It's my happy hour book. The book Jay went and bought after he saw me reading it at the bar. The book that launched him on his spicy romance novel journey. The book that was the basis of our first conversations. *Our* book.

He's looking back at me over his shoulder, gauging my reaction. My eyes fill with tears, and of course one escapes and rolls down my cheek. He sits up with a smile.

You better believe I'm his goddamn girlfriend.

Y

December 1995

Jay's eyes pop open. His first thought is *Santa*.

His second thought is, *What time is it?* He can see light behind his curtains in his bedroom. But Gunny told him he couldn't get out of bed until the clock said seven. He rolls to his side and looks at his nightstand. The clock says 6:47. He does the math in his head.

Thirteen minutes.

He rolls onto his belly and puts his face in his pillow. He listens. He hears no sounds.

When the thirteen minutes are up and the digital clock finally rolls over to 7:00, he tosses back the covers and hops out of bed. He opens his door carefully and peeks out into the hall.

Silence.

He goes back into his room and pulls on his slippers, because his mother hates the sight of bare feet.

He walks down the hall and out into the great room. The apartment in Manhattan is fully decorated from top to bottom in Christmas swag. There's a tree by the floor-to-ceiling windows sparkling with what must be ten thousand white lights. All the decorations are red. They are all the same size. Different shapes but the same size. The family doesn't decorate the tree. The decorator decorates the tree. The whole apartment really. Actually, it was a team of people, and they arrived one morning and swarmed the place during the first

Monday in December, and by the end of the day, it was Christmas. Perfect.

Gunny told Jay before she left yesterday after feeding him lunch that when he woke up this morning, there would be a stocking hanging on the fireplace mantel filled with presents from Santa. But now the mantle is bare. There were presents under the tree, all wrapped in matching silver paper with red-and-green glossy bows. About a half dozen. But there is no stocking.

Jay walks closer and pokes around a little, but he doesn't see a stocking anywhere. *Hmm.* Gunny promised. She always keeps her promises.

When she left yesterday after his grilled cheese and tomato soup, she had a strange look on her face. She hugged him hard at the door, swept his hair back from his forehead, and kissed his cheek. "Merry Christmas, little man," she said to him. "Remember what I told you. Don't get out of bed until seven."

He nodded solemnly. When he knew what the rules were, he always obeyed them. Sometimes it was hard to tell, though. Sometimes he got it wrong, and he didn't even know why. Never with Gunny, though.

Gunny let herself out of the apartment wracked with guilt, on her way to spend Christmas Eve and Christmas Day with Jack and his family in Queens. They were engaged now, and Jack told her she had to insist with Mrs. Wells that she was not working through the holiday. Before, it hadn't mattered because she had no family. But now, Jack was her family. His family was her family. But she was so worried about Jay. Irene Wells had been acting strangely for months. Ted Wells was barely around, even less than usual. Things weren't right.

But she left anyway because after all this time with the family, she knew she couldn't solve that pyramid of problems. She did her best to make Jay feel loved and included and safe, but when push came to shove, he wasn't hers.

She told Mrs. Wells that she had put together a stocking for Jay. She told her where she hid it. She knew that Mrs. Wells's personal shopper had bought some clothes for Jay; that's what was wrapped under the tree. But Gunny wanted him to have toys and books and candy. LEGOs. She'd even gotten him all the *Toy Story* characters. They had gone to see that movie three times since it came out at Thanksgiving.

Jay heard Gunny tell his mother about the stocking. Even at seven years old, he knew there wasn't really a Santa. There was no time in his world for fantasies, but he played along with Gunny every year because he knew it made her happy to see him happy.

Not seeing the stocking hung up means he has to go pull it out from its hiding place in the little closet just inside the kitchen door. So he does, and he sits right there on the floor and carefully unpacks the treasures one at a time, inspecting each item before laying it on the floor next to him. When he is done, he smiles. Then he pauses and listens again. He looks at the kitchen clock. His stomach tells him it is breakfast time. The clock says it is 7:40. Where are his mother and father?

He carefully repacks his stocking and lays it aside. He pushes himself to his feet and walks back down the hallway toward the bedrooms. He stops outside the master, taking a couple of deep breaths before he carefully … so carefully and slowly … turns the knob.

He pokes his head in. It is dark. He can make out the outline of the bed against the wall, but no light comes in through the blackout shades. He sees a lump under the blankets. His stomach felt funny.

Jay tiptoes into the room, leaving the door ajar so he can see where he is going. He walks over to the bedside and stands there with his belly pressed against the mattress. The bedside table is cluttered with two empty wine bottles, a wine glass, two water glasses, a box of tissues, used tissues, and a spilled bottle of pills. The white label said "zolpidem."

He can see his mother's hair poking out from under the blankets, but that's all he can see. The rest of her is buried. She is very still. He holds his breath and listens.

There it is. Faint, but he can hear it. Breaths in, breaths out.

His father's side of the bed is empty.

Jay retreats from the darkness and carefully closes the door behind him. He makes his way back to the kitchen and opens the refrigerator. He can reach pretty much anything he needs, so he takes out some jam and bread, and closes the door. He gets the step stool and drags it to the pantry, climbing up to reach the peanut butter. He makes himself a sandwich and eats it carefully. He can't reach the plates, but he can reach the napkins.

After eating, he goes to his room and puts on a pair of khaki pants and a button-down blue shirt. He tucks in his shirt and adds a leather belt. He combs his hair and brushes his teeth. Back in the kitchen, he retrieves his stocking and brings it to the living room, where he again carefully unpacks it on the floor beside the gorgeous Christmas tree. He opens all the boxes holding the *Toy Story* characters and takes them out, lining them up in order of his favorites— Rex first, then Buzz, then Woody.

He will play quietly until Gunny comes for him, he thinks. It will probably be soon. Gunny always comes for him.

I smell coffee.

It smells so good.

I open my eyes. Jay is sitting up next to me in the bed, holding a mug and using his hand to waft the steam coming out of it toward me.

"Is that for me?"

"Good morning. Merry Christmas."

I sit up, and he hands me the mug. He picks up another one sitting on the nightstand next to him.

"Cheers," he says, and we clink.

I sip. He makes it exactly how I like it.

"Merry Christmas," I say back, leaning in to give him a kiss. "What time is it?"

"Early. Like seven," he says. "No one else is up yet." We used to do Christmas at my suburban house on the cul-de-sac, but this year's chain of events led everyone to decide that we should do Christmas at the beach house. Bitty flew in, and she, Harley, Keith, and Matty are all ensconced in their bedrooms. Chickie was over last night for Christmas Eve and will be back late morning for presents, food, drinks, and the annual viewing of *Die Hard*. Matty will leave this afternoon to go see his mom.

Jay puts his mug back on the table and reaches down to the floor next to the bed. He pulls up a—wait, what?—Christmas stocking. A big, red velvet Christmas stocking, all lumpy and bulgy. *Is that ... is that* my *name in glitter along the top? Sweet Jesus, it is.* Clearly handwritten, based on the wobbly lines.

"Santa came," he says, handing it to me with what appears to be a shy smile. Oh, good Lord, this man.

"Jay! I didn't ... I didn't ..."

"It's OK, babe. You didn't have to do anything. I mean, if you asked my parents, they'd tell you I shouldn't have one because I'm on the 'permanent naughty list.' Right? It's fine. I wanted to do this for you. I wanted your Christmas to be special."

"I mean, I did get you presents," I continue to try to alleviate my instantaneous guilt over this situation. "They're under the tree."

He kisses me. Hard. "Katherine," he whispers, brushing my hair off my forehead. "It's OK. I wanted to do this."

I haven't had a Christmas stocking in decades. My mother told us that Santa's rule is that once you either graduate from high school or turn eighteen, whichever comes first, you stop getting a stocking. So through our adult lives, we just never had them. It made sense, because Santa is for kids. Christmas, for all intents and purposes, is for kids. Celebrating Christmas all these years with my grandchildren-less parents and childless siblings always did come across as a little forced. We'd get together, open some presents, eat some food, and go back to our respective homes.

Am I going to cry?

"Are you crying?" he asks me.

"Maybe?" I say, blinking a thousand times. "This is so sweet. I don't know what to say."

"Don't say anything," he replies. "Dive in. I'm super proud of this stocking."

"Should I dump it out? Or take things out one at a time?" I ask. In my family, Harley and I always carefully unpacked our stockings, while Bitty was a dumper.

"*One at a time,*" Jay whisper-shouts at me. "What kind of savage *dumps out* their stocking?"

I giggle and reach in. Five packages of Classic ChapStick, three in each package. I look up at him.

"I know you don't like the flavored ones," he says.

Next, I pull out a small plastic bottle. I turn it to see the label and read aloud, "#LubeLife Water-Based Watermelon-Flavored Lubricant."

"Jay!" I say, immediately turning bright red. I can feel the flush work its way up my face all the way to my hairline. He shrugs and laughs.

"Something to think about," he says. "Maybe when we play 'Watermelon Sugar.'"

"Whose stocking is this?" I ask, giving him a shove.

"Keep going," he says. Out come Hershey's kisses, the almond ones, then those little Ghirardelli dark squares with the sea salt, and then

Swedish Fish. These are all my favorite candies, and again I have to blink a million times because the fact that he knows all this makes my eyes sting.

Then out comes a paperback, *Puck Me Secretly*. I look at him, eyebrows raised.

"Hockey romance! I think you're going to love it."

Next comes a plain white box, and Jay shifts around on the bed next to me, settling himself and then pulling me close to his side. I open the box and pull out what looks like a sheet of instructions.

Puzzled and slightly alarmed, I open the paper and read aloud, "The Rose Toy Clit Sucker with Thrusting Bullet Vibrator." I look at him, and he has his eyes glued to my face, waiting for my reaction.

I grab the down comforter and yank it up over my head, slamming myself as far down the mattress as I can to hide. I can hear him laughing. Then he joins me under the blanket.

"Do you like it?" he says, trying to keep a straight face.

"Oh. My. God. I am going to die," I say.

"Babe, it has ten levels of suction. I can't wait to see the different faces you make."

"Wait, I thought this was *my* stocking."

"Oh no, Katherine. This one is for both of us. I'm hoping you'll join me on the 'permanent naughty list.' Now come on, there's one more thing in there."

He flips the duvet back and picks up the stocking, holding it out to me once again. Glitter sprinkles the sheets. I shove my hand in, all the way to the bottom, where I feel an envelope.

When I open it, I see two tickets. Tickets for Taylor Swift's March show at TD Garden. I look more closely.

"Pit?" I say, looking up at Jay's truly radiant face. "We are going to Taylor, and we are in the pit? How? How did you do that? These tickets are a fortune! Actually, I thought they were all gone!"

Another shrug. "I know a guy," Jay says. "He helped me out. I thought it would be fun. We can dance it out right in front of Taylor. Swifties for life, right?"

"Do you love her because I love her?" I ask him.

"Why can't it be both?"

I throw my arms around him, then pull back just enough to kiss his entire face. A thousand kisses. Everywhere I can reach while still keeping my arms circled around his shoulders. "This is amazing. You are amazing. This is the best Christmas I think I have ever had," I say.

He smiles at me, this beautiful smile that goes all the way into his eyes, stretching to both sides of his gorgeous face.

"I was hoping you'd say that," he says, then pulls the duvet back over us and grabs that white box.

16

Chickie is drunk.

She was drunk when I arrived about a half hour ago, and I am still sipping my first margarita. We are lying on her bed, allegedly watching *Bridgerton*, but she is holding a hand over one eye, and I am scrolling my phone.

"I see two *Bridgertons*," she says.

"Dude, you are shit faced," I reply. "I'm shutting this off. You won't remember any of it anyway."

"I *am* drunk." She sighs, sitting herself up straighter. Or trying to anyway. I reach over and grab the pillows behind her, plumping and readjusting them to help her stay upright.

"Do you think I'm an alcoholic?" she asks me.

"Do *you* think you're an alcoholic?" I answer, wondering where this is coming from and where it's going.

Another sigh. "No. Maybe. I don't know. I drink. Sometimes a lot. I read something that said even if you don't drink every day, if you drink to get drunk, then you're an alcoholic."

"Do you drink to get drunk?"

"I feel like I drink, and then I end up drunk," she replies after a moment of thought.

I ponder that. "Sounds accurate. I mean, we don't set out to get drunk. We set out to go out. To have a good time. And alcohol has always been a part of that for us. And quite often, we end up at least a little drunk, and some of the time, a lot drunk. We have been various degrees of drunk, a lot."

She turns to me and sighs. "I hate January. It's a stupid month. Full of false promises of new beginnings. Plus, it lasts forever. The weather is always shitty. Also, I'm a terrible person."

Hmm. Not sure what the hell is going on tonight. I have a feeling whatever it is, it's a lot.

"Because …?" I prompt.

"I was happy when your shit blew up."

I choke on the sip of margarita I was taking. "Say that again."

"I was happy when your marriage ended."

I turn my body so I am facing her. She is steadfastly not looking at me.

"Explain," I demand.

"I need a drink," she says, trying to swing her legs over the side of the bed, away from me. I grab her arm. "No way, Chickie. I will get you some water. You sit there and explain what exactly you mean when you say you were happy when my thirty-year relationship and twenty-five-year marriage went up in flames."

"M'kay," she says.

She waits until I return with her water, and she chugs half the glass. I settle back down beside her. My cocktail is on the bedside table. I have no interest in drinking right now.

"Do you know why I keep the restaurant open all year?" she asks.

"Don't change the subject," I say sternly.

"I'm not! This *is* the subject. Do you know why I keep the restaurant open? It barely breaks even from November to April. Like, by a thread. Enough money comes in to pay the bills. I take no salary for those months. Do you know why?"

Two things:

1. What are we actually talking about?
2. I had no idea that she lost money during the off season by staying open. Her father must spin in his grave all winter.

"Why?" I prompt again.

"Because if I didn't, I would die of loneliness or alcohol poisoning, whichever came first."

"Chickie …"

"Shut it, KK, and let me finish. I actually do have a coherent mother-fucking thought right now even though I can tell you think I don't."

I say nothing.

She pokes me in the chest. "You are my best friend," she says. "You have been my best friend since we were toddlers. But if you add up the time that we actually spend together—summertime—then it's only one hundred fifty-nine months. That's the math for sum-mertime besties. June, July, August. One, two, three. Three times fifty-three. One hundred fifty-nine. See? And when you divide that by twelve months, that's really only thirteen years. Well, 13.25 because one time I did the actual fucking math, but you know, we can round down for this conversation."

I remain baffled. And silent.

"So. We've been friends since we were two. And we're now fifty-five. So that's fifty-three years. Only it's really only thirteen years be-cause we are summertime friends. And yeah, yeah, we text and FaceTime and dance it out and whatever in the off season, but you aren't *here*. You're *there*. And you have that whole life. That *nine-month* life. That's the majority of it, you know? That's four hundred seventy-seven months in case you were trying to figure it out. A clear fucking majority of time being not *here*. Being *there*. With *him*. And *them*. Whoever *they* are, because I don't honestly know. I just don't know. I was never invited to be *there*. Because I'm just *here*."

"Oh Chickie." I breathe out.

She holds up her hand, her palm inches from my face. "Don't you dare fucking say anything right now, KK. Don't you dare. Don't you think you are going to apologize for living your life. Because that's what it was, right? You lived your summertime life, and you lived your other life. And honestly, I did too. After my dad died, I kept the restaurant open through the winter so I didn't die of alcoholism, and I fucked the meat delivery guy every once in a while to keep my pipes flushed, and it is what it is.

"But then it all turned out to be a big, fat lie, and you threw him out, and you were *here*. Suddenly *here*. In the not summertime. In my time. And yes, I hate him and want to kill him for what he did to you. And yes, I'm so sorry you had to go through that, but if I am being honest—and you know me, I'm honest to a fucking fault—I was so happy. Because you were here. Full-time. Off season. And I wasn't alone.

"That's why I'm a terrible person. Because I was happy that your sadness meant I wasn't alone."

She takes my hands in hers and squeezes. "And then you found Jay."

I end up sleeping over at Chickie's, mostly because shortly after she dropped several life bombs on me, she passed out. I was nervous to leave her alone and hell bent on finishing what I felt like was three-quarters of a conversation.

I wake up early and pop out to get both Dunkin' and McDonald's because I'm not sure what her hangover needs are going to be. I let myself in with my key when I get back.

She's sitting at the kitchen table, absorbed in her phone. I know she's playing her solitaire games. It's all part of an anti-Alzheimer's strategy that she came up with around our fiftieth birthdays to—and I quote—"keep my brain from turning to mud." She's got me doing it too, especially since I watched my mom fade away.

I lay everything out in front of her—the Dunkin' hash browns and the stuffed biscuit bites, bacon, egg and cheese on an English muffin, the medium frozen coffee, and the medium hot coffee, light and sweet. Plus, the McDonald's large Diet Coke with light ice; bacon, egg, and cheese McGriddle; Egg McMuffin; and sausage biscuit with egg.

"Oh jeez, KK," Chickie says, surveying the bounty. "I wasn't that bad."

"Well, I wasn't sure if we were going to treat the hangover, eat our feelings, or both," I reply, laying out a metric ton of napkins and a half dozen straws. "Do you want hot sauce?"

"Nah," she says, pulling both the frozen coffee and the Diet Coke toward her. "I'll just eat them plain. Which do you want?"

"Oh, no honey, you pick first. I had less than one margarita last night. I was too blown away by your true confessions to drink."

She hangs her head. "Yeah, about that. How about we just skip the postgame analysis?"

"No way," I reply. "How much do you remember?"

"I think all of it unless I ended up actually setting something on fire. I know there were metaphorical flames."

I reach over to her and hug her shoulders. "Listen. I love you. You love me. Bottom line is that. So ultimately there's nothing to worry about. But I do want to talk through some of this, if you want to."

She shakes her head. "I don't really want to. What I felt ... what I feel ... about you, Jay, your asshole ex, us ... that's all it is—my feelings. I can't expect my feelings to influence you and the way you live your life, nor do I want them to. That sure as hell isn't fair to you. And it's selfish of me. My expectations are not supposed to be your reality."

I nod. "OK, I guess I can see that," I say. "But should we talk about you feeling so alone? I mean ... the meat delivery guy?"

"Chuck."

I spew my iced caramel macchiato across the table.

"His name is not Chuck."

She stares at me for a second and then lays her head on the table. Her shoulders begin to shake.

"Wait," I say, barely able to get out the words through my laughter. "You never put that together? That the meat delivery guy's name is Chuck?"

Her whole body is shaking. She gently bangs her forehead on the table a couple of times before raising what are now tear-stained cheeks to me.

"Chuck," she wheezes. "Fuck my life."

It takes a good five minutes to recover from that. When we have pulled ourselves together and I have cleaned up my macchiato mess, I sit next to her and pull my chair close.

I can't not pick the scab that's delicately laid over what she said last night about our friendship. I should leave it, but that's never been me.

"I always thought you wanted to come back here and run the restaurant with your dad. I got the feeling last night that wasn't really the case."

She sighs. Then she eats all the Dunkin' hash browns and drinks half the Diet Coke. I am watching food heal a human right before my eyes.

"I feel like … I don't know, in my fifties, I feel like I am triggered by everything," Chickie says. "I used to go through life unencumbered by what was going on around me. I just did my thing. But for the last ten years, I feel like I feel *everything*.

"The thought of a specific day or month or even a year that's tied to a memory or an experience—it triggers me. The idea of seeing someone else having or doing something that I think I might want—it sets me off. It depresses me. Depression isn't me. Or it never was. But now I feel so fragile all the time, and I don't know how to deal with it, how to make it stop. I feel like I live my life on a sheet of cracked glass.

"And I've always understood the reality of our relationship, that I had one life and you had two lives. It never bothered me until all of a sudden it did. You know? When I realized you were still here in the fall, it just set me off to thinking about how I had gotten shafted for all those years because of the choices I had made, because of the expectations that were laid on me by my father, by the restaurant. My obligations, you know? And you can't ignore your family obligations. Certainly not in my family.

"But it's not like we even ever really talked about it," she continues, unwrapping the McGriddle and examining it closely before laying it on the table. "It's not like my dad sat me down after I graduated from high school and said 'Chickie, I'm going to let you go to college and have four glorious years of freedom and the chance to become your own person, but then you will come back here, and I will crush the life out of you.' I mean, we never had that conversation. It was just understood. I understood. So I did it. In reality, the choices I thought I had made weren't really choices."

She picks up the Dunkin' frozen coffee and stirs it with the straw. It's partially melted. "Did you get this from the Front Street Dunkin'?" she asks.

"Of course I did," I answer. "They are the only ones who know how to make a good frozen coffee."

She nods.

"So weird," she says, "that there is zero consistency among Dunkin' frozen coffees."

I smile, since this is one of the many "same-old, same-old" conversations we have about things.

Now it's my turn to pick up the McGriddle, but I don't want to eat it either. Instead, I think about the weight of family. I never felt like our parents laid expectations on us, other than to be good people and be kind. But certainly there were no instructions to carry on a legacy.

We had none. People like Chickie and Jay—they grew up with lots of expectations laid on them. Chickie inherited a multigenerational family business that was beloved in the community. The expectation was that she would carry it on, simply because she was next.

And it seems as if Jay's parents have practically disowned him because he rejected the expectations they had for him. He talks about how he struggled to figure out his path forward, first with those expectations, and then without them. And the only way he could see to get out from under that pressure was to live the most basic life he could imagine, working paycheck to paycheck, going town to town, putting no more into life than he was willing to take out.

He was being crushed, like Chickie. It just looked different.

I suddenly appreciate how lucky I am. Even after my own shit storm.

I realize Chickie is staring.

"I know you don't want me to say, 'I'm sorry,'" I tell her, "so I won't."

"Can we leave this now?" she asks. "Can we just forget everything from the last twenty-four hours?"

I lean in and hug her to me. "OK," I say. "Except we have to find you a new fuck buddy. What's the produce delivery guy's name?"

17

Yes, I'm going to Chickie's high school reunion. As is Matty. And no, it won't be weird. We know everyone from her class because we spent every summer with them. Hell, I lost my virginity to Brad Wiley, also a member of the class of 1985. (News flash: Brad has not aged well.) Made out with a whole bunch of other '85 boys, too. Probably half of the guys in this room have touched my boobs. It was summer at the beach.

So we all three go to the reunion at the Holiday Inn one town over, held in what they call (with a straight face) their "banquet room." A DJ plays only songs from 1981–85, per order of the class president. Oh, and the reunion's on Groundhog Day. Why? Because it's funny. They also have one every year. Why? Because it's February, and what else is there to do?

Man, do we get shit faced. So much tequila. Margs, shots, straight from the bottle. So much.

ME. We are drunk.

SUPER-HOT SURFER GUY. No shit.

ME. Guess what there are none of right now.

SUPER-HOT SURFER GUY. People with common sense, good decision-making skills, and clear vision?

Me. Fucking Ubers.

ME. Fucking class princess Alynn Fucking Monroe fucking took them all, and by all I mean both of them.

ME. Can you come get us?

ME. Oh shit, are you mad?

ME. Is this text broken? Is my phone even on?

SUPER-HOT SURFER GUY. Wait for me in the lobby. It's cold out.

We are literally in a pile of each other on a lobby couch when Jay arrives. He takes us one at a time outside to his car—Chickie first, then Matty, then me. I get to ride shotgun because, as I shout to the bodies in the backseat, *"I am the girlfriend, bitches."*

Jay brings us all to my house, and again one by one he brings us inside. When he carries me in last, I see Chickie and Matty on the big couch in the family room, covered in blankets. Jay has carefully positioned them on their sides so they don't choke to death if they vomit in the middle of the night, and he strategically places various plastic trash cans by their heads, just in case.

He's such a great guy.

He carries me up to my bedroom, lays me on the bed, takes off my shoes, peels my dress up over my head, tugs a T-shirt onto me, and rolls me under the covers. I am a tequila-infused rag doll.

He strips down to his boxers and climbs in on the other side. I feel him tug me over against his chest, making sure I too am on my side. He smooths my hair back off my face.

"Thank you, Jay," I murmur, almost passed out. "You're such a great guy."

"Go to sleep, Katherine," he says. A minute goes by, and when I don't answer him, I hear him whisper against the back of my neck, "I love you."

Wait. What?

August 1985

Dockside is jumping. The outside deck is packed, the inside dining room is packed, the bar is three deep, plus all the high tops are full. It's a ninety-minute wait, and people are actually waiting. The hostess station is in chaos.

KK and Chickie are sweating buckets bussing tables. Matty is working the hostess station, but he's not great under pressure. His madras shirt is soaked through with his sweat, which stems partly from the suffocating late-summer humidity and partly from his sheer terror at fucking things up. He has already double-booked two tables today. Chickie's father reamed him out both times.

Chico Madeira runs a tight ship. He has a seasonal staff that arrives every spring green as hell and in need of training, discipline, and the instilling of fear. Working at Dockside is like joining the marines. A third of the newbies wash out in the first two weeks and go crying over to Twister's ice cream stand, where the living is easy and you build up the biceps on your scooping arm.

But at the restaurant, the money is amazing, and those who stick it out can go back to high school or college or wherever with a fat and sassy bank account.

At seventeen, the friends are old enough to wait tables, but Chico won't let them. Hell, he doesn't even pay Chickie. He doles out an allowance, keeping her on a short leash. Matty and KK make minimum wage, and they get a teensy percentage of the tips the front of the house staff pulls in. They split that tiny pot with the kitchen guys, all of whom are assholes.

They clear tables, stack dirty dishes by the sinks, wash glassware behind the bar, and run and run and run. Except today. Today Matty is hosting with Karla and Debbie, two girls who go to high school with Chickie. Chickie hates them, which is why she strongly believes her father hired them and gave them the cushiest job at the restaurant. They get to wear dresses and nice sandals and smile at people and carry around menus.

Chickie is out on the deck, clearing a table of ten that just vacated the premises. They had three—*three*—toddlers with them, one of whom cried the entire time, one of whom threw everything he could reach onto the floor, including dozens of french fries, and one of whom sat on his mother's lap and sucked his binky through the meal. Chickie loved that one. She kept slipping him oyster crackers.

Anyway, this table and its immediate surroundings are disgusting, and it will take a few minutes to clean it off, then break it back up into smaller tables. Large parties are a bitch. And they usually tip like shit.

KK is behind the bar, madly washing wine glasses. Everybody wants Chablis on a humid day. Or sangria. Ugh. Lipstick stains are the bane of every glass-washer's existence, and today is no exception. KK has the extra bleach-soaked rag at her sink, using it to swipe the lipstick before she plunges it into the scalding mix of hot water, soap, and the cleaning solution that supposedly sanitizes it. After holding it up to make sure the lipstick is gone, sending water running down her arms and soaking her already- sweat-soaked polo, she dips it into the second sink to rinse it. The glasses go upside down onto the drying rack, although it's so busy that the bartenders are grabbing them, still wet, right from the rack. There's been zero chance to slide any of them onto the holders that hang from the ceiling.

Suddenly Matty is at her side, yanking on her shirt, his eyes huge. Like, bugging-out-of-his-head huge.

"Mama," he whisper-shouts. She can barely hear him over the buzzy hum of tourists getting shit faced. He yanks again.

"Matty, stop. You're going to make me drop a glass." KK glances up at his face and freezes. "What? What the hell is wrong with you?"

"Mama. Bathroom. *Now.*" He yanks again and makes his way down the bar toward the opening.

KK looks at all the dirty glasses, at Matty's rapidly retreating back, and at the ten or so clean glasses she has on the rack. She sighs and decides to risk it. She follows her friend.

She sees him go into the ladies' room.

Once she's inside, he throws the lock on the door. "Matty," she says, "people are going to want to come in here."

"I need a minute," he shrieks and hides his face in his hands. He slumps against the wall.

KK quickly checks the two stalls to make sure they are empty and then grabs his shoulders. "What happened?"

He drops his hands and looks at her. Tears fill his eyes and are about to spill down his face.

"Matty. What. Happened?"

"Lou in the kitchen came out and told me to go into the storage pod to get cans of crushed tomatoes. As many as I could carry. Apparently, there's a run on shrimp fra diavolo today, and they keep running out. He handed me a box and told me to fill it with the cans and bring it back. They were too slammed to go themselves."

"So this is about tomatoes?" KK asks.

"No!" Matty cries, and the tears burst the eyelid dam and run down his cheeks. "No! Oh my God!"

KK takes a deep breath. "Matty. Matty. Look at me. Let's breathe. Right? Like we do. In through our nose. Right? Out through our mouths. In. Out. In. Out. OK, good. Now. Tell me."

KK wipes his cheeks with her thumbs and holds his face in her hands. Their eyes are locked on each other. If someone harassed him, she would kick his or her ass.

Matty takes in one more breath. "So I go out to the pod, and the door is a little open, which is weird. But I don't really think about it, and I just pull it open all the way, and you know how it's so heavy, and when you pull it hard, it just swings all the way open all by itself? So yeah, it did that, just swung all the way open all by itself, and I'm standing there, and the pod is all lit up with the sunlight. You know, because it's sunny, and the door is wide open."

He stops and takes another breath.

"Keep going," KK says encouragingly.

He starts crying again. "And all lit up there inside the pod is Chickie's dad, and his pants are at his ankles, and he's … he's …"

Oh Jesus, KK thinks. *Oh no. No. No. No. No. No.* She wraps her arms around him and pulls him into her. "Who?" she asks.

"Maureen," he sobs. "He's fucking Maureen. She's like bent over one of the shelving units, and her skirt is up over her butt, and he's fucking her from behind. And when the light hits them, they both look over at me, and they freeze. They just freeze.

"And she's holding on to the shelves where the cans of crushed tomatoes are."

KK pulls back from Matty, holding him at arm's length. "Wait," she says. "What?"

Matty huffs a breath. "She was in front of the tomatoes. I couldn't get the tomatoes."

"Oh Matty," KK says, pulling him back in for another hug. "Come on. Let's wash your face off, OK? Pull yourself together, and we'll go get that box, and we'll go back and fill it with the cans of tomatoes. They'll be gone. It will be safe. And I'm going to guess it will be safe from now on. Chico will have to find a new place to be his disgusting self."

Matty nods. "OK, Mama. Thank you. And we won't tell Chickie, right?"

KK pushes him toward the sink. "That's right, baby. We won't tell Chickie a thing."

🍸

CHICKIE. SOS.

CHICKIE. Mama, I need your help ASAP.

CHICKIE. Code fucking red.

It's Valentine's Day, and I am on the giant old couch in the family room watching *Love Actually* on demand. Don't tell me it's just a Christmas movie. It's timeless. Also, Laura Linney's character, Sarah, is the saddest character in all of rom-com history. I will fight you on that.

Chickie is blowing up my phone, which is weird because she's working tonight. Dockside is full for dinner reservations, and I know she expected the bar to be busy because I helped her with a social media campaign a few weeks ago.

I came up with Gal Pal Val(entine's Day).

I know, it's weak, but in my defense, I've been out of work for a few years. My tagline game has lost its edge.

But anyway, the promotion was two-for-one cocktails and half-price apps in the bar all night on Valentine's Day for the single ladies. Bring a gal pal, drink cheap, eat cheap, and have fun. She ran it on Facebook and Instagram.

My phone rings. It's Jay.

"Hey what's up?" I answer, and through the line I hear what can only be described as chaos and bedlam.

"Hey, Katherine, uh, Chickie wants to know if you can come down and help me in the bar. It's pretty packed here, and Susie was sup-posed to come in and help, but her baby has croup or something, so I'm totally slammed."

"Me? How can I help?"

"Yeah, so listen, I can't really hear you, and honestly I'm desperate, so can you just come?" he asks, and the line goes dead.

Hmm.

I change into jeans and a long-sleeved black T-shirt, put my hair in a ponytail, and head down to the bar. I have to park two blocks away, and when I walk in, I am hit with a wall of sound. It is loud in here because, holy shit, it is wall-to-wall women. Interspersed with men. Hungry-eyed men. It's like the two-for-one drinks were the chum, and the sharks have arrived.

I see Jay behind the bar, and he looks … frantic? Frazzled? Definitely sweaty. Also gorgeous. I catch his eye, and he gestures madly for me to join him.

"Oh, thank God," he says. "Can you first just bus tables and wash glasses? I'm almost out of everything." He hands me a tray. "Thanks, babe."

He turns back to the bar to fill orders that are being shouted at him from all sides. I see that the dining room servers have taken to making their own cocktails and pouring their own draft beers because Jay simply can't keep up.

I fight my way through the crowd and begin snagging empties off table after table. I sweep dirty napkins onto plates and pile as much as I can on a tray before making my way back.

Rewinding forty years, I start washing the glasses in the bar sink and placing them upside down on the drying rack. As quickly as I put them up, Jay snags them for drinks. I hear Chickie's father's voice in my head: *"As long as there are no lipstick stains on the rims, they're clean."* Mentally crossing my fingers we don't poison anyone tonight, I go back out to collect more.

Pretty quickly, I have the tables cleaned up. Jay then has me doing waters and sodas for his orders. There's no table service in the bar tonight; people have to come up to order. A few patrons, mostly male, are cranky about it, but it's the only way to survive this tsunami.

We fall into a rhythm behind the bar, me assisting when I can, collecting dirty dishes when needed, and washing, washing, washing. As the night goes on, I become increasingly aware of how many women are blatantly hitting on Jay: stuffing twenty-dollar bills in the tip jar with prolonged eye contact; touching his hand, his wrist, his forearm as he delivers drinks; licking their lips, blowing him kisses, winking. I never understood what it meant in my spicy books when they say somebody is eye-fucking somebody else, but now I get it.

Jesus Christ. Is it like this all the time? Or just on fake holidays? I start to feel old. And invisible.

As he sees me seeing all this unfold before my eyes, he subtly and then not so subtly begins touching me as he squeezes by to serve customers up and down the bar. A hand on my waist, a tap on my ass, a touch on my shoulder—he is giving me near constant reassurance that he knows what's happening, and he doesn't care. He's not interested in them. He sees me.

Then a particularly gorgeous young thing with especially giant hair and a concerning amount of lip liner scrawls her number on a bar napkin and pushes it toward him. I stand there, practically in front of her, watching as he looks at her, grabs the napkin and crumples it in his fist, then takes my chin in his other hand and kisses me. With tongue.

I peek over at her and her open-mouthed friends. Jay releases me and moves up the bar to take some orders without looking back at her. The girls stare at me. I give them a big smile and two thumbs-up.

"I know," I say to them. "Sometimes I can't believe it either."

18

KK taps lightly on the door, which is ajar. She pokes her head through. "Hello?" she calls.

"Come in!" a voice says cheerfully.

She pushes the door open with the full laundry basket she is carrying. It is close to overflowing with clothes.

"Good morning," she says. "I brought today's laundry! It's quite a load."

The elderly woman sitting in a chair by the window looks over, her face blank for a moment before recognition settles in. "Mother! Our work is never done, I guess."

Margie Rhinehart lives in the memory wing of a long-term nursing facility outside Boston. Once a week, KK comes to visit. She is the only one left who does. Her father stopped going the day after Margie no longer recognized him as her husband. Harley stopped going the day after she thought he was her husband and tried to kiss him on the mouth. Bitty has never been, because she lives in Chicago and in her own little world of what KK imagines is utter fucking perfection.

Margie thinks her daughter is her mother, KK's namesake, Katherine ("Call me Kay"). It hurt for a while, but honestly she's gotten used to it now, and since they started the laundry thing, the visits have been a breeze. KK actually enjoys these walks down her mother's scattered, shattered, dementia-colored memories. Sometimes Margie spills some really old tea, and it's fascinating. Like who knew Margie smoked? Marlboros, for God's sake. She apparently quit when she was pregnant with Bitty.

It was a CNA who came up with the laundry-folding activity after Margie got really bad. This young woman worked the overnight shift when Margie would get combative and upset. One night when the CNA was called in to help restrain Margie, she had a basket of clean towels with her. She rushed into the room and put the basket in a chair next to Margie as she freed her hands to help hold the old woman down. Margie's eyes locked on the basket, and she immediately calmed.

"Do you need help with that?" Margie asked the aide, whose name was Clara.

Clara and the nurse and the orderly who had been fighting Margie seconds before all froze. Clara looked from the basket to Margie's face and back again. "Why yes, I do," she said. Margie smiled and held out her hands. "There's always a mountain to fold with all these kids, isn't there?" she said, waving her hands in a gesture to have the basket brought to her.

And since then, it is the laundry that calms Margie's ravaged mind. For KK and her mother, it is the laundry that gives them one last connection.

Over time, KK has tweaked the equation. Towels were the start, but they weren't enough. KK scoured thrift stores and came up with a basketful of family laundry, from baby onesies to little kid cartoon character T-shirts to shorts and dresses and pants. Sizes infant through teen. Margie loves all of them, and as she folds, she remembers stories from when her kids were those sizes, those ages. She talks KK's ear off.

KK puts the basket on Margie's bed and then goes to the chair and helps her mother up. Margie shuffles to the bedside, and KK pulls the chair along behind her, seating her in front of the basket. Then she tips the basket over and dumps the pile of clothes onto the bed.

"Oh Mother, you always make me laugh when you do that," Margie says delightedly, clapping her hands and picking up an armful of clothes. She holds them to her nose and breathes deep. "I love the smell of freshly dried laundry. I do love the clothesline," she says.

KK smiles, knowing full well these clothes have never been near a clothesline. They've been washed only once after their purchase from the thrift stores. None of it matters, though. Mom is happy.

It does bother KK that she can't call her mother "Mom" when they're together. It upsets and confuses her because Margie thinks KK is Kay. Their grandma didn't live with them year-round, but she did come to the Cape house for the whole summer every year until she died. KK was five when Grandma passed.

"Well, what's new?" KK asks as she starts to pull out the socks and put them in front of Margie. Margie likes to start with the socks.

"Oh gosh, you know I'm a little worried about Bitty," Margie says. This is the first time this has been brought up. KK leans in a little.

"Really? Why?"

"She's so serious all the time. She's so focused on her schoolwork, and I worry that she doesn't have any real friends or even any fun. And Rod just encourages it. He tells me she is focused on her future success and that I should be quiet, but I want her to enjoy life and have fun like the other kids do."

"I'm sure she's fine," KK says.

"I hope so," Margie says. "You know KK has Matty and also Chickie in the summertime, and they are thick as thieves, those three. They love each other so much. And Harley is part of it, too. They take care of him and watch out for him. I worry that Bitty doesn't have that. But Rod tells me I'm overreacting."

Margie focuses on pairing the socks and folding them together in neat, little bundles that she piles up like logs in the bottom of the basket. After a few minutes, she starts talking about what they might have for dinner and whether she needs to go to the store. KK smiles, nods, and says, "Mmm-hmm" at the appropriate times, but her thoughts are on Bitty. Far-away Bitty.

Y

March is coming in like a lion, so the beach has been packed with surfers from all over to take advantage of the unusually good waves. Jay has been spending a lot of time on the water, popping into my house for a quick shower and then heading to Dockside for work. Because it's such a skeleton staff and a relatively short workday, everyone works all six days the place is open. Just Sundays off. Chickie is starting to get short tempered.

"I'm always like this in March," she says to me one morning at my kitchen counter. "You've just never seen it."

Ouch.

She senses my inner wince and puts a hand over mine, squeezing. "I didn't mean it like that," she says. "March is just when I start to turn into a real bitch. Before my summertime, raging-lunatic bitch."

"Ah yes," I say, squeezing back. "I know that girl well."

My phone shows an incoming FaceTime—it's Bitty.

"Hey, Bit, great timing. Chickie is here with me," I say when I answer.

My sister is in her kitchen in her Chicago apartment, sitting at her kitchen counter. And she's clearly either crying right now or has just stopped. Chickie leans into my phone to get a better look.

"Bitty, are you crying?" she asks. "Seems early for tears for you, no? Have you even had coffee yet?" It's only eight a.m. in Chicago.

She wipes her face with her palm, rubbing at her cheeks and swiping at her eyes.

"I had the worst date last night, you guys," she says, heaving a huge sigh and propping the phone up on her counter so she can go hands free. We watch as she pours coffee into a (circa 1990 Dockside) mug.

I yank my Mark Bittman cookbooks across the counter so we can lean my phone against them. We perch our asses on the stools and wait.

Bitty sighs. "Second date from Tinder. First date was coffee. He seemed nice. He asked me to dinner. Garth. Tax attorney. Sixty."

Chickie and I nod. Got it.

"So we spend ninety minutes at this nice restaurant. We drink. We eat. He talks."

"He talks?" I ask.

"Yeah, he talks. And talks and talks and talks. About himself. His career, his golf game, his art collection."

"Didn't he ask you anything about yourself?" Chickie says. "Did you exhaust the topic of you on the coffee date?"

Bitty shakes her head and takes a sip from her mug. "Oh God, no. That date was pretty short. It was midafternoon, and we met during work, so it was more of a 'Are you a serial killer or super weirdo?' kind of interaction. Not a ton of sharing on either part, but enough to know we wanted to try to get to know each other better with a second date.

"Or, I guess in retrospect, he wanted *me* to get to know *him*."

We all take sips from our mugs. This story is slow going, but we give Bitty the space she needs to share it at her own pace.

"So literally ninety minutes of him, him, him. And then as we finish dessert, the bill comes. He leans across the table, puts his hand over mine, and says, 'I took a Viagra before I left the house, so our timing is perfect.' And he squeezes my hand and then sort of turns his gaze down to his lap. Then he looks back up at me and … and …"

Chickie and I are breathless with anticipation. "And *what?*" we say together. Then we look at each other and laugh.

"He wiggles his eyebrows. Like a goddamn cartoon character. Like up and down, up and down, up and down."

She starts crying again. It does seem like an overreaction to the situation, but I nudge Chickie under the counter so she'll stop chuckling.

"Bitty, sweetie, what's going on? Why are you so upset? You didn't sleep with him, did you? Or did you?" I say.

"No, I didn't sleep with him. I told him I had an early morning and was going to grab an Uber home. I left him sitting at the table, and I actually walked three blocks over from the restaurant so he wouldn't bump into me on his way out while I was waiting for the car."

"So why so sad?" Chickie asks.

"It just seems so hopeless," she says. "I'm just so sick of listening to men. I feel like I have spent decades of my life professionally and personally listening to men drone on and on. About themselves. About work. About topics I know a million times more about than they do, and yet they endlessly lecture me. School me. Explain to me. I'm tired of it. Just exhausted."

We all look at each other through the small phone screens, and I feel helpless and sad. Helpless because my big sister is in Chicago, and she's depressed, and I'm in Massachusetts and can't give her the hug she needs. And sad because Lord knows we have all been there, and it never ends. Men never stop talking. At us. They never stop talking at us. I spent thirty years with a man who talked at me. Chickie's father spent her whole life talking at her. It is exhausting.

Bitty's eyes focus on Chickie and me, and then she looks away, off toward something in her kitchen.

"What sweetie?" I ask.

Her gaze returns to her phone screen.

"What?"

"What else is bothering you?" I say. "I can tell there's something else. What's going on?"

She shrugs. "I don't know. Seeing you guys sitting there together, having coffee, makes me homesick. I miss you guys. All of you. I see the photos on Instagram of you guys all doing stuff together. It's like the old summer days at the beach when we were kids, and it makes me lonely."

Chickie nudges my knee with hers.

I smile into the phone. "It sucks being with her all the time," I say, whacking Chickie on the arm. "She's got a filthy mouth and zero patience. Plus, she works twenty hours a day."

Chickie cocks a thumb in my direction. "Trust me, Bit, I never see this one. She's too busy getting railed by a millennial to even go get coffee with me. Plus, I work twenty hours a day."

Bitty smiles and wipes her cheeks. "Yeah, right. I don't know what it is lately, but I just feel like being almost fifty-eight years old is like pushing a boulder up a never-ending hill. I mean, I have an acupuncturist for my headaches, a pelvic floor therapist for the fact that I can't sneeze while walking without pissing myself, a nutritionist who keeps me flooded with antioxidant juices and low-carb prepared meals, a psychologist for my anxiety and depression, and a massage therapist for my neck. It doesn't take a village to keep me going; it takes a metropolis."

I lean back on my stool. I had no idea Bitty had this much going on. She always looks perfect to me. She's the CFO of a Fortune 500 company in Chicago with a penthouse apartment, a seven-figure salary, ridiculous bonuses and stock options, and great hair.

We hide so much from each other when it would probably eliminate half the outside help we hire if we just opened up and shared.

Misery loves company, right? Nothing more miserable than a bunch of women in their fifties.

"Speaking of getting railed by a millennial," I say, "why don't you change the age range on your dating app to men between thirty-five and fifty? Go younger! See what happens. I mean, I've been enjoying myself. Ten out of ten would recommend a millennial. At the very least, he won't have to pop a pill and set a timer."

Bitty blushes. "I couldn't do that. I'd be mortified. Plus, who would swipe on me? No one."

"Ha, Bit, you should've seen this one when Jay started flirting with her at the bar," Chickie says. "Like two seconds away from full cardiac arrest every time he looked at her, never mind when he talked to her. And when he walked away from her behind the bar, her eyes were glued to his ass."

"I thought you were in the kitchen all the time!" I say, giving her a hard enough shove that she has to put one foot on the floor so she doesn't fall off her stool.

"So, (a) I would peek out all the time because it was slow in there, and (b) I have spies everywhere."

We all three laugh, and Bitty looks a little more relaxed. She changes the subject.

"How was Taylor Swift?" she asks me. Jay and I went to the concert at TD Garden two nights before.

"Oh my God, amazing," I say. "Being in the pit was so fun. It was crazy."

"Ask her about the ride home," Chickie says, giving Bitty a huge overdone wink.

Now I blush. "Oooooo," Bitty says. "How was the ride home?"

"Fine," I reply.

"Mama!" Chickie says. "Tell her."

"OK, fine. Jay got us a limo, well, more like a luxury SUV sort of thing, so we wouldn't have to worry about driving and parking, and if we wanted to drink when we were there, plus it would be late when it got over, and we'd be too tired to drive. So, you know, to be safe."

"*Get to the actual point*," Chickie yells at me.

My face is purple and very hot. I feel sweat on my forehead. Bitty leans way into her phone screen. "KK?" she says. "What is the actual point?"

I cover my eyes with my hands. "So we maybe had a 'No Way Out' moment or two on the way home," I mutter.

"Bullshit! It was full-blown 'Show us the monuments,'" Chickie yells, tipping her head back to unleash her signature belly laugh.

I keep my eyes covered, but I spread my fingers slightly so I can see the phone. Bitty is staring straight into it with a really serious look on her face.

"Guys, I have to go," she says. "I need to go update my dating app profiles. What range did you say? Thirty-five to fifty? Wait, how old is Jay? Thirty-four, right? Yeah, I've gotta go. I'll talk to you later."

She clicks off. Chickie throws her arms around me and laughs again. "Thanks for coming to our Ted Talk," she says. I hug her back.

19

My phone dings. I pull my readers down off the top of my head and perch them on my nose.

MATTY. Holy shit, you are on TikTok again.

MATTY. *Link*

I'm out walking. I pause for a minute and click the link. My TikTok app opens, and there we are, in the pit at Taylor Swift.

I immediately smile. It was shot during "Lover." The minute we heard the opening notes of the song, Jay held his arms out wide to me, and I jumped. He cradled me, his hands under my ass, my legs wrapped around his waist and my hands at the back of his neck. He was slow-dancing me in a very middle-school-ish way, turning us in a slow circle as we sang the lyrics to each other at the top of our voices.

We were wearing our matching Taylor tour T-shirts that he insisted we buy from the merch booth when we walked into the Garden. Eighty dollars *each* for the long-sleeved T-shirts. I argued, but he insisted we buy them and that we put them on that minute. "When dorks go to Taylor," he told me.

The video is probably less than a minute long, just us lost in the "Lover" moment together, staring into each other's eyes and singing, "Have I known you twenty seconds or twenty years?" as he sways me back and forth. I am struck again by how happy I look and how clearly in love with him I am. And I think … I think … that he's in love with me. I mean, I know he whispered it that time when he thought I was passed out after the reunion, but neither of us has have ever said it aloud to each other. But we look happy together. We look … together.

The caption says, "I think it's them! #capecodkaraokecouple! OMG so cute. Come on TikTok do your thing! Who is this unicorn couple?"

Remember when the ocean tried to kill me? Turns out that was nothing compared to the universe's bitch slap.

Once they figure out who we are—and honestly, kudos to those TikTok girlies who can out-sleuth Enola Holmes when it comes to outing both of us—it doesn't take long for the trolls to emerge. Everybody has something to say about our relationship, and it is no longer good. We go from #cougardreams and #socute to #WTF and #GILF (which I didn't get at all, but Matty translated it for me into "Grandma I'd Like to Fuck") and even #EW, which doesn't stand for anything except … ew.

They crawl all our social media. Someone screenshots a post of mine from a few years back when I was in the throes of the worst of the menopause symptoms, a closeup selfie of my face (because why the fuck wouldn't I do that?)—red, blotchy, sweaty, with huge circles under my eyes. I captioned it "Well-played menopause." Apparently, all my social platforms were set to public. Filed under "too little, too late," I made everything private. The damage was done.

They paired that portrait with a capture from Jay's Instagram when he was surfing in Portugal back in 2019, and he was tanned, ripped, gorgeous, and smiling on the beach with perfect crunchy hair.

And then come the articles, the analyses, the mainstream shredding, in which we move off brutal comments, stitches on TikTok, and memes on Twitter into a relentless breakdown of the mechanics of our relationship. Headlines like "Are Millennial Men into Menopausal Women?" "Who's Putting the 'Man' in Menopause?" and "Wait—Are Hot Flashes Hot?"

An Instagram DM from some producer at *Rise*, that network morning show, asks us to come on to talk about what they call "the twenty-first century May-December romance trend that has everyone talking." Everything about that makes my skin crawl. It's a no from me.

Chickie keeps switching my phone to airplane mode to get me to stop obsessing over all of it, but I can't.

I. Can. Not. Stop.

Jay keeps telling me he doesn't care what idiots on the internet say, whether they were commenters on TikTok or morons at *Men's*

Health. He keeps saying the opinions of strangers don't affect us. Matty, Chickie, and my siblings keep telling me the same thing.

Except they affect me. It's like all those whispers of self-loathing I'd been filling my head with for the last four decades have suddenly come to life. Every bad thought I'd ever had about myself is now validated and realized a thousand times over. I am old. I am ugly. I am gross. I am unlovable. Ha! I knew it.

Then one afternoon we are in my kitchen. Jay is getting ready to go into Dockside, and his phone is face up on my counter. He left it there and went into the bathroom to brush his teeth. When it starts vibrating like crazy, I casually flip it around. The home screen flashes briefly with hundreds of notifications. Then the screen goes black.

A bad feeling settles in my already unsettled gut.

When Jay sweeps back into the room, he encircles my waist with one arm, pulling me in for a minty toothpaste kiss. "Come to happy hour?" he asks.

I shake my head.

"Katherine, come on," he says. "We can't stop living our lives because of this ridiculousness. We just have to ride it out. Something else will pop up soon, and everyone will forget about us."

"I won't forget," I say.

He shrugs. "I'll have you set up if you decide to come," he says, giving me another quick kiss. "I hope you do."

But I don't, and when he gets home, I pretend to be asleep. He climbs in beside me, and soon I hear his breathing go deep and slow. He's out.

I carefully slide out from under the covers and creep over to his side of the bed. His phone is charging on the nightstand. I unplug the cord, take a deep breath, and swipe up, quickly turning it toward him. Face ID engages, and the home screen appears.

Apparently, Jason fucking Bourne has not learned her lesson.

I quickly disappear into the bathroom, closing the door behind me and sinking to the floor, leaning up against the glass shower wall. All his social apps have massive numbers of notifications next to them. I tap Instagram first.

There are hundreds of DMs. An endless list under regular messages, nearly all of them marked as read. Next to the little "requests" are hundreds more. I tap on that. *Oh sweet Jesus.*

It's endless porn. Messages from woman after woman, with titty pics, crotch shots, lingerie shots, ass shots, mouth shots, tongue shots. Acid rises in my throat. Every single one of them says—and I'm paraphrasing here—"Why would you want to fuck that old bag of dust when you can have my hot, wet, young, flexible, tight pussy?"

Switching back to the regular messages, it's pretty much the same. Message after message inviting Jay to fuck, get fucked, get blown, get jacked off, get engaged, or get married. I want to throw up, but I don't want to lose my access to this torture chamber, so I swallow the bile back down.

I swipe out of Instagram and go over to text messages. I don't know how all these people got his cell number, but holy shit. Message after message. Dirty pic after dirty pic. Filthy solicitations, one after the other. He's read them all, except for the several dozen that arrived after he went to bed. Even as I am looking through them, more are pouring in. The phone never stops vibrating in my hand.

In and around and included in all these solicitations are horrible comments about me. How I look (ugly), how I must feel (wrinkly), how I must fuck (badly). Hitting him up and tearing me down simultaneously.

As far as I can tell, he hasn't answered any of them. But he's read them all. They are there. He hasn't deleted them. He hasn't told me about them. There's clearly messages from people he knows too, men and women, asking him, "Dude, WTF?", "Man, you like 'em old now?", and over and over "Does she have $$$?"

And then my eyes fall on the text from "MOTHER."

It begins with "Jason," and I am immediately flummoxed. I had no idea his name was Jason. I thought his name was Jay. Why wouldn't I know this?

> Jason, your father's assistant has forwarded him some links to various online publications that we find quite off putting. Your father sent them to Irene, who printed them out for me. I'm sure you won't be surprised to learn that we find these items upsetting.

> So far, the good news is no one has made the leap to connect you with us. We are hoping that remains the case. That being said, we are also hopeful that this humiliation is the wake-up call you need to

ELISSA BASS

get your life back on track. Your father is actively looking for appropriate openings for you, as we are assuming this will be the impetus to get you back to New York, where you belong, and back to your career. It is time to leave that ridiculousness behind you. Stop embarrassing yourself and us.

Feel free to let Irene know when we can expect you. She can assist with arrangements. In the short term, you can stay with us.

And suddenly it's last August, but instead of me screaming "Get out" at him, it's my brain screaming "Get out" at me. I drop his phone on the bath mat and haul myself to my feet. Somehow remembering to be quiet, I go back to the bedroom and get my phone off my charger and make my way downstairs. I have to hold onto the banister the whole way down because I feel like I might pass out. I grab my All Birds by the back door and my purse from the kitchen table, and I quietly unlock and open the front door. I don't bother to close it behind me.

I make my way to my car, get in, and start it up; and this time it's me backing out of the driveway, gravel flying.

This time it's me.

During the two-hour drive to Harley's, I have to stop seven times to throw up. By the time I get there, it's nearly two in the morning, and I am so exhausted and dehydrated that I can't stop my hands from shaking. My legs are shaking. My whole body is shaking. I am dressed only in pajama pants and a long-sleeved T-shirt. My feet are bare. My shoes are on the seat next to me.

Outside their condo, I pull to a stop and turn my phone on to call Harley. He answers after three rings. "KK?" he says. "You OK?"

"I'm outside," I say.

"Outside where, honey? What's going on?"

"Outside you," I say, and then I drop the phone on my lap and start to sob.

A couple of minutes later, my car door is yanked open, and Harley's arms are around me. "It's OK, honey," he says soothingly, unbuckling my seat belt and trying to gently haul me out of the car. "I got you. It's OK."

Harley carries me inside while Keith hovers around us. I want to tell them what is happening, but I cannot seem to form words.

They bring me into their guest bedroom, and Keith pulls back the covers. Harley tucks me in and then holds me up while Keith puts a glass to my lips.

"KK," he says. "Drink this. Come on. Just drink this, and then you can sleep."

So I swallow some water, and they lay me down onto the pillows. I curl onto my side into the fetal position. Sobs wrack my body. Harley sits next to me, patting my shoulder over and over. I close my eyes, my chest heaving.

The next thing I know, the mattress is shifting. Without opening my eyes, I know Matty is here. He crawls into bed with me. He puts one arm under me and one arm over me and pulls me into his chest. He holds me in a death grip.

"I'm here, Mama," he whispers. "I'm here."

"Matty … Jay …," I start.

He shushes me. "Later, Mama. We'll figure it out later. Just sleep."

When I open my eyes, Matty is inches away from my face, his wide eyes staring at me.

"Hi," he says.

"Hi," I croak. "I'm so thirsty."

He sits up and reaches over to the nightstand, bringing a glass of water to me. I raise my head, and he helps me drink.

"What time is it?"

"Nine," he says.

"A.m. or p.m.?"

He smiles. "A.m."

"I should get up," I say, attempting to sit up. I'm so weak. Like a newborn kitten. Except not cute. Catastrophic.

The bedroom door swings open, and Harley comes in, carrying a tray. Keith is again hovering behind him, a worried look on his face. He puts the tray down on the nightstand. There's a cup of steaming tea, and a plate with scrambled eggs and applesauce. I look up at him and give him a watery smile.

"Our sick plate," I say.

He nods, smiling. It's what our mother used to make for us when we were kids after we were sick. It's our literal comfort meal.

"I had to run out and get applesauce because who just has applesauce lying around, right? No one. Not us, anyway," Keith says, rambling and nervous. "But Harley said you had to have it."

"Thanks guys," I say, pushing myself up.

Harley puts the tray on my lap. Matty tosses back the covers on his side and gets out of bed.

The three of them look at me. I blink back at them. I'm so dehydrated I have no tears left. My eyes feel like sandpaper.

"KK, can you tell us what happened?" Harley asks.

"Jay has been blowing up all our phones looking for you," Keith adds.

I wasn't even sure where my phone, bag, or shoes were at this moment.

"We told him you were here and that you're fine," Harley says. "We also told him not to come."

"Thank you," I say. I pick up the spoon on the tray and start to eat the applesauce. It's cool on my throat. It feels nice. They watch me, like mother hens. I love them so much.

"Did you guys know that Jay's real name is Jason?" I ask.

They look at each other. "No," Harley says. "Why?"

"It is. His real name is Jason. Which I never knew. Don't you think it's weird that I never knew that? It made me wonder what else I don't know. And then I realized there's a ton I don't know. Like, basically, everything. I don't know everything about Jay. I just know the Jay from, like, October to now. I know like six months of Jay. That's not much, right? I mean, he's thirty-four. There's no history there. There's no … I don't know … context?"

"KK, honey, I'm confused," Harley says. "What are you talking about?"

"I looked at Jay's phone," I explain. "I noticed that he had like a zillion notifications, so after he went to sleep, I cracked open his phone and went through everything."

"Oh Mama," Matty whispers.

I nod. "I know, right? Stupid. Like, what did I think was going to happen? Anything good? Experience should have told me, 'No, Katherine Kristina Rhinehart, nothing good will come of you creeping your boyfriend's phone.' But nobody ever accused me of being smart. I'm dumb. And pathetic. Remember? That's me. Dumb and pathetic."

I sip the tea. It's lemon ginger. Mom used to make us English breakfast tea with lots of milk and sugar.

"Putting aside the hundreds of disgusting solicitations and nude pictures and gross propositions he's gotten—and trust me when I tell you there were things in his messages I can never unsee—it's clear from reading the ones that came from people he knows that he's never told anyone in his life about me. About us. I am invisible. Not a part of him. Not a part of his life. Not important enough to share. Nothing.

"I only exist in the little bubble over the beach house and Dockside and town. Outside of that, I am nowhere. Nothing. He keeps me a secret. I'm not even sure *secret* is the right word. Because a secret implies you care enough to keep it hidden, right? So not a secret. Just … nonexistent. Invisible.

"Like he is ashamed of me. Of us."

Harley sits on the end of the bed. "I don't think you're being fair, KK."

"You know what," I say. "I don't want to do this right now. Can I just be by myself please?"

Harley stands up, and the three of them leave without saying a word. I push the tray off my lap and lie back down. I curl onto my side and stare at the wall. I fall back asleep.

When I wake up, I see my phone on the bedside table. I turn it on. There are multiple missed calls and a slew of texts from Jay. I ignore them. Instead, I text Chickie.

ME. Did you know Jay's real name is Jason?

I hear nothing back from her, so I assume she's decided to stay out of this.

20

After another day at Harley and Keith's, we caravan back to the Cape. Matty and I are in my car, and Keith and Harley are in theirs. They will get me settled at the house and then drive back to the city together. We have confabbed with Bitty via FaceTime multiple times over the last forty-eight hours, so she is in the loop as to my current state of affairs and mind. There is no plan, but at least I'm not hysterical anymore.

We are driving through town on the way to the beach house, Matty chattering away in the passenger seat when he suddenly says, "Hmm. What's going on at Dockside? There's a fire truck. And the police."

I slow the car and look over my shoulder to the Dockside parking lot. There are actually two fire trucks, an ambulance, a police cruiser, a police SUV, and a police car that says "CHIEF" on the side.

Without thinking, I jam on the brakes, throw the car into park in the middle of the street, and jump out my door. I can hear Matty yelling my name, but I am running full speed across the street and through the parking lot. The restaurant isn't open yet. It's not even midmorning, so whatever is happening, it's not someone choking on a fish bone.

I tear around the side of the building to the door to Chickie's upstairs apartment. There are two paramedics and a stretcher there.

"What's happening?" I ask them. They are young, I don't recognize them, and I know they don't know me. They look at each other and stay silent.

I push past them and run through the open door and up Chickie's stairs. The door at the top is also wide open.

"Chickie!" I call as I rush inside, stopping abruptly.

The apartment has a long hallway that leads to a huge living room/kitchen at the end, overlooking the water. Lots of windows and bright sunlight. Off the hallway are three doors. The one on the left is the bathroom, and the two on the right are the bedrooms, Chickie's and the spare. Chickie's bedroom door is directly across from the bathroom.

I can see firefighters standing around at the end of the hall, in the living room. As I come in, shouting her name, someone pops out of the bathroom. It's Mike Ponce, the town's police chief. He was a couple of years behind Chickie in high school. We know him well. He's one of the boys who touched my boobs.

"KK," he says, beginning to come toward me, his latex-gloved hands outstretched.

"Mike," I say, panic and bile rising in my throat. "What's happening? Where's Chickie?"

I notice him carefully step over a pile of dried something on the rug as he makes his way to me.

"KK," he says again, reaching out to grasp my arms.

I push past him, shoving him against the wall. "Chickie!" I yell. "Chickie!"

I stop, looking down at what is clearly a pile of dried vomit. I look right into Chickie's bedroom and see her unmade bed, covers thrown back like she had to get up quickly. The little lamp on her nightstand is knocked on its side. There's another dried pile of puke on the rug by the bedside.

"Chickie," I whisper. I look to my left into the bathroom. There's a man in there, kneeling beside a pile of bed sheets.

What the hell is happening?

I feel hands on my arms, this time from behind me. It's Mike.

"Where is Chickie?" I ask him, turning my head so I can see his face. "What is happening?"

His eyes flick from mine to the bathroom floor, to the pile of sheets stretched from the side of the bathtub toward us in the hallway.

It's not a pile of sheets.

"Mike," I say. "Mike."

"KK, I'm so sorry," he says into my ear. "We aren't exactly sure what happened. It looks like she was sick and fell and hit her head. Maybe a couple of days ago."

My brain stops. My heart stops. My breathing stops. I feel like I'm underwater. Everything is muffled. There's activity all around me, but I can't really see or hear it.

Way, way far away I can hear Matty's voice, calling my name as he comes up the stairs. Like he's a million miles away. Maybe Harley, too? I'm not sure.

My eyes lock on the sheet on the bathroom floor. I yank my arms out from Mike's gentle grasp and drop to my knees. I crawl into the bathroom.

The man who is in here looks up at Mike for guidance, then rises and steps backward so he is standing in the tub.

I crawl right over that sheet so I am hovering above it. Carefully, oh so carefully, I pull it back. I see her hair. I see a cut, a gash almost with dried blood on it, in the middle of her forehead. I see her eyes, open and empty. I see her mouth, her slightly parted lips a pale blue.

"Chickie," I whisper, moving close to her ear. "What are you doing? Come on, it's time to get up. I'm here. Let's get up. We'll go get Dunkin', OK? We'll go get frozen coffees from the Front Street Dunkin'. Come on. Let's get up."

I feel Mike kneel down next to me and put his hands on my shoulders. I try to shrug him off, but he won't let go.

"KK," he says. "She's gone. You can't stay in here. We're waiting for the coroner to come. Come on, KK. You have to come with me."

ELISSA BASS

I look back at him. "I don't understand," I say. "What is happening?"

In the doorway I see Matty and behind him, Harley.

"Matty," I say, looking at his face. I move my eyes over to my brother. "Harley, help me. Help us. Chickie needs help."

Matty turns away, a loud sob bursting from him. Harley steps inside the doorway and puts his hand on the sink to steady himself. Mike stands up and goes to him, speaking low into his ear. Harley nods and rubs his hand down his face. He comes toward me.

"KK," he says. "Honey, we need to step outside this room, OK? Come with me. We need to wait outside. They need to finish here. We can't stay in here."

He helps me to my feet and puts one arm around my waist. He lifts my arm and puts it around his shoulders. We start to walk toward the hallway. Baby steps. I look back down at her.

"Haw," I say. "I don't like this."

"I know, honey. I know. I don't either. Come on. It will be OK. Let's just step outside."

He leads me back to the door that will take us outside, and as we are about to go through, a man carrying a large briefcase comes in, pushing past us. He's pulling latex gloves out of the top of his case. When he is past us, we leave Chickie's apartment and go down the stairs to the parking lot where Keith and Matty are, their arms around each other. Those two guys with the stretcher are still waiting.

When we get around the corner and out of sight of all that, Harley stops. He looks at me.

"Haw," I say to him. "I don't feel good."

Then everything goes black.

$$\mathbf{Y}$$

The next week is a blur. Everyone is at the beach house—Matty, Bitty, Keith, and Harley. Matty is feeding me Valium like they are Tic Tacs, and I am numb. The restaurant has been closed since Chickie died, and Harley and Bitty are seeing to the arrangements.

Why do they call it that? Arrangements. It's weird. I want to Google it, but I don't have the strength.

Matty keeps an eye on me, and he cries only when he thinks I'm asleep. We've been sharing a bed. I don't let him use Jay's pillow, though—I clutch that to me every night like it's my blankie. Keith has been cooking up a storm, but no one really eats. I'm not drinking because of the Valium. I'd rather be in a narcotic haze than a tequila buzz.

Every once in a while, one of them tells me that Jay has texted, asking about me, asking whether he can come over. My phone has been off since I arrived at Harley's. Since that last text I sent Chickie, asking her whether she knew what Jay's real name was. The text she didn't answer.

Because she was dead.

And I keep telling them no. Jay cannot come over.

Chickie is dead.

April 1974

Beach Grandma is gone.

That's what Rod and Margie tell the kids. They gather them around the kitchen table, and Rod says, "Grandma Kay is gone."

She had many names. Rod called her "Grandma Kay." Margie called her "Ma." Bitty, KK, and Harley all called her "Grandma" when they were with her, but when making reference to her, she was "Beach Grandma." They called Rod's mother "Other Grandma," but even as young as they were, the kids knew to keep that to themselves.

Grandma Kay is gone? This puzzles KK. What does it mean—gone? Where did she go? Mommy and Daddy aren't saying. They look super sad though.

KK adores her grandmother. She is her namesake, which means she is named for her. They share a first name. KK knows this fact automatically makes her Grandma's favorite, even though no one ever says this aloud. But at seven years old, KK knows some things, and this is one of them.

She loves her grandma's hair. It's snow white and in little puffs all over her head. She goes to the hairdresser once a week, and he makes those little puffs. Grandma makes an amazing lemon meringue pie. The meringue is a mile high.

Her hands are gnarled beyond belief from arthritis. KK sometimes wants to hold her hand, but Grandma says she can't because it hurts. So she offers the little girl a belt loop on her trousers. "Hold that," she says, wrapping KK's little fingers around it. And they walk around, with KK's arm practically straight up in the air so she can reach that belt loop, her fingers curled tightly over it.

Rod and Margie think they're doing the right thing when they tell their kids Grandma is "gone." They never actually say "died." Or "dead." They just say "gone," perhaps thinking it is easier for them to understand. Bitty is nine and can likely grasp the concept of death just fine, but Harley is only five and so sensitive to boot.

Of course, Harley has the inevitable follow-up question: "When is she coming back?"

And they say "never." She is "never coming back."

That answer scares the crap out of KK. She wants to ask them what they did that made her go away, but she doesn't. She's too afraid. She worries that if she knows, if it turns out it was something that specifically she did that caused Grandma to leave … well, KK knows she will never recover from that.

Later that night, when KK is supposed to be reading in bed before lights out, she creeps downstairs and sits outside the living room. Her mother is crying, and her father is saying over and over, "It's OK. It will be OK." Her mom is sad, KK knows. They are all sad.

And then after lights out, after everyone has gone to bed and finally fallen asleep, KK's eyes pop open in the dark, and she knows beyond a shadow of a doubt that her whole family is dead. She climbs out of bed and goes across the hallway to her parents' door, which is ajar. She pushes it open, steps inside, and stands by the mattress. Her parents are two big lumps under the blankets. They are both breathing rhythmically, her father snoring lightly.

KK leaves their room and goes to Bitty's and listens to her sister breathe for a few minutes, then to Harley's room, where she watches his chest rise and fall under his Bugs Bunny blanket.

Then she returns to her room and gets back under her own covers. She closes her eyes. *Where did Grandma go?*

Mike Ponce comes by. He tells us that Chickie had an aneurysm. He says she probably died sometime Saturday night. The restaurant workers told him she left a little early that night, asking the bartender (Jay) to close up. It looked like, based on what was in her kitchen, she cooked some pasta but didn't eat much of it, since it was sitting in a bowl on the table. There were also an open bottle of wine and a half-filled glass.

The likely scenario, Mike tells us, is that she went to bed and then woke up with excruciating pain in her head, pain that caused her to vomit over the side of the bed onto her rug. She was able to get up and make her way into the hall, where she vomited again. Once inside the bathroom, she fell, hitting her forehead on the side of the tub. The cut I saw was superficial, though. It was what happened inside her brain that killed her.

She would've died pretty quickly after that, Mike says. Alone. On her bathroom floor.

When the meat delivery guy arrived Monday morning with the week's order and Chickie wasn't there to let him in to put everything in the walk-in freezer—and she wasn't answering her phone, but her car was in the lot—he called the police.

Yep. It was Chuck.

Her body is at Cleary Funeral Home now, Mike says. They are waiting to hear from us. She listed Harley and me as her emergency contacts. Officially she has no next of kin. The aunt in Maine is like twice removed or something.

"I'm so sorry, KK," Mike says to me before he leaves, crouching down to look into my eyes as I sit at the dining room table with the others, where we have all gathered to hear his report.

Join the fucking club, buddy.

21

Chickie's service is lovely.

I hate when people say that. It's a funeral. How can it be anything but terrible?

But it is lovely. The Pee Wee Little League team that Dockside sponsors comes in their uniforms, their little green shirts with *Dockside* in bright yellow letters across the front. They shuffle their five-year-old selves to the front of the church along with their coaches and sing, "You Are My Sunshine." There isn't a dry eye in the house.

Except mine. My eyes are dry. Dry as bones. Dry as dust. Dry as parchment.

Harley speaks. The mayor speaks. Then it's Matty's turn.

"So when we were kids, Mrs. Rhinehart would sometimes drive us down to Waylands' Wharf after supper so we could 'dive for treasures,'" Matty says, standing behind the podium at the front of the church. He looks majestic in his pale-gray suit and magenta striped tie. "We called them treasures, but it was pretty much junk that people dumped off their boats into the harbor or lost when they were swimming, you know?

"So anyway, one evening we're swimming and diving, and Harley comes to the surface with a gun! A really old, rusty Roy Rogers six-shooter-type pistol. So when we got back to the house, Mrs. Rhinehart calls the police and tells them we found a gun in the water at the harbor. And then Officer Murray arrives, and he and Mrs. Rhinehart are standing on the front porch, and the gun is on the table, and all us kids are sort of hanging off the railings and sitting on the steps listening. And Officer Murray is not happy with Mrs. Rhinehart; we can tell that right away."

Then Matty turns to the side a little bit at the podium and says in a really deep, gruff "cop" voice, "So they found the gun and gave it to you, and you came right home and called us."

And then he turns and faces the other side and says in a high-pitched "Mrs. Rhinehart" voice, "Actually, they gave it to me and then swam for quite a while more, and then we went to get ice cream, and then we came home, and I called you."

Matty faces the other direction with a deep, gruff voice. "Really? Where was the gun?"

He turns with Mrs. Rhinehart voice. "In the trunk of my car."

Turns. Cop voice: "Really?"

Turns. Mrs. R. voice: "Well, it certainly doesn't look like it was used to commit a crime in the last week. And it clearly doesn't work. So I thought that was OK."

Turns. Cop voice: "You were driving around with kids and a gun in your car."

Turns. Mrs. R. voice: "Yes."

Matty faces front, looking at the audience, many of whom are laughing into their tissues.

"And then," he says, "Chickie stands up from where she was sitting on the steps, walks over to Mrs. Rhinehart, plants her little self in between Mrs. R. and the cop, and adopts the classic Chickie pose we all know and love."

He steps away from the podium, plants his feet wide apart, puts his curled-up fists on his hips, tilts his head to the right, and adopts a ferocious scowl. He looks exactly like an angry/protective Chickie. *Oh my heart.*

He steps back to the microphone. "And she looks him right in the eye and says very sternly, 'Officer Murray, you know ice cream is the priority!'"

The congregation erupts in laughter and applause. Except for me.

I took half a Valium before we left for the church and feel as though I'm watching everything through a mist and hearing everything through a slight buzz. My tongue feels like it is filling up my whole mouth, and my lips feel chapped. I reach into my pocket for my ChapStick, but instead, my fingers wrap around the pill bottle.

Chickie.

It is Chickie. Inside an old pill bottle. In my pocket.

According to her wishes, Chickie was cremated. The day after I knew it was done, I went to the funeral home and found the funeral director, Fred Cleary, in his office. He had gone to high school with Chickie. If I remember correctly, they went to prom together. They made a nice couple, but for some reason it never worked out. Too bad, since they both stayed around. Although Fred was, you know, a funeral director.

He was surprised to see me and even more surprised when I told him what I wanted. But he didn't argue. I handed him the pill bottle, and he disappeared for a bit. When he returned, he gave it back to me, and I left.

In my car in the parking lot, I twisted the cap off the bottle and peered inside. Chickie's ashes filled it almost to the brim. "Hi," I whispered. "I got you." Then I put the cap back on, made sure it was secure, and drove home.

So here she is, with me, in the church. In my pocket. I clutch that pill bottle like it's a rosary.

Even though the service is in a church, it isn't religious. We just needed a space big enough to hold everyone, because Chickie knew everybody, and everybody knew Chickie. And it's the end of March in a beach town, and what else is there to do on a Saturday afternoon?

When it's over, we ride in the motorcade to the cemetery. Even though she's been cremated, she has a space in the family plot. Generations are buried there. Part of the town's fabric. Don't mess with tradition. Meet those expectations.

I grasp the pill bottle and keep my head down. Matty is on one side of me, and Harley's on the other, holding me up. I need a drink and the other half of that Valium. I feel so dry.

Just a fraction of the people who were at the church are here at the cemetery. Chickie's family plot is pretty large, and it's up on a small hill with a nice view of the ocean in the distance. They are all here: her grandparents, her parents, some aunts and uncles. And then there's the space for her. There's already a headstone.

Jesus. I feel a sharp pain in my side, like someone's stuck a knife between my ribs. I clutch that pill bottle in my pocket with all my strength.

Then—I don't know—there are words; there's shuffling. Someone places the urn with her ashes into the hole, there's more shuffling, and Harley and Matty each take an arm and turn me toward the limo.

"Katherine."

I don't plan on stopping, but Harley and Matty stop. I lurch forward a little before I come to rest as well. But I don't turn my head.

"Mama," Matty whispers in my ear.

"I know, Matty. But I can't. Please, can we just leave?"

Bitty is ahead of us, and she realizes we are no longer right behind her. She stops and turns. Her eyes widen. She points her chin to the man I know is standing behind us. I give her a very small shake of my head. *I can't. Don't make me.*

"Katherine." His voice is anguished and closer than it was. "Please."

And suddenly I have clarity. I need to cowboy up and just take care of this. I can't rely on my old cloak of invisibility. Shit, thanks to the internet, it doesn't even exist anymore. Everyone has seen me, no matter how much I wish they hadn't.

I need to do what needs to be done. I turn around and look up, staring straight into those werewolf eyes. He looks beautiful and terrible all at the same time. Exhausted. Sad.

Join the fucking club, buddy.

That pain in my ribs is excruciating. Now it feels like a rabid animal is gnawing at my side.

"No," I say. I realize it comes out like a wheeze, so I square my shoulders, shaking off Haw's and Matty's hands from my arms. "No," I say louder. "*No.* You don't get to do this. You don't get to be here. You don't get to pretend that this matters. That *I* matter. That we are something. Because we aren't. We are nothing."

He steps toward me. His eyes are red. He's so pale. A little voice way in the back of my head tells me to open my arms to him, to invite him to me. But there's a louder voice in the front reminding me that, while I may have invited him into my life, he never showed me the same courtesy. It took the rest of the world—it took thousands upon thousands of strangers—to show me the truth.

"Don't say that," he pleads. "You know that's not true."

"You know what's true, Jay? Here's what's true: I didn't even know what your real first name was. I've never been to your apartment. I've never slept in your bed. I've never met your family. I've never seen your family photos. I don't know any of your friends. Does your family know about me? Do your friends know about me? I'm not on your Instagram. I'm hidden on your camera roll, locked behind your password. There's no proof, right? No proof of us. No proof of our life together. Outside of you and me, I don't exist. I'm invisible."

"That's not …" He starts, but my eyes slice across his face, and his voice dies in his throat.

"I told you things about me, about my life, about my feelings that I had never told another soul. Not one person. I shared secrets with you. *Secrets.* I let you in—I brought you in—hell, you forced your way in, but I have not stepped one foot into your life. Not one. Never been invited.

"Was I a project? A challenge? A way to kill some time? Did you think, *Hmm, can I melt her? Can I open her up? Can I give her an orgasm?* Congratulations on that achievement, by the way. All thanks to you and the miracles of modern medicine, right?"

I take a breath, but oh no, I don't stop. I. Am. On. A. Roll. My voice gets louder.

"I'm in my third act. You're still in your first intermission, right? Isn't that what this was? Intermission? Your time to take a break and 'clear your head'? 'Find your space'? That's what you tell your parents, your Wall Street buddies, your old girlfriends. We are so far apart. How could it possibly work? How could you possibly want me? There's so much out there that's better. Younger. Fresher. Easier. Right?

"I look at life through a rearview mirror. I've left far more behind than what remains in front of me. I'm at the stage where it's *all* about the goodbyes. You haven't even finished all your hellos. All those DMs to answer. So many great offers to consider. So. Much. Pussy.

"We were in a bubble. A nice, safe, private bubble. Well, the bubble has popped. The world popped it. We're *done*."

And then I pull out my last grenade, and without a second thought, I yank the pin and hurl it at him.

"What was it, Jay? Really? You couldn't save Jasmine, so you thought you'd save me?"

His face jerks back as if I slapped him. I can feel Harley and Matty flinch beside me.

Muttering, "Jesus fucking Christ, KK, " Bitty grabs my arm, spins me around, and, with a hard shove to my back, sends me through the open door of the limo. They climb in after me, the door slams, and we drive away.

I don't look back. I don't want to see the carnage I have left behind.

I'm on the living room couch, in the usual penance position. It's dark outside, and it's dark in here because I can't get up to turn on the lights. It took me hours, but I finally stopped crying. I don't even know if I was crying for Chickie or Jay or me or my life. Bitty, Harley, and Matty didn't want to leave me at the house after we drove away from the cemetery, but I insisted. Vociferously. I told them I needed to be alone for a while.

I hear a car. I hear footsteps on the porch. The doorknob turns. Then it rattles.

"Seriously?" Jay calls. "Seriously, Katherine? You locked the fucking door?"

I'm quiet. I have all the shades pulled so he can't see in, but I'm guessing he's guessing I am on the couch. He doesn't have a key because, well, I never lock the door.

He knocks. Then he pounds. "Katherine!" he yells.

I pull myself off the couch. I grab the bottle of Chickie off the coffee table and tiptoe to the door. I lean up against it. I press my cheek against the wood. But I don't say anything.

"I know you're there," he says. His voice is quieter, but it comes through clearly. "I know you are. Open the door. Let me in. We can talk about this. We can make it work. I know you are heartbroken about Chickie, but don't do this to us. I've given you space. I've given you time. Don't shut me out. What they think doesn't matter. What they say doesn't matter. *We* matter. To each other. Please. Open the door. Let me hold you. Let me be with you. Let me love you."

The tears are pouring down my face, but I smother my sobs with my hands. I don't want him to hear me. Did I mean what I yelled at him at the cemetery? Of course not. I love him with my whole heart. But it can't work. The world won't let it.

"Katherine," he says, his voice breaking. He's crying. "Don't do this to us."

"Don't tell me what not to do," I whisper into the wood. And then I turn and go upstairs. I crawl into bed, and I grab the pillow that smells like him and hug it to my body. I push my face into it and take deep breaths.

After a while, I hear his car go down the driveway. And then it's really quiet.

22

I sit on the back porch swaddled in fleece blankets. The ocean breeze is cold. *Fuck you, April. Stop pretending you're spring.*

ME. Hi,

The phone on the cushion next to me dings.

ME. I need you to answer me.

Ding.

ME. I can't do this.

Ding.

ME. No. I refuse to accept this.

Ding.

Me. I'm scared. I don't know what to do.

Ding.

Me. Everything is fucked up, and the only one who can tell me how to fix things is you. We need to dance it out.

Ding.

Me. Chickie, please don't be gone. Please. You're my anchor, remember? I can't. I can't without you. I don't know how. I'm adrift. I'm at sea. I'm texting you fucking boating metaphors, and now is when you text me back, setting me straight.

Ding.

Me. Please.

Ding.

I sit there for a bit, but I'm starting to get cold. Then I put down my phone and pick up the other one next to me. I tap in the password and open texts. There's a long list of unanswered messages from lots of different people. The newest are the ones I just sent.

I tap and type a reply to the last one that came through.

Chickie. You can do this, Mama. I've still got you.

My phone dings next to me. It's stupid, I know, but in a weird way it helps. I put down Chickie's phone and push myself up off the loveseat. I need to take a shower.

Y

Chickie has left me the restaurant.

Apparently, the year we turned fifty, she asked Harley to make her a will. She never told me, and he never said anything because of attorney-client blah fucking blah.

Then he called me yesterday and said the will was in probate, and so it was official. Dockside belonged to me. She left me a letter, too.

He brings it to the house, but I won't let him in, so he sticks it in the mailbox. I wait an hour before I go outside and get it.

I stare at the envelope on the kitchen counter for two hours before I open it. It's one page. Typed.

> Dear KK,
>
> I'm dead.
>
> I know this because you are reading this letter.
>
> I mean, I don't know you are reading this letter because I'm dead, obviously, but you know what I mean.
>
> Yes, I left you Dockside. It's yours.
>
> And yes, I know you don't know one single thing about running a restaurant. Except that you know from listening to me for more than thirty years that it sucks.

ELISSA BASS

Don't sell it. Unless I lived to be ninety, which means you are also ninety, and then, Jesus Christ, please sell it. You're too old for this shit.

But if I don't make it to ninety, then keep it.

And for fuck's sake, don't be scared. You can do this.

You are my family. And this is my family restaurant. I need the peace of mind in my afterlife that Dockside is safe. You will keep it safe. Just like you always kept Matty and me safe. For my whole life, you were my safe place. My heart. My home.

I love you, Mama.

I hold this piece of paper against my shattered heart, and I rest my head on the kitchen counter.

"Don't be scared."

I've always been scared. Scared my family isn't breathing when I wake up in the middle of the night. Scared I won't be successful in my career. Scared no one will love me. Scared of being alone. Scared of being in love. Scared of being myself. I'm not sure I know how to be anything but scared.

But more than anything, I want Chickie to have peace in her afterlife, and I have a strong suspicion that she will somehow know if I don't at least give it a try.

Y

May 1998

"Mama, I swear to God, if you don't close your eyes and lift your chin right this goddamn minute …"

The room falls silent. Matty has morphed into Mateo and not in a good way.

Chickie snorts. "KK, you better do what he says, or you'll be walking down that aisle with kabuki makeup."

KK smiles, then forces her lips together, tilts her chin, and closes her eyes. Matty puts his fingers under her jaw and raises her face another two millimeters before spraying her full on from an aerosol can inches from her skin.

KK chokes.

"*Hold your breath!*" Matty shrieks.

"Well, you didn't say *that*," KK replies.

Matty steps back. "Never mind," he says. "I'm done. Let the setting spray dry for a second. Keep your mouth closed."

KK hears the door open and shut. "Who's here?" she asks. "Can I open my eyes?"

"It's Dad, honey," her father says. "It's almost time to go."

KK opens her eyes. Her father is standing just inside the door, looking dapper in his black tuxedo. She looks around the room. Chickie and Matty are standing a few feet away from her, their arms around each other's waists, admiring their work. KK is stunning from top to bottom. There has never been a more beautiful bride.

"Where's Mom?" she asks her father.

"She was just seated. Everyone's seated. It's time for the bridesmaids to line up."

Matty shrieks again and leaps toward KK. He grabs her hands.

"I'm not going to touch any part of you because you are absolute perfection right now, but just know that I. Love. You. So much! We all do! Right, girls?" He turns to face to Chickie and Bitty. Bitty is standing farther back, basically in the corner apart from everyone else. She has kind of a weird look on her face, but Matty doesn't have time for her bullshit right now. He gestures to them both.

"Let's go!"

KK doesn't have a maid of honor because she couldn't decide between Chickie and Matty. So she has five bridesmaids, including her sister and two friends from college. They all head for the door, then rush into the hallway and toward the doors that will lead them into the church proper. It goes college friend, college friend, Bitty, then Chickie and Matty side by side.

Suddenly, this little room where they were all crowded a minute ago is nearly empty and very quiet. Her father steps to her side. "Ready?" he asks quietly.

She turns to him. "Am I?" she whispers.

He fixes her veil, pulling the sheer fabric over her face. Her eyes are a little shiny. "You tell me, honey."

"Forever is a long time, Daddy."

He purses his lips, and for a second his eyes flick away from his daughter's. Then he finds her gaze again.

"Yes, it is, honey. It's … forever. So this is your chance to change your mind. Once we step down that aisle, you are committed to this new path."

Now it's KK's turn to avert her eyes. Her dad puts a hand on her shoulder. "KK? Are you ready?"

She sighs, shrugs, and tosses her head—carefully so she doesn't mess up Matty's meticulous styling—and plasters a smile on her face.

"Ready," she says. "Here we go."

"KK?

"Honey, you OK?"

It's Harley. I heard a car come down the driveway, but I didn't turn around to see who it was. I couldn't. I feel frozen in place, sitting cross-legged on the dead, brown lawn in front of the storage pod. The pod's door is open. I hauled out a bunch of boxes and opened a few of them before I just simply couldn't function and sank to the grass.

Photo albums. My life in pictures. My old life in pictures. And if a picture is worth a thousand words, there are millions of stories in front of me.

I feel his hand on my shoulder, and then he sits down on the grass next to me. "KK, how long have you been out here?"

I turn to look at him and shrug. Seeing him—his face full of worry, his brow furrowed, his eyes moving from my face to the boxes and back again—makes me pull in a sharp breath. It's quite possible I haven't taken in any oxygen in a while. "I'm not sure. What time is it?"

"It's two, sweetie."

"A.m. or p.m.?"

He smiles. "P.m."

"Why are you here?" I ask, trying to regain some focus. "Shouldn't you be at work?"

"I was at work. Mrs. Cravats from across the street called me. She was concerned because she said you've been sitting out here since early this morning."

It's a two-hour drive from Boston, which means I was sitting in the yard for quite a while before the nosy, old bat called him. I feel bad that he had to leave work and come all this way.

"Where's Matty?" Harley asks. "I thought he was with you."

"I sent him home. I'm fine."

"KK, you are not fine. Saying it out loud doesn't make it so."

"I'm manifesting," I whisper, looking down at the ground.

A tear drops out of my eye and plops on my sneaker.

I'm wearing Jay's Carhartt beanie, Jay's Beachcomber hoodie, Jay's gray sweats, rolled four times at the waist so they don't fall off. I am swimming in Jay.

"Have you talked to Jay? You know, since the—"

"Shit show?" I finish his sentence and shake my head.

"Well, I was going to say 'cemetery,' but yes. He hasn't reached out?"

"Oh, he's reached out. He texts and calls. A lot. Sometimes he comes by and knocks on the door."

"You don't answer?"

I shake my head again. More tears. Lots of them now. *Goddamn it.*

"Why?"

I just shrug.

Harley points to the giant pile of white fabric on my left. "What's that?"

I reach out and finger the material. "My wedding dress."

"Oh, KK. Honey. Come on."

"Remember that day, Haw? It was fun, right? We all looked so good. Fan-fucking-tastic. Endless possibilities stretched ahead, not just for me and him but for all of us. So hopeful."

"It was a great day, K. You were beautiful."

I look over at him. I can barely see him; my eyes are so full of tears. "They should tell you," I say.

He tilts his head. "Who, honey? Who should tell you what?"

"*They.* They should tell you. They should tell you that nothing lasts. Nothing is forever. You won't always look this way. You won't always feel this way. You won't always have that person. They should fucking tell you that everything ends. So you can be ready for it. Because when it starts, when all the ending shit starts, you aren't ready. It really fucks with you, you know?"

I grab at the wedding dress and haul it onto my lap. "Love, honor, cherish, sickness, health. Bullshit. Temporary at best. The only thing true in those vows is death. That's the only guarantee. But they trick you into thinking that all the rest of it is real, too, you know? That it will all last. That you will always look this way and be this way and feel this way. Except you don't. Everything falls apart. Everything ends. Everyone leaves. Everyone dies."

I wipe my face with the satin.

"Remember when Mom got sick? It was the craziest feeling, like all of a sudden we swapped places, and I was the parent, and she was the kid. Like she needed me for the most basic things, and she asked me the most basic questions. Questions I had spent my whole life asking her. And all of a sudden, my mom was gone, and I had this kid in her place who depended on me.

"But now, who could I ask for help? Who could I ask for advice? There was no one. It was the loneliest feeling. And then when Daddy died, I just felt like the last barrier between me and the end was gone. You know? Like your parents' job is to protect you, and then they're gone, and you have no protection. So you just wait around for the other shoe to drop. For your turn to go."

Harley is quiet. He can tell I'm not done. And I need to get this last part out, because this is what's been killing me, what's been eating at me endlessly.

"I can't remember my last conversation with Chickie," I sob. "I can't remember what we talked about. My last text to her was me being mad about not knowing Jay's real name. And our last actual conversation? I can't remember no matter how hard I try.

"She needed me, and I wasn't there. She was dying, Haw, and I wasn't there for her. She was all alone. Was she scared? Did she know? Did she want me? Did she call my name? I wasn't there for her. She was …"

I'm heaving sobbing now. Harley scoots across the grass until he is right next to me, and he wraps his arms around me and pulls me into his chest. He holds me so tight that I have trouble catching my breath.

"And you know what? I didn't get a chance to say it all. To say everything. I didn't tell her I love her. I didn't tell her she's the most important person in the world to me. I didn't tell her that her friendship literally kept me alive at certain points in my life. Why didn't I say those things? Why didn't I? All those years I should've been telling it to her every day. All the time. But I didn't.

"This is why they should fucking tell you in advance. Like, when you turn twenty-one or something. Because that's when you're all cocky and excited for the future, right? Like, oh yeah, what's next, Life? Bring it on. I'm going to conquer everything. Youth is like a suit of armor, you know? You're impervious to loss. But they should tell you when you turn twenty-one that, in fact, life is just going to chip away at you endlessly and take things from you and take people from you. If you had that heads-up, you wouldn't make mistakes. You would make sure everyone knows."

My brother squeezes me.

"Everyone does know, KK," he whispers in my ear. "I know. Bitty knows. Matty knows. Keith knows. Chickie knew. We all know that we love each other, that we hold each other up, that we are each other's everything. That's how it works. You don't say it out loud all the time, because who's got time for that? No one. Life is busy, and you are busy living it. Is it all awesome? No, it isn't. A lot of it fucking sucks. And yes, a lot of it is loss. But before you ever have a single loss, honey, you have a gain. You gain love. You gain support. You gain friendships and memories and feelings.

"And if things didn't ever change, then you wouldn't ever change. You wouldn't grow. You wouldn't be better. And you know that over all these years, we've all gotten better. We are so much better people than we were way back then. Were we great on your wedding day? Yes, we were. Fan-fucking-tastic. Are we better today? Oh my God, yes. So much better."

He pulls me even tighter, and I wiggle up onto his lap and wrap my arms around him, too. I sob into the crook of his neck.

"I miss her," I whisper. "I miss him. I miss ... me."

"I know, honey, I know. Grief is brutal. And you are deep in it. It's been like whiplash for you. First the internet and then Jay and then Chickie. That's more than anyone should bear at once, huh? But let's come out on the other side together, OK?"

He lets go of me and pulls his face back from mine so he can look into my eyes.

"Let's put these boxes back in the pod and leave this for another day," he says. "Oh, except for your wedding dress. Let's take that out back and burn it. Then we can have some lunch. I have sandwiches in the car. And then we'll call Matty and ask him to come back for a bit. OK?" He gives me a smile. At this moment, he looks so much like our dad that the sight catches my breath in my chest.

"I love you, Haw," is all I can manage.

"I know, KK. I always know. Just like you always know that I love you, too. Come on, let's go."

23

February 1996

KK knocks on the hotel room door. Nothing.

She knocks again, hard enough to make her knuckles sting. Nothing.

She slaps her flat palm against the door. Slap. Slap. *Slap*. She hears shuffling behind the door, then the chain being slipped, then the bolt being thrown, then the knob being turned. Everything feels like it's happening in slow motion. She feels queasy.

The door swings open, but no one is there. She sees Matty's back as he retreats into the room. At least she thinks it's Matty. Awfully thin. Pajama pants barely hanging on slim hips. There's no ass to speak of. Shoulders are narrow.

She steps inside and closes the door quietly. Why does she feel the need to whisper?

She walks into what is a standard hotel room: two queen beds, desk, dresser, TV, armchair. The floor-to-ceiling curtains are drawn, but she knows there's a view of Boston Harbor on the other side. Right now, there are twinkling lights since it's nighttime. It's almost midnight, in fact. She got in the car as soon as she received Matty's text. She came right away, but from the suburbs, the trip it still took almost an hour.

He throws himself on one of the beds face-first and lies still. He might well be smothering himself in the pillows. KK is unsure what to do.

She sits on the edge of the mattress and gently puts her hand on his back. "Matty?"

She is whispering. Why is she whispering?

"Matty," she says, louder and more firmly.

She feels him sigh. He rolls over so he's on his back, and her hand is now on his belly. She can see his ribs through his thin T-shirt. *Jesus.* His face is … gaunt? Sunken? He looks like the Robert Downey Jr. character in *Less Than Zero*. What was his name? Oh, right. Julian. He looks like Julian.

He tries to smile. "Hi, Mama," he says, his voice a croak at best. KK sees a bottle of water on the nightstand and grabs it. She puts her hand behind his head and lifts, offering the bottle to his lips. He drinks.

"Hi, Mama," he says again, this time sounding a little more like himself.

"Jesus, Matty, what the fuck?" she says.

"I'm home!" he says weakly. He lowers his eyes. "I'm home," he whispers.

"This isn't home, Matty. This is a shitty hotel room. Why are you here? Does your mom know you're home?"

He shakes his head. "I couldn't let her see me like this. She thinks I'm still in LA. You're the only one who knows I'm here."

"Have you eaten? I'm not going to lie, Matty. You look like shit. You're scaring me."

He smiles. Sort of. "Thanks, Mama. You, on the other hand, look beautiful as always."

"I'm calling room service," KK says. "And Chickie."

She reaches for the bedside phone, but he grabs her hand. "Don't," he says.

"You need food!" she says.

He releases her. "Fine, get me food. But don't call Chickie. I need to get myself together before anyone else sees me."

"You want to tell me what happened? I knew you were sad about the breakup with Sean, but … this seems extreme."

He sits up. She helps him adjust the pillows behind him, and he clasps her hands in his.

"It was bad," he says, his eyes filling with tears. "Really bad. We had a terrible fight, and he threw me out. So I was sort of bouncing around, you know, from house to house. Friend to friend. Except it turns out, I don't have too many friends. Turns out they were all Sean's friends. Or they just wanted a free haircut."

"Oh, honey, I'm sorry. That's a lot to deal with."

"Yeah. Ha. A lot. Coped with coke. Lots and lots of coke. Spent lots and lots of money. Pretty much all of it."

"How long was this going on?"

He closes his eyes. "Six months? I don't know. I lost track. Eventually I lost all my work. I realized I basically had enough for a plane ticket home, so I bought one. I booked this room on the last credit card I have, and I'm sure it's maxed out. I feel like such an idiot. Like a child. Like I can't be trusted with sharp implements or life decisions."

Tears are snaking their way out of his closed lids.

KK pulls her hands out of Matty's grasp and clasps his face in her palms. "Matty, look at me."

He doesn't.

"Open your eyes, baby. Look at me."

He shakes his head. Her hands are wet from his tears. She squeezes gently.

"Open," she commands.

He raises his lids.

"I love you," KK says. "I am here. I am not going anywhere. We will get this fixed. We will get you better. We will fatten you up and get that shine back. And if I have to, I will fly to LA and throat-punch Sean. At the very least, I will get all your stuff and bring it home. Because you are home. Where you belong. Where you will stay. OK? You hear me?"

She gives his face a gentle shake. "You hear me? You're home."

He lays his hands over hers, and she gives his face another shake. "OK, Mama," Matty says, heaving a big sigh. "I hear you. I'm home."

"Did you ever watch all our videos from that night when I slept over and we drank that bottle of tequila?" Matty asks while brushing out my wet hair. We are upstairs in my bathroom. After Harley's call, he arrives, unpacks his gear, and starts on me immediately. He's already done the color, and he's getting ready to cut. This is his love language.

I meet his eyes in the bathroom mirror. He's looking suspiciously innocent.

"No," I say. "Weren't they all just our various soliloquies on the magnificence of *Desperately Seeking Susan*?"

"Hmm," he says, shrugging. "Probably." He tips my head down—somewhat aggressively, I might add—and I hear the scissors start snipping at the back of my neck. "The bangs are growing out nicely," he says.

When he's done cutting, he hands me the blow-dryer with the diffuser and instructs me to tip upside down and dry my hair.

"I need a bevvy," he says, and he closes the bathroom door behind him when he leaves.

I have known this man my whole life. There is apparently a video on my phone I need to watch right this very minute.

I know immediately which one it must be. It's a little over three minutes long, and it's Matty's big, giant, beautiful face taking up the whole screen in the little thumbnail. I can practically count his pores.

Tap.

"Mamaaaaaaaaaaaahhhhhhh," he whispers into the camera. "You are so beautiful when you sleep." He turns the camera a little, and there I am, flat on my back in the bed, my mouth hanging wide open, a little bit of drool oozing out of the side, snoring like a chainsaw.

He turns the camera back to himself, and he's having silent hysterics. His whole body is shaking.

"Girl," he says. "We have had a time tonight. Good thing I had that little nappy a bit ago. But then you went down like a redwood. I had to carry you up these stairs. Thank God I do all that Pilates. I needed my core to get you up here in one piece.

"Listen. I need to tell you some things. And you need to hear them. Because you are a good listener, my gorgeous girl, but sometimes you don't fucking hear. You need to *hear* me.

"I'm glad he's gone. I mean, I'm so sorry that it was such a hurtful train wreck. I'm so sorry that happened to you the way it did. I wish you could have extricated yourself from him in a way that didn't beat you down even more, make you feel even worse about yourself, but I'm not sorry he's gone. I'm glad he's gone.

"Because he beat you down. He made you feel bad about yourself. He isolated you. You know what he did, Mama? He quieted you. *You*. The brightest, shiniest, brassiest instrument in the band. He quieted you.

"And I apologize because I watched it happening for all these years, and I never said a word. I thought it wasn't my place. Chickie watched it. She knew. But we sort of agreed, years and years ago, probably at your wedding, that we wouldn't intervene unless it was a crisis. And it never reached a boil, you know? He just kept it on simmer all those years, just enough to chip away at your shine but never enough for us to blast the secret signal in the sky and come save you.

"And I'm so, so, so sorry that we never did. Because we should have."

Matty stops for a second and wipes his eyes. My sweet man, my sweet boy, whom I protected and fought for all those years when we were growing up and he was trying to become his perfect self, is crying. For me. For what he thinks he didn't do for me, what he thinks he should've done. We are always so good at disappointing ourselves.

He blows out a big breath.

"And I'm also really sorry that—speaking of listening but not hearing—that I kind of ignored everything you were saying about your menopause. I mean, really. I thought you were being dramatic. You know? Because who talks about menopause? *No one*. And we should. We should talk about it! And science and medicine should fucking talk about it and study it and do research and figure out how to fucking fix it. Or make it better. I don't know. I'm guessing you can't actually fix it. Right? But *something* for fuck's sake. Do they even study it in medical school? Are there books? Wait, I'm going to make myself a note in my phone to Google some shit tomorrow so I can be smarter. Because smarter is better, right?

"Mama," he says, pushing his face right-up-into-the-camera, "you are the fucking bomb. The bomb. You own the place. The world! You own the world. But you stopped believing you did. And *most* of that was because of 'fuckwad' and his fucking subversive dismissal of you all the time. God, remember that Christmas party in the Seaport at that fancy bar, and you looked fucking amazing, and all he asked was why you couldn't walk faster in those pumps. *Those were fuck-me pumps.* You looked amazing! I mean, yes, that was twenty years ago, but I'm still mad about it."

He realizes he's kind of whisper-shouting at this point, and he looks over at passed-out me to make sure he hasn't woken me up. I remain unconscious. And drooling.

"Anyway, I wanted to make this because even though we've had an amazing day today, and I do feel like my gorgeous butterfly is coming back to life a little, I didn't get to say all this because, as much as we love each other and are there for each other, sometimes it's just really hard to say shit out loud. You know? I know you know.

"I love you, Mama. My KK. My beautiful girl. You are everything. To so many. For so long you were the universe's piñata, but now it's time for the candy. We started bringing back that shine today, Mama, and I know it's going to get brighter and brighter. Kisses."

And he makes those signature Mateo lip-smacking noises like a hundred times into the camera, getting closer and closer (and I'm remembering this is actually my phone, and I wonder how germy it was for the next few days after this), and then the screen goes black.

My shine. I forgot I had shine. I forgot *to* shine. Can I still?

Chickie's ashes have been holding court in their pill bottle from my kitchen windowsill. From this spot, she can see the back porch and the ocean stretching out at the bottom of the hill. She can see the kitchen and through to the front hall. I'm assuming ashes have eyes in the back of their heads or whatever, 360-degree vision.

And yes, I have 100 percent personified my dead friend's ashes. I talk to them all the damn day.

I try to stop when Matty comes back. He's essentially moved in. I keep asking him about his clients and their dark roots, but he keeps telling me to shut up and mind my own beeswax. We are seven again, apparently.

But yesterday morning, he caught me having coffee with the ashes. I thought he was still asleep. I get up before the sun these days. My eyes just pop open between 3 and 4 a.m., and then I'm up. I'd think it was the menopause, but I know those estrogen patches are still working their magic. It's grief. Like Harley said, I'm deep in it.

So I'm sitting at the kitchen counter, and I'm drinking my coffee from the "For Fox Sake" mug Chickie bought me for my forty-seventh birthday. It has a picture of a fox on it instead of the word *fox*. Get it? You know I can tell you exactly what gift she gave me for which occasion, dating back decades. I remember them all.

Anyway, there I am, drinking the coffee and talking to the ashes, relaying today's forecast from my weather app, when Matty walks in. He gives me a side eye as he pours his coffee. Straddling a stool at the counter next to me, he casually asks, "To whom are you speaking?"

"To whom?" I reply, cocking an eyebrow.

"Grammar matters, Mama," he says. "So tell me, to whom?"

I sigh. He pushes his shoulder up against mine. "Spill," he commands.

"Chickie."

"Chickie?"

"Yes, Chickie."

"Like, in heaven?" he asks.

"No, like on the windowsill," I say. I point to the window over the sink. The pill bottle is nestled between two succulents in clay pots.

"Chickie is on the windowsill," he says, laying a cool palm across my forehead. "No fever," he says.

I shake his hand off me.

"I'm not sick. I have a small amount of Chickie's ashes in that pill bottle. And I talk to her. To them. To the ashes."

He pushes himself off the stool, walks around the counter to the sink, reaches over, and snags the bottle. He pries off the lid.

"Be careful!" I shout.

"I *am* being careful," he snaps back, peering into the bottle. "I've never seen someone's ashes before. They are … lumpier than I thought." He gives the bottle a little shake. "Hmm. There's … stuff."

"I know," I say. "I Googled it because I thought the same thing. All the squishy stuff burns up, but the bones don't really. They are more pulverized than anything. So it's coarse. Thick. It took me a little while to get used to it, but I actually like it now. She's got substance."

"Does she talk back?"

I laugh. It might be the first time I've laughed (or even cracked a smile) since the shit started being fed into the fan.

"No, honey, she doesn't talk back. She just listens."

He pops the lid back on, checks to make sure the seal is tight, and brings the bottle over to where I'm sitting. He sits back down on his stool and takes a swig of his coffee.

"You know, she didn't want to be buried in the family plot," he says. It's not a question; it's a statement.

I look at him in surprise.

"I did not know that. How do you know that?"

"Oh, she told me once. A long time ago. We were at the beach. We were smoking a joint, lying on the sand, talking about everything and nothing, and she mentioned that her father told her she had a place in the family plot, and he was having a headstone prepared for her and everything. It freaked her out that her dad was being pro-active about her burial, having the headstone carved with her name and her birth date. It would even be installed in advance."

I take a sip of coffee and pick up the pill bottle. "She never told me that. I didn't know anything until Harley told me how the arrangements were going to work."

"Yeah, she was mad. Going on and on about how family expectations dictated everything about her life, even her death."

Whew. Family expectations. Expectations in general.

I feel like the universe is trying to tell me something, but I can't quite hear it.

"So what did she want to do?"

"Oh, it was great," Matty says, tugging his stool closer to the counter and smiling. "She wanted to be cremated. Then she wanted to have a huge barbecue with a band and kegs, and she wanted everyone to wear khaki shorts and Hawaiian shirts. She wanted toasting and cheering and laughing and singing along. The band would be required to play 'If I Can't Have You,' you know, by Yvonne Elliman? And then everyone would troop down to the beach and sprinkle her ashes in the ocean and do a shot of tequila."

I knew none of this. None. These were my best friend's final wishes, and I was clueless. How could that be? Why didn't she tell me?

"Why didn't she ever tell me?"

Matty shrugs. "Don't know. Maybe because she knew it wouldn't ever happen because it wasn't what her family wanted her to do. I mean, we were high as fucking kites that day. I think it just all spilled out. She never mentioned it to me again. And honestly, I forgot all about it until just now."

We sit in silence and sip our coffee. I finish mine, get off my stool, rinse out my cup, and put it in the dishwasher.

I put my hands flat on the counter opposite Matty, who is staring at the pill bottle. I meet his eyes with mine.

"Well, let's go make her final wishes come true," I say.

"Fuck yes," he says, jumping off his stool.

We scramble around to gather everything we will need to bring down to the beach. We briefly debate calling Harley and Keith to join us but decide that would only make Bitty feel bad for missing it, and we definitely don't want to put off doing this. Chickie has waited long enough to be properly laid to rest.

We don't have barbecue, but I do have a rotisserie chicken.

And no keg, but I have some Narragansett tall boys.

Matty rummages through Harley's closet and finds khaki shorts and a Hawaiian shirt, and I find the same in mine. I mean, who doesn't have that outfit lying around in case of an emergency?

Tequila, duh. Shot glasses, duh.

We can find the song on YouTube when we get down there. Luckily, it's not a windy today, so we won't freeze to death. We decide to walk, like a funeral procession of sorts. We load everything into a couple of totes.

And last but by no means least, we have Chickie in her pill bottle. The realization strikes me that this is the last vestige of my friend, and I am about to literally toss it away. Can I do this?

Matty sees my hesitation.

"It's what she wanted," he says quietly. "Let's do this for her."

He picks up the totes with one hand and grabs my hand with the other. We head out the back door and down the porch steps toward the path to the beach. When we get there, we make our way over the rocks on the jetty to the tip. We unpack the totes and lay everything out.

"We are gathered here today to celebrate the life and times of Charlene Marie Madeira," Matty proclaims to the sky. "Our beloved Chickie."

We each take a bite of a chicken leg and then throw the bones into the ocean. I grab the Gansetts, and we clink them together before I punch a hole in the bottom of each one. "Cheers!" I shout, and we both pop the tops of the cans, beer gushing into our mouths.

I realize too late that tall boys were a mistake. That's a lot of beer. Choking, I pull the can away from my lips. "I feel like I just waterboarded myself," I wheeze. Matty is a champ, however, and finishes his with a flourish, crushing the can in his hand when he's done. He rips a belch that echoes off the water.

Then Yvonne Elliman's beautiful voice comes out of Matty's phone, singing "If I Can't Have You."

We must've seen *Saturday Night Fever* a dozen times during the summer of 1978, memorizing the dance steps to recreate them on the back porch of my house and singing all the songs at the top of our lungs as we rode our bikes around town. We were far too young for that movie at that time, but back in those days, no one cared. We just bought our tickets and walked right in. Popcorn, Milk Duds, and John Travolta's perfect hair and blue balls.

Matty and I do our best on the big flat rock at the end of the jetty to dance like we used to. He spins me out and pulls me back in, dips me, and hip bumps me. We are laughing and holding each other, and even though this is essentially a funeral, for the first time in what seems like such a long time, I feel at peace.

We've checked off all the boxes on Chickie's last wishes list except for one. So I lie on my belly on the smooth rock. If I stretch out my hand, it will be inches from the water. Matty lies down next to me.

I open the pill bottle. Matty reaches out his hand to me, and I move mine toward him so we both grip the bottle. Both holding Chickie.

"It's OK, Mama," he says. "It's time for us to let her go."

"I don't want to, Matty. I can't."

"You can, KK. You can. We can. We do this like we do everything, right? Together."

"But it's always been the three of us, and now it won't be. Maybe we can just keep this little part of her, you know? Just this little bit so that it will still be us three. So nothing changes."

Matty squeezes his fingers around mine. His hand is warm. His eyes are wet.

"Everything changes, honey. You know that. But what will never change is what is in our hearts, the love that we have always had for each other. And we owe it to her to give her what she wanted.

"You know, you've always asked me why I started calling you 'Mama' all those zillion years ago when we first started playing together. I mean, I didn't even understand why I did it for the longest time. It was weird, but it just felt natural to me.

"When I met you, I felt so safe and warm. Like I was home, you know? And in my four-year-old brain, I guess I equated those feelings with being mothered. So to me, you were Mama. Chickie and I used to talk about that, about you, and about how you had this amazing ability to make people around you feel safe and loved. Like you were the safe harbor. No matter what was going on, if we could find our way to you, it would be OK. She always knew you would take care of her. This is that. We can do this. For her. For Charlene Marie."

You would think with all the tears I have shed since last August that I would be a sobbing mess right now, but I'm not. I'm oddly … serene? His words and the feel of his hand over mine soothe me. My heart has been shattered into a million pieces a zillion times over the last nine months, but in this moment, maybe some pieces are joining back together. I don't begin to understand why letting go of my last physical connection with Chickie is having this effect on me, but it is.

We look at each other, and then we look at the little pill bottle. Without saying a word, we tip our hands toward the water and watch the ashes fall. With no breeze, they drop straight down, disappearing beneath the surface.

We silently watch until the last trail of them goes. Matty releases my hand, and we both push ourselves up off the rock. Still not saying anything, we hug each other. Hard. So hard. I let go of Chickie, but I'm not letting go of Matty. Not now, not ever.

We fill the shot glasses with tequila, clink, and toss them back.

Then we pick up all the stuff, put it all back into the totes, and turn to make our way carefully off the jetty, quickly discovering we're a little tipsy after shotgunning the beers and tossing back the tequilas.

Out of the corner of my eye, I see him standing by the path to the parking lot, holding his board and watching us. He must've been on his way out to surf when he saw us performing our odd little ceremony.

I stop. Matty stops because I do, then looks where I'm looking.

"Want to …?" he starts.

I look at him and shake my head. Then I look back at Jay, who holds up a hand, palm facing us, in a tentative wave. My heart thumps in my chest, and all my organs feel like they are being squeezed. I give him whatever version of a smile I have these days. I take Matty's hand.

"Let's go," I say.

24

He can see her in the distance. She's so far away that she's almost blurry. Or maybe he has tears in his eyes; he's not sure. She's far enough away that she doesn't hear him when he shouts her name. Or maybe she does hear him, but she's ignoring him. She gets farther and farther away until she's just a dot on the horizon, and then, like the last seconds of a sunset, she's gone.

Jay's eyes pop open. He takes a second to focus on the ceiling above him, to calm his breathing. He's had the dream again. The Jasmine dream.

It's been a while since he was notified that she was dead. He never dreamed of her until then, until that lady from the city called and told him that the woman he had reported missing had been found dead in an underground parking garage. That's when the dream started.

It wasn't really a nightmare. It wasn't scary. There were no monsters. But he always woke up gasping.

Maybe he was the monster.

He sits up and tosses the blankets to the floor. He looks around the bedroom. He knows the living room is a mess of sealed boxes, his surfboards in their bags, his old lacrosse duffle stuffed with clothing. He's packed and ready to go. He just needs to load the truck.

He rented one of those small U-Hauls to cart his belongings to Narragansett. The apartment he found is furnished, so he's selling all this stuff, all these pieces of furniture, to the woman who bought his condo. She loves his taste. At least that's what the Realtor told him.

Whatever.

He hates all this shit. Shiny and black. So much glass. God, what was he thinking?

A big part of Jay hates himself for giving in after spending his whole life fighting against his parents' expectations. Majoring in economics at Bates, getting his MBA from Columbia, taking that job at that despicable hedge fund. Why? Why did he acquiesce?

He deserves his misery, he thinks. He fucking deserves it. But all that ends now.

If only he could take all the money he has made over these last few years and all the money he was making from the sale of this condo and give it away. But the part of his brain that has been responsible for talking sense into him for his whole life (that voice in his head with the Jamaican accent) tells him he needs to hang onto it. He doesn't want to end up like Jasmine, for God's sake. No one does.

His father is livid. Jay almost liked watching Ted's face morph back into its old expression—a mix of disgust, disappointment, disdain, and dislike. Eh, let's be honest. It's not dislike. It's hatred. Ted thought he won the war, but it turns out he only prevailed in a battle. A singular skirmish. Jay dropped a nuke at the dining room table last weekend when he told Ted and Irene that he had quit his job and sold his apartment and was moving to the beach.

Ted did that thing—his signature move—where he stands up and leaves the room without a word. Irene did that thing where she chugged the remainder of the eighty-seven-dollar bottle of cabernet. And Jay did that thing where he hears music in his head as he leaves the apartment. This time for the last time. Of that he was sure.

He tried. He wishes someone would give him credit for that. He wishes Carl was still alive to give him a clap on the back. He wishes he could call Gunny and talk things through with her. But she's busy with her family and her life. She loves him—he knows that—but it's time to move on. Move ahead. Figure shit out.

Maybe he'll create an inspirational Instagram account. Hang on, baby, Friday's coming.

He isn't afraid to be alone because really he's been alone since the day he was born. A revolving cast of characters has come and gone, taking care of his needs in the moment. But his needs changed, his characters changed, and here we are.

It's time for him to be the change.

My phone dings.

Jay.

Don't click on it. Block his number. Leave it.

I click on it.

It's a playlist. It's called "Manifesting Katherine."

Don't click on it. Block his number. Leave it.

I click on it.

There are twenty-three songs.

"Lover." Both the plain Taylor version and the duet with Shawn Mendes. "Falling Slowly" from that movie. Harry Styles's "Falling." One Direction's "What Makes You Beautiful." The Greg Laswell version of "Girls Just Want to Have Fun." I smile at the memory of the night Jay played that song for me and we slow-danced on the back porch while he sang in my ear.

The Chainsmokers, both "Closer" and "Call You Mine," which was the next song we planned to do at karaoke. We were making actual karaoke plans. Then there are Ariana's "God Is a Woman" and "Boyfriend." A sob bursts from my throat at the memory of that night on that stage, bringing the house down at that bar and ending up on TikTok. Fucking TikTok.

"One Call Away" makes me laugh because Jay can't stand Charlie Puth, but he knows I love him. More Taylor, "Don't Blame Me."

Then Aidan Bissett, "Tripping Over Air." I found that one on TikTok. I liked to sing it loud, right in his face, when we danced in the kitchen.

I'm smiling and crying simultaneously. Harry, "Adore You." Shawn and Camila, "Senorita." The Miley version of "Like a Prayer." Halsey's "Darling." For once I got to introduce Jay to something. He'd never heard Halsey before. "Slow Dance." "10,000 Hours." Selena's "Who Says." The Sydney Rose cover of "Home." Pink's "Fucking Perfect." Ray LaMontagne's "Trouble."

I haven't played music since Chickie left me. I carry the phone upstairs and climb into my bed, pulling the covers over my head. I grab Jay's pillow—I still haven't washed the case, and his beautiful scent lingers—and hug it to me. I hit PLAY.

As the first song starts, my phone dings again.

JAY. Ready to dance it out whenever you are, sweetheart. ♡

I take the casserole dish out of the oven and carry it over to the kitchen table, where I place it on a trivet. The bacon and the bagels are already out. Harley, Keith, and Matty are seated, sipping their proseccos.

I scoop the chili pepper puffed eggs onto each plate and pass them around. They each add their own bacon and bagels.

"This smells amazing," Keith says, smiling at me.

"Cut the shit, you guys," I reply. "What's going on?"

Keith and Matty both look at Harley, who clears his throat, shoves a huge bite of egg casserole into his mouth, and promptly starts to choke.

I sit down and glare at them.

"Why are we having brunch?" I ask them.

Harley, who has pulled himself together, reaches across the table to take my hand. "We need to talk about the restaurant," he says. "And also the pods in the yard."

We hired someone to empty Chickie's apartment. We didn't sort anything or throw out anything; we just hired them to put every single thing in boxes and into a storage pod, which now sits in the beach house front yard next to the other storage pod.

I am officially that crazy neighbor lady. When the summertime people come back, they're going to lose their minds.

"Why?" I ask.

"Because we can't just let everything sit, KK," Harley says. "We have to move forward. You have to decide if you're opening the restaurant for the season—there are people counting on you for that. If you aren't going to, we need to let them know so they can make other plans and find other jobs. We've continued to pay them, but we're running out of money, and they are running out of patience."

"I don't know anything about running a restaurant," I say.

The three of them look at each other again. I want to throttle them all.

"What?" I say sharply.

Harley takes another huge bite of casserole and then shoots Matty a deep and meaningful look that clearly says, *You tell her. I'm afraid to.*

Matty grabs his champagne flute, guzzles it empty, refills it, and chugs again. He breathes in a big breath and then whooshes it back out.

"Chickie was training Jay," he says.

"I don't know what that means," I reply, filling my coffee mug from the carafe on the table and dumping in some oat milk creamer.

It's now apparently Keith's turn to spill something. "Well, she was training him on everything to do with the restaurant," he says. "The purchasing, inventory, payroll, scheduling, mechanicals. She asked me to show him the bookkeeping right before she … she …"

"Died," I finish for him. "Right before she *died*."

"Ahem, yes," he says, turning red. "That."

"Why was she doing that?" I ask, looking specifically at Harley, who was her lawyer.

"He asked her to," Haw tells me. "He told her he wanted to move up, maybe take over the day-to-day operation from her. Run the place for her so she could step back a bit."

"Why did he want to do that?" I ask, thinking I am starting to sound like a toddler with endless questions.

Now it's Matty's turn. "Um, I think he was making plans to stay here. You know, like permanent? Like, to be with you."

"She didn't say anything to me," I tell them. They blink back at me. "He didn't say anything to me. Why didn't *she* tell me this? Why didn't *he* tell me this?"

Blinking. More blinking.

I grab my champagne flute and the bottle of prosecco, and I shove back my chair. I turn my back on the three blinking idiots, and I go upstairs to my room.

My bedroom door cracks open, and Keith pokes his face around. I am lying on my bed. I smile at him, and he comes in and sits on the bed.

He looks at the bizarre collection of things I have on the mattress around Jay's pillow. There are the framed photo of Chickie and me on Block Island, the Taylor Swift concert ticket stubs, a bar napkin with tic-tac-toe on it from one night at Dockside when Jay and I were bored. There are my Christmas stocking with most of my glitter name worn off, some candy wrappers, a couple of gummy edibles covered in lint, a box of tissues, a lot of used tissues, and an old stuffed bear I found in my storage pod. My parents gave it to me when I had mouth surgery when I was six. I threw up all over the back seat on the drive home from the dentist, and my dad brought me the bear.

I sit up with an apologetic smile. "This looks completely insane, I know. It helps me sleep."

I shove it all down toward the foot of the bed and pat the mattress next to me. He lies down and turns on his side to face me.

"I want to tell you something," he says.

Keith and Harley have been together about fifteen years. They got married in 2010. Matty became an ordained minister with the Universal Life Church online and performed the service. Bitty and I were the witnesses/bridesmaids. Then we all had a nice brunch.

He's quiet and reserved, which makes him a good fit with Harley, who is also quiet and reserved unless he's had a boatload of tequila. They are what I would call a thoughtful couple. They listen to each other, they take care of each other, and they take nothing for granted.

While both Matty's and Harley's sexuality were fully accepted by our family—including our parents when they were still alive—Keith was not so fortunate with his. He hasn't spoken to his father since he came out in college, which makes it difficult for him since his parents are still married. His mom calls him when his dad isn't home, but Keith isn't allowed to call her. It causes too many problems. He hasn't spent a holiday with them in decades, and I honestly can't remember the last time he saw his mother in person.

He reaches out and pushes my hair off my cheek and tucks it behind my ear. Then he grabs my hand and knits his fingers with mine. He sighs.

"Keith," I start, but he takes our joined hands and presses them against my lips. I guess he wants me not to talk.

"You know how Matty talks about how he knew he was gay in the womb?"

I nod.

"I never had that luxury. I had no idea what I was—other than confused—up until I was about fourteen, when I went to a pool party at Mary Anne Riley's and her sister kissed me behind the cabana. With tongue."

"Did you like it?"

"I didn't *not* like it. But I didn't like it either. I was Switzerland. I sure as hell didn't feel anything like what other boys had described in the locker room when they were talking about kissing girls.

"A month later, I went to a birthday sleepover at Jacob Parilla's, and his brother kissed me in the garage, and I had my first boner."

He smiles at the memory. I smile with him.

"So you knew you were gay," I say.

"No, I really didn't. Because I didn't know what gay was. It didn't exist in the world I lived in. I lived on Missionary Position Avenue in Straight Town, Heterosexual USA."

Keith actually grew up in the northwest corner of Connecticut, Litchfield. He tells me that he never kissed another boy in high school, never thought about who was cute, who he liked. He just pushed it all down because that was the circumstance in which he found himself.

"In college, I met out gay men," he said, "and I kissed my fair share of them. Then, during my junior year, I fell in love with Tommy Virello."

I've never heard this story. I'm sure Harley knows it, but I don't know how far outside that tiny circle it's been told.

"I was so in love," Keith says. "I lost my virginity to him, and we were dating seriously. When I came home for Christmas, I wanted him to come with me. I told him I wanted to come out to my parents and introduce him at the same time."

He pauses, and it's my turn to brush my fingers through his hair. "Oh Keith," I murmur, my heart getting ready to break for his twenty-year-old naive self.

"Yeah," he says. "I told my parents at dinner the first night. I put my hand over Tommy's and said, 'Mom, Dad, I introduced you to Tommy today as my friend, but the truth is, he is my boyfriend. We are in love.'

"Silence. For about twenty seconds. Then my dad stood up from his chair, took two steps toward me, and punched me in the face."

I make a noise that's part gasp, part scream. Keith's face shows no emotion. I begin to cry.

"I fell out of my chair onto my back, and my dad threw himself on top of me and just kept punching me and punching me. And my mom was screaming, and Tommy was trying to pull him off. But then he turned and started whaling on Tommy.

"We finally were able to drag ourselves away after my father basically exhausted himself by beating the shit out of us. We ran upstairs, grabbed our bags, and left. We walked to the bus station and bought tickets back to school. We were covered in blood. People kept asking us if we needed an ambulance or the police. But we just said no."

When they got back to UConn, he says, they each went to their separate dorms.

"I would see Tommy after that, in the dining hall or around campus, but we never spoke again," Keith says. "In his defense, it was pretty early in the relationship to get his nose broken for me.

"The next time I had a relationship, it was when I met your brother."

He unclasps his hand from mine and sits up, leaning back against the headboard.

"I never really knew acceptance for who I was," he says. "Even in college, where I allowed myself to be openly gay, even when I was in love with Tommy, it wasn't real. It wasn't authentic. Because my family didn't know. And then, when my family did know, my father tried to murder me. So I was always terrified to be me. And I was scared for anyone who wanted to be with me."

I pull myself up, reach down and grab my bear from the foot of the bed, and join Keith up against the headboard.

"Help me see your point," I say.

"I'm shit at this," he says, smiling, but I clasp his hand and squeeze it, because he is laying himself out to me in a way he never has before. I want him to know not only that I appreciate it but also that he is safe.

"When I met Harley, I knew right away he could be it. And more than anything, I wanted to keep him—keep us—safe from harm. Harm in all its forms, whether it was discrimination or hate from strangers or hate from my own family. I was so afraid that an outside influence, an outside judgment, would destroy us like my father had destroyed what I had with Tommy.

"I drove Harley crazy with not wanting to tell anyone about us, not wanting to show affection in public, not wanting to meet his family or friends. I just wanted us … safe in a bubble where no one could hurt us. Or him. Or me."

Bubble. Aha. I have connected the dots.

"It's not a stretch to apply that kind of thinking to Jay, KK," he says, reading my thoughts. "I have a unique perspective here. And I think he was truly trying to protect what you two had, in its early stages, because he was scared what would happen to you if the world was allowed to see it. I don't think he was hiding you out of shame. I think he was protecting you out of love.

"When he met you, you were pretty fragile. And I think circumstances have shown that he was right in a much bigger way than anyone could've expected."

He pats my thigh and gives me a side hug before sliding off the bed and heading toward the door.

"Keith," I say, stopping him. "I'm sorry that happened to you."

He gives me a smile over his shoulder. "Me too, honey. Me too. But it did, and I survived, and I found the love of my life. It's the climb, right?"

The door clicks shut behind him, and I gather all my comfort items back around me and lie down. I close my eyes.

It is the climb.

25

It's a nice day. It actually feels a little like spring. I tell Matty I'm going out for a bit. He gives me a raised eyebrow, but I don't give him details or an invite.

My muscle memory kicks in about twenty minutes into the drive, and I pretty much zone out for the next two hours until I click on my left blinker and make the turn onto the cul-de-sac. *My* cul-de-sac.

I'd been listening to Taylor the whole drive up, mostly "cardigan," "mad woman," "my tears ricochet," and "hoax." I might be fifty-five years old, but that young woman speaks to me. *"I didn't have it in myself to go with grace."*

I park on the street a couple of driveways up from my own. I know no one will be home. I mean, I know *he* won't be home because he'll be at work, and if he has a live-in woman, I'm assuming she works too. Although if she is home, it won't matter. I'm not knocking on the door.

I spy a HelloFresh box on the porch, and I can't help but snort. He probably has no idea how to turn off that service, so it just keeps showing up every Monday like clockwork.

I feel like this is another goodbye I have to make, another bottle of ashes I need to pour into the ocean of my life.

If I'm being honest, this cul-de-sac, this life I led here, feels like a million years ago and a million miles away. I haven't been here since last July when I packed up the car and drove to the Cape for my month. But I never came back, and soon after, all my stuff arrived on my front lawn in a storage pod. There's no part of me left here. Just ghosts. And a little regret.

I feel no sense of loss. Not like the feelings I've had about Jay, about Chickie, about my place in the world. I do feel sad that so much time passed here that wasn't good. I mean, I know I smiled and laughed and did things and conversed with people during the years here, the years with him. But seeing it all in the rearview mirror, I understand that it wasn't good. It was just … existing.

I think about Chickie's friendship calculations, her math adding up how much time we had together versus how much we didn't. It dawns on me that she got it totally wrong, because she excluded the most important part of her equation—quality. The quality of time spent together—all those summers, those Junes, Julys, and Augusts—added an nth degree to the sum total. It was all quality time, all rock solid, made up of foundational experiences. What we did together back in those days, over those summers—that's what made us who we are today.

When someone is there for so many of your firsts, well, that's in-calculable, right? But it adds up. Chickie missed that part of the equation. I wish I had thought of it when we were having that conversation. It would've made a difference to her.

Why do we convince ourselves that what we have is what we deserve? Why do we settle? I know now why I settled; it was because I was always afraid. He was my shield. He showed interest, and I thought that was enough. I thought it was what I deserved. So I took it. Signed the paper, made the vows.

We bought this house because someone told him a cul-de-sac was the perfect place to raise kids. I had two miscarriages in the first two years of our marriage, and then we just stopped talking about it. After a while, I didn't care anymore. That's what I told myself. But was it true, or was it simply how it was?

It's funny because the Rhineharts were a happy family, and we all had happy childhoods. Our parents loved each other, they loved us, and we loved each other. Harley found love, but Bitty and me? Not so much. And no kids among all of us.

Bitty almost got married once. In her early forties, there was a man, but then one day there wasn't a man, and we didn't mention him again. We sure are good at burying the bodies.

I stare at the house, and I get it. That's all it is. A house. A building with rooms. I slept there. I ate there. I got drunk there. I cried there. I once threw a plate across the kitchen to try to get his attention there. He didn't even look at me. He just took his car keys and walked out the door.

Foreshadowing, I guess, except that time he came back.

It's crazy that we haven't spoken since the night I cracked open his phone. Haven't seen each other. And focusing on it now, I realize I haven't missed him. Not one single thing about him—physically, emotionally, intellectually. He was long gone from me before that night. And I was long gone from him. I thought he was what I deserved until I learned that, in fact, he wasn't.

My phone dings.

MATTY. Mama, when will you be home?

I smile. No questions. No digging. He knows when I'm ready I will tell him what I did today.

ME. Two hours.

MATTY. Perfect. I was feeling domestic, so I am making Caesar salad, chicken Milanese, and fettuccine Alfredo for dinner.

ME. From scratch?

MATTY. Oh yeah. I'm wearing an apron. And I've started drinking.

My kitchen will be a shambles by the time I get back. I start the car and put it in drive. I queue up my music, and, needing a different vibe for the return trip, I choose "Reputation." I hit shuffle, and "Dress" comes out of the speakers. *OK, Universe, I am starting to hear you.*

Looking at that bright yellow door I painted five years ago—he hated yellow—I fully understand that the beach house is my home. It's where all the pieces of my heart are, where my family lives. It's where I am my true self.

Y

"Mama, mama, mama, MAMAMAMAMAMAMA," Matty is screaming from upstairs. I'm in the kitchen with my coffee, wishing I had Chickie's ashes to talk to. Wishing I had Jay to dance with. Wishing I was thirty-four years old. If wishes were horses … He pounds down the stairs and literally skids into the kitchen on his fleece-socked feet.

"Jay is on TV!"

He flips on the small screen I have in the kitchen and grabs the remote. *Rise* is on. The camera shows one of the hosts, Helen Something, sitting on a sofa.

"They went viral on TikTok with their upside-down May-December romance," she begins. Images of Jay and me, stills and video from the karaoke and the Taylor concert TikToks show on the screen.

"And then the backlash began."

I let out a little scream as a giant, full-color billboard of my "well-played menopause" Instagram selfie and Jay's gorgeous body shot from the beach in Portugal fill the screen. Next come shots of all those goddamn headlines and hideous reader comments, tweets, and memes.

So. Much. Hate.

I might faint. I definitely wobble. Matty puts both hands around my waist and pulls me into him, holding me up.

"Jesus," he says.

"Turn it off," I beg, shutting my eyes. "Please."

"How did this couple's unusual relationship become a national debate on older women dating younger men? Here to talk about it, the May half of that relationship, Jay Wells. Welcome."

I open my eyes. Matty and I both suck in a breath. The camera pans back, and he looks so beautiful sitting on the couch next to Helen on the *Rise* set. He's wearing a V-neck sweater, a deep midnight blue ("That's cashmere," Matty whispers), dark jeans, and his beat-up Blundstone Chelsea boots. His sleeves are pulled back from his wrists, and his forearms look delicious. His hair is … perfect. Why wouldn't it be? Longer in the back than when I last saw him, well past the collar of his sweater, brushed over his ears on the sides. One rogue curl flops down onto his forehead.

"They did a great job on his makeup," Matty says, giving me a side eye and reaching out one hand to squeeze my tight fist, which is resting on the counter. His other hand continues to hold firmly to my waist, his arm around my back.

"Thank you, Helen. Thank you for having me," he says with a shy smile. My eyes fill with tears. I miss that face. I miss that voice. I miss him.

Helen leans forward and pats Jay on the knee, smiling brightly at him.

"Helen *Handsy*," Matty shrieks, startling me so hard that I knock over my coffee cup. We both glance at the liquid spreading across the counter, heading to the edge, and neither of us does anything to stop it. Our eyes focus back on the screen.

Jay visibly flinches and casually adjusts himself on the couch to move a little bit farther away from her.

"So Jay, tell us about your relationship with Katherine Rhinehart. She's in her midfifties, and you're in your midthirties. How did you meet?"

Jay rubs his palms on his jean-clad thighs and takes a breath. ("He's nervous," Matty whispers.)

"Well, I had just moved to Massachusetts to start a new job bartending at a restaurant on the outer Cape, and I was surfing one day when I saw her on the beach. Katherine was out walking. And she just immediately captivated me. But it really was just a fleeting thing. I was heading out of the water, and Katherine was leaving the beach. So it was like a minute, but it was funny, because my stomach did this little flip."

("His stomach did a little flip," Matty whisper-shouts in my ear.)

"And then, shortly after that, I saw Katherine at the restaurant. She came in for happy hour. She was good friends with the owner. And she came in a bunch of times, and we struck up conversations, and Katherine and I became friends."

("I love how he keeps saying your name," Matty says.)

"Really?" Helen says, leaning in again. ("Helen," Matty says loudly, "back the fuck off our man.") "How did you end up dating?"

"I liked her, and she liked me, so we started spending time outside happy hour together, and it all just clicked," Jay says. "We had a million things in common, and a lot of things not in common, and it was fun getting to know all that about each other. Like any relationship."

"And the age difference didn't bother you?" Helen asks, tilting her head. ("Is she … smirking?" Matty asks, outrage in his tone.)

"Well, no, why would it?" Jay asks her.

There's what feels like an interminable pause as Helen appears flummoxed by her guest asking her a question—a perfectly logical, reasonable question.

"There's been a strong reaction to your relationship because it's unusual for a man to date a woman so much older than he is," she says, smiling so all her teeth are showing, but somehow it doesn't seem genuine.

"There has been a strong reaction," Jay says, leaning forward slightly and resting his edible forearms on his thighs. ("Good God, he is scrumptious," Matty says.) "Which is insane. I mean, why? If it were reversed, if I were fifty-five and she was thirty-four, hell, I'd be getting high fives in the locker room. But instead, I'm getting strange looks and people asking me if she's rich. And she's getting shredded. Katherine is gorgeous, she's smart, she's funny, and she and I share interests. Why wouldn't we be together? And why does anyone else care?"

Helen's eyes flicker off her interview subject over to something or someone off camera. She leans back slightly. "Sexual intercourse can be difficult or unenjoyable for menopausal and postmenopausal women," she says.

("That doesn't feel like a question," Matty says. "It feels like a line from her memoir.")

Jay gives his perfect head a shake, his hair moves gorgeously under the lights, and then he looks straight at Helen.

"Sex can be challenging in any relationship. One partner can give too much, the other not enough. One or both may not be attuned to the other's needs. Expectations can be too high. Execution can be low. Needs can differ greatly. Interests may not align. You can have terrible sex at fifteen, twenty-five, thirty-four, or eighty. You can have amazing sex at all those ages, too. You get out of a sexual relationship what you both put into it, and I'll be honest with you, Helen, the sex Katherine and I had was the best of my life."

("Holy shit, Mama, did you hear that?")

Helen blinks. Is she clenching her thighs together? I have to remember to Google how old she is after this.

"You said 'was.' Are you no longer together?"

Jay presses his lips into a flat line. "We are not together," he says. "All this craziness, this internet reaction to our relationship, has been really hard, especially for Katherine. She has had truly terrible, hurtful things said about her—and to her—by complete strangers. Judged, insulted, mocked. None of it makes sense. Two videos of us minding our own business and enjoying each other's company out on dates made a lot of people collectively lose their minds. So it's been a struggle.

"On top of that Katherine suffered a horrific loss recently, unexpected and heartbreaking, so we are just taking a little time to breathe. It's what people who love and respect each other do for each other. And the bottom line is, we love and respect each other. When she's ready"—he turns and looks directly into the camera—"I'm here for her."

Rise goes to a commercial.

"I don't know about you, Mama, but I just came in my pants," Matty hollers.

Join the fucking club, buddy.

26

KK. I'm not coming.

Matty and Chickie sit up at the same time when their notifications show them the text. They lock eyes.

"No fucking way," Chickie says.

"Abso-fucking not," Matty agrees.

"Abso-fucking?" Chickie asks.

"Whatever," Matty says. "I'm flustered. Text her back and tell her to get her ass in the car."

"You text her back."

"No, you should. It's your house. She'd be your guest."

"Chicken shit," Chickie grumbles, opening her phone. She taps away furiously.

Matty's phone dings. He looks down, and his eyes go wide.

"So I see you went straight to violence," he says.

"It's the only way to get through to her these days," Chickie replies, shrugging. "It's like she's half dead."

"Well, we all know who has committed that semi-murder."

Matty stands and goes to the kitchen table in Chickie's apartment above the restaurant. She has taken the weekend off because the three of them had planned a mini reunion. Matty was slammed during August when KK was at the beach for her month, and Chickie always has difficulty carving out quality time during the high season. So they didn't see each other then. They planned this get-together for the weekend after Indigenous Peoples' Day, when it begins to slow down.

And now KK is backing out.

"I knew she was going to do that," Matty says.

"I don't know what the hell is up with her," Chickie adds. "She's been like this for a while. Even when she's here in August, she doesn't want to do anything. She blew me off almost every time I tried to get together the few times I tried."

Matty's eyes glisten. "Maybe she's sick, and she doesn't want to tell us. Maybe she has"—his voice drops to a whisper—"cancer."

"Oh, good Lord, settle down. Make us some margaritas and blow your nose. She's not sick."

"Well, she does say she doesn't sleep very much anymore. She says the hot flashes are terrible at night, and she's really restless. And sweats like a lumberjack."

Chickie raises an eyebrow at him. "Lumberjack? They sweat a lot?"

"In my dreams they do," he says and winks at her.

They both look at their silent phones.

"She's ghosting us," Matty says, handing Chickie a margarita with a perfectly salted rim.

"Dammit," she says. "She's a master at this. Lulls us into a false sense that she will, in fact, follow through with the plan, then cancels at the last second and ghosts us. The perfect crime."

"Should we go there tomorrow?"

"Ugh, no way. I can't even imagine the look on his face if we pull up to that house. The cul-de-sac would never recover. The horror!" Chickie throws back her head and puts her hand on her forehead.

"If she doesn't have cancer, then what the hell?" Matty says, flopping down on the couch. The sun has just set, and the sky outside Chickie's apartment is aflame with reds and purples.

"I've tried asking. She just says, 'Menopause.' And then I say, 'What does your doctor say?' And she says, 'Nothing. Ride it out. Yeah, it sucks.' And I say, 'What does Todd say?' And she says, 'I don't think he even notices anything is wrong with me, except he gets really pissed when I wake him up at night with my sweating.'"

"Aren't there, like, herbs and stuff?" Matty asks.

"I guess," Chickie says. "My menopause was easy. One of the very few things I can thank my mother for, I guess."

Matty snorts. "An admittedly short list."

"Yeah, but I think my dad's is even shorter. Just the restaurant, and even that I don't want more times than not."

They are quiet.

"I know you knew," Chickie says.

Matty looks up. "Sorry? What?"

"Honey, it's OK. I know you knew about my dad banging all the waitresses. And the hostesses. And the line cooks. And probably the cleaning lady. I know you knew."

"How? We never told anyone."

"Wait. Who's 'we'?"

Matty grabs his margarita and downs the whole glass. "What 'we'?"

"You said 'we.'"

"I did? I must've meant the royal we."

Chickie leans forward. "KK knew about my father? Banging everything that wasn't nailed down?"

Matty quickly rises and begins frantically mixing a new cocktail. He is banging and clanging the shaker and the ice, and viciously squeezing limes. He meticulously salts the rim.

"Matty," Chickie says in a frighteningly low voice.

He pours his drink into his glass and swallows it whole. "Oh God, Chickie, yes, KK knew. I told her. Because I saw him. I saw your dad. In that stupid storage pod, fucking that terrible Maureen. Remember her? She was so gross. I have never been able to look at canned tomatoes since that day.

"And honestly, we only ever knew about that one time, although we certainly suspected there were others. But eww, we just tried not to think about it. And we never ate off any surfaces in the kitchen."

"She never said anything to me."

"Well, we sure as shit didn't know that you knew!" he says. "And we wanted to protect you and not have you be upset or mad. Even though your mom was long gone by then, we thought it would upset you. God knows it upset me. It's still one of my anxiety nightmares."

Chickie picks up her phone and then puts it down again. Picks it up and puts it down. And then one more time.

"I'm not going to beg her to come," she says to Matty. "She's a big girl, and she can make her own decisions. If she doesn't want to see us, that's her call."

She tips her glass back and empties its contents down her throat. "Let's get drunk."

Matty has badgered me nonstop for three days, and so tonight we are going out. I agree to have drinks and dinner in Provincetown, and he makes a reservation at a—quote, unquote—nice place. He insists on styling me, and since I know this is how he shows he cares, I let him. He even has a dress and shoes for me, although that was a fight.

"Dude, I am not wearing that." My back is turned toward him as I stand in my walk-in closet, searching for an outfit among my hangers. I am ignoring the dress he is holding up.

"*Do not* call me 'dude,'" Matty replies, yanking me out of the closet by my elbow. "And yes, you are. You will look ahh-mazing."

"It has no back. I cannot wear something without a back. My front does not support no back. My boobs will be at my knees. Not to mention my back fat."

"Honey, please. Do you think for one second I would let your boobs touch your knees? I wouldn't even let them touch your belly button! This is the latest in fashion technology—look. Built-in support! It's fabulous. And you do not have back fat. Those are lines of demarcation. Seriously, shut the fuck up."

"It is a tiny scrap of fabric!" I say, touching the hem of the dress. Although it is a gorgeous cranberry color, it does have draping to it that I think might hide what I hate and accentuate what I like. It has molded cups inside the front that do look like they will provide the support I need for my bulgy, lumpy, postmenopausal boobs. The halter style accentuates my shoulders. And on top of everything else, the material feels lovely as well. Soft. Comforting almost. Then I notice my dirty white Chucks on the floor.

"With sneakers?" I ask him, tilting my head. "You hate sneakers."

"I am about to get really, really insulted at all of this questioning of my taste," he says, adopting a half haughty, half wounded tone.

I hold up my hands in surrender. "Dress me, baby," I say. He claps his hands together and yanks my sweatshirt up over my head. An hour later, I am dressed, haired, and make-upped.

Matty is driving so I can overindulge. Or at least that's what he says. He hates driving, but again, I'm not going to argue anymore. He wants to do this for me, and I let him.

But instead of driving to Provincetown, we get on Route 6 in the wrong direction. "What are you doing?" I ask him.

"I have a stop to make," he says. "It will only take a minute."

Twenty minutes later, we are in the parking lot of the karaoke bar.

"What's going on?" I ask. "And actually, now that I think about it, why are we dressed like we are going to prom?"

Matty has decked himself out in shiny black pants, a red button-down shirt open at the neck, and—I kid you not—a white dinner jacket.

"I left my wallet here," he says, opening his door and unbuckling his seat belt.

"When?" I ask incredulously.

"Um, before," he says. "The last time I was here." He has gotten out of the car, and he leans back in his door. "I come here. I *do*! Come in with me. I have to find the manager, and it might take a minute. I don't want you waiting in the cold."

I shake my head, unbuckle my belt, and climb out of the car. In this dress, it is a challenge not to flash my coochie to the world. I need to be mindful.

It's early for karaoke, so the parking lot is about half full. We go in the front, and Matty says something into the bouncer's ear. He looks at Matty, and then his eyes flick to me, and he motions us in. No cover charge for wallet retrieval, I guess.

The music is pounding, and the bar is busy. People are scattered around at high tops and milling around on the dance floor in front of the stage. Matty grabs my hand and pulls me toward the center of the room.

"Where's the manager?" I ask him.

"I think I saw him over here," he yells back to me. "Hang on right here."

We come to a standstill, and suddenly, shit gets weird.

The bar goes silent. Like, pin drop quiet. I realize there is empty space all around Matty and me, as if everyone took five steps back. A spotlight appears on stage, and another one shines down on us. And then a guitar intro comes blasting out of the speakers. Someone somewhere starts to sing.

It's Jay. He's singing Walk the Moon's "Shut Up and Dance," one of our favorites from dancing it out.

And then there he is, sauntering onstage.

In that blue fucking suit.

My heart stops. Matty grabs my shoulders, kisses me hard on my cheek, shouts, "Please don't kill me for this," and takes off toward the stage. Suddenly Bitty, Keith, and Harley are standing behind Jay, wearing the same outfit as Matty. Doing a dance? Yes, definitely some kind of choreography is happening behind Jay. Matty leaps up the stage stairs in a single bound and joins them.

What. Is. Happening?

Jay's eyes lock onto mine. And as he sings, looking absolutely swoon worthy on that stage, the crowd around me joins in, singing and dancing but keeping their distance.

I realize from the lyrics that I am wearing the outfit from the song, "a backless dress and some beat-up sneaks."

I catch Matty's eye, and he gives me double finger pistols. My brain struggles to comprehend what is unfolding before me, a romance-novel-worthy grand gesture, one that took a lot of thought, coordination, and planning.

My family did this. My real family. My blood family and my heart family.

Jay makes his way down the stage stairs and shimmies his way across the floor to me, singing and shaking his hips and his ass and being entirely ridiculous. I think I'm smiling and laughing and crying all at the same time. He never breaks his stare.

"This woman is my destiny ..."

He's right in front of me, and suddenly he's standing still. He moves the mike away from his mouth. His beautiful mouth.

"Hi," he says.

"Hi."

He looks around us. The four idiots up on stage are still dancing, and now they are singing the song. We are surrounded by cell phones held up by cheering and singing karaoke fans.

"We might be headed for TikTok." He smiles, dropping the mike on the table next to me and pulling me in close.

"You think?" I say, wrapping my hands around the back of his neck.

"You OK?" he asks.

I nod.

"I want to kiss you," he says.

"Do you want me to say, 'Go ahead'?" I ask.

"Yes," he says.

So I do.

EPILOGUE

Jay

I've asked her to marry me five times.

Each time, Katherine has given me a sweet but firm no. But just like her goddamn front door, she keeps leaving open the possibility.

On the upside, we have amazing sex afterward.

We made it through our first summer running Dockside. Business boomed. We operated at about two hundred miles an hour pretty much the whole time. It's quiet now, as we are getting close to Indigenous Peoples' Day, and the tourists have thinned out.

We have plans in place for the winter season. We'll be closed Sundays and Mondays because Katherine and I know we will need that break. We aren't Chickie, as we have proved a hundred times a day through the high season.

And we're going to have karaoke on Tuesdays.

We created a nonprofit arm of the business called "Second Helpings." We partner with the local agencies who help the food insecure.

Instead of tossing out the restaurant's unused food, we donate it to either the food bank or the community meal center, depending on what it is.

We also plan to offer cooking classes over the winter to teach people how to make low-cost healthy meals with only a few ingredients. Our chef is excited about it, and Katherine was able to land a corporate sponsor, the local hospital, to cover the expenses. We have lots of ideas on how to expand and get other restaurants onboard to help even more once we are established.

Bitty, Harley, and Keith spent a lot of time at the beach over the summer. It's a six-bedroom house, so they decided their old arrangement of each having a month was dumb. Harley and Keith came down just about every weekend and even helped at Dockside, monitoring online reservations and seating people. Bitty decided enough was enough, quit her job, sold her condo, and moved back. And yes, for a while we had *three* storage pods on the front lawn. There's a metaphor in there somewhere.

Matty lives in the apartment upstairs from the restaurant. After Chickie died, he said he couldn't be so far away from Katherine, so he closed his salon and moved here. He drives into the city to take care of his super-super-super-rich clients. He even hired an assistant to lug all that crap he used to bring to Katherine's.

He has a salon here now. Lots of his old clients who aren't wealthy enough to warrant house calls actually make the drive to see him. And he has Katherine's old seat at the bar reserved. He holds court there; that's for damn sure. Chickie's handmade "Reserved, Assholes" sign is framed and hangs on the wall.

I can't help but smile when I think back to those happy hour days. Katherine looking like she was going to keel over if I even glanced at her, reading her book so hard, sipping her wine with such forced casualness. I wanted to peel back all her layers.

Even though it's been a year, I still catch her looking at me every once in a while like she's trying to answer the question of why I am with her, why I love her. If she asks me, I'll tell her, even though I hope I show her every single day.

She settles me. My whole life I felt like whatever it was I was doing wasn't right. Everyone else's expectations were set on me, and I was never allowed to create them for myself. Unfulfilled. Lost. The only time I ever felt at peace, sure of myself, was when I was sitting on my board on the water, waiting for a perfect wave. When I'm with Katherine, I have those feelings. Settled. Certain. Peaceful.

I'm going to propose again today. And while my last five attempts were sort of spur of the moment, with no ring in hand, this time I have a plan.

First, I'm taking her to the tattoo shop. I've already talked to Danny, and we've settled on the art for the inside of her left wrist. It's a heart that's been sewn up the middle with red thread. At the top, the thread continues through the eye of a needle that hovers above it. At the tail end of the thread is a cursive *J*.

I have a matching one on the inside of my right wrist that he did a couple of days ago. It's hidden under a bandage; I told her I cut myself in the restaurant kitchen and the urgent care nurse told me to keep it covered for a few days. My thread has a cursive *K* at its end.

After that, we're going to the beach where I first saw her and where we had our first date. I've got Yetis filled with coffee and a bag of pastries already in my car. And I've got the ring box in my pocket. Matty helped me design it with a jeweler friend of his.

I can't decide whether I'm doing the down-on-one-knee thing. I've been practicing it in front of a mirror, and I think I look like a fucking dork every time. She almost caught me the other day. I had to pretend I was looking for something under the bed.

I don't have a speech, really. I thought about writing some stuff down, but I know I just want to put my arm around her, look into her eyes, and tell her that she fills my heart and holds my soul. She quiets me in the best way.

She has continued to text Chickie's phone, which she keeps in her nightstand. She thinks I don't know, but I do—first, because we still pay the bill on the plan; and second, because the phone is still connected to the Mac in the restaurant office so I can see all the texts; and third, because sometimes in the middle of the night, I hear it ding, and I know she's turned away from me in bed, texting Chickie because something is bothering her.

Don't get the wrong idea; I'm not spying. I just check every once in a while to make sure Katherine is OK. It's how I know that the last time she turned down my proposal she texted Chickie that she thought she might be ready, and she hoped there would be a sixth one.

Here we go.

KK

I used to talk to Chickie when her ashes sat on my windowsill. I used to take her with me in my pocket when I left the house. She was always my anchor, and that little pill bottle with her dust in it served that same purpose. When Matty and I let her go, I felt seriously adrift for a few days.

But like all that time ago, when I thought I couldn't go on without her and I texted her phone like a complete psycho—and then texted myself back from her phone like it was time for the men in white to come get me—I do that to this day when I need her strength. Her humor. Her love. Her ride-or-die support.

So now I sit on the jetty where we released her ashes, out on the farthest rock. It's big and flat, and after a day of sunshine, it stays warm for a long time. I know this because sometimes I sit here for a long time. Jay lets me be. They all do. They get it. I'm really OK. Sometimes I just need Chickie.

I pull out my phone. The sun is really low, and the October breeze is cold. I won't stay much longer.

> Me. I said yes.

> Me. But you knew I would.

> Me. And I know you're happy for me. Even when you weren't, you were.

I know that back at the house, her phone is dinging in my nightstand drawer. I keep it fully charged. I know Jay knows it's there. He gets it.

> Me. I can do this. I'm not scared.

I shove the phone back in my pocket and push myself up to standing. I need to get off the rocks before the sun goes all the way down. Don't want to break a hip.

Here we go.

PLAYLIST

"Crazy for You," Madonna
"Love Me More," Sam Smith
"You're So Vain," Carly Simon
"Best Friend Song," Rozzi
"Wagon Wheel," Darius Rucker
"Boyfriend," Ariana Grande and Social House
"Bang Bang," Jesse J, Ariana Grande, Nicki Minaj
"Started from the Bottom Now We're Here," Drake
"Lover," Taylor Swift
"Lover," Taylor Swift and Shawn Mendes
"Falling Slowly," Glen Hansard and Markéta Irglová
"Falling," Harry Styles
"What Makes You Beautiful," One Direction
"Girls Just Want to Have Fun," Greg Laswell
"Closer," The Chainsmokers
"Call You Mine," The Chainsmokers
"God Is a Woman," Ariana Grande
"One Call Away," Charlie Puth
"Don't Blame Me," Taylor Swift
"Tripping Over Air," Aidan Bissett
"Adore You," Harry Styles
"Senorita," Shawn Mendes and Camila Cabello
"Like a Prayer," Miley Cyrus
"Darling," Halsey
"Slow Dance," AJ Mitchell (feat Ava Max)
"10,000 Hours," Dan + Shay & Justin Bieber
"Who Says," Selena Gomez
"Home," Sydney Rose
"Fucking Perfect," Pink
"Trouble," Ray LaMontagne
"Shut Up and Dance," Walk the Moon

ACKNOWLEDGMENTS

My parents were both journalists and writers, and they put a love of words in my DNA. So the biggest thanks go to both of them for meeting in a newsroom, falling in love, making a life together, and gifting me with the desire to tell people's stories.

Thank you to Margaret, who was the first to set eyes on this story of mine when it was only fifty pages, and tirelessly coaching me through it.

And to Karen, my Karen, who served as muse and beta reader and honest-feedback giver from the start to the finish. She saved KK's story several times. She's read it almost more than I have, and her enthusiasm never waned.

To my husband and kids, who—once I was brave enough to show them the manuscript—provided unending support and cheerleading.

Deep gratitude to Jill, the best copy editor in the world. You made my story razor sharp.

But thank you most of all to those girls/women and boys/men who make up my foundation—those who are never afraid to be honest when I need it, to be fearless when the time is right, and to always hold my heart gently in their hands. I couldn't do any of it without you.

ABOUT THE AUTHOR

Elissa Bass was born into a family of journalists and writers, which made dinnertime interesting. After a long and award-winning career in journalism, she started her own communications business, continuing to tell others' stories while attending her two kids' high school soccer and basketball games. She lives in southeastern Connecticut with her journalist husband and texts memes to her now grown children every day.

Made in United States
North Haven, CT
26 April 2024